S0-AWN-006

Amy Tan was born in Oakland, California in 1952, two and a half years after her parents emigrated to the US. Though her parents hoped she would become a neurosurgeon by trade and a concert pianist by hobby, instead she became an administrator of programmes for disabled children and later a reporter and editor. She visited China for the first time in 1987 and found it was just how her mother had said: 'As soon as my feet touched China, I became Chinese.'

Amy Tan lives in San Francisco with her husband. *The Joy Luck Club* is her first novel.

Amy Tan

THE JOY LUCK CLUB

Minerva

A Mandarin Paperback

THE JOY LUCK CLUB

First published in Great Britain 1989
by William Heinemann Ltd
This edition published
by Mandarin Paperbacks
Michelin House, 81 Fulham Road, London SW3 6RB

This edition first printed in Australia 1993

Mandarin is an imprint of Reed International Books Limited

Copyright © 1989 Amy Tan

A CIP catalogue record for this title
is available from the British Library
ISBN 0 7493 3602 1

The author wishes to thank the following publications in
which some of the stories in slightly different form, have
already appeared: *The Atlantic, Grazia, Ladies' Home Journal,
San Francisco Focus, Seventeen,* and *The Short Story Review.*

Printed in Australia by Griffin Paperbacks

To my mother

and the memory of her mother

You asked me once
what I would remember.

This, and much more.

ACKNOWLEDGMENTS

The author is grateful to her weekly writers' group for kindness and criticism during the writing of this book. Special thanks also to Louis DeMattei, Robert Foothorap, Gretchen Schields, Amy Hempel, Jennifer Barth, Mary Clemmey of the Abner Stein Agency, and my family in China and America. And a thousand flowers each to these people whom I have had the joy and the luck to know: my American editor, Faith Sale, and my British editor, Amanda Conquy, for their belief in this book; my agent, Sandra Dijkstra, for saving my life; and my teacher, Molly Giles, who told me to start over again and then patiently guided me to the end.

THE JOY LUCK CLUB

THE MOTHERS	THE DAUGHTERS
Suyuan Woo	Jing-mei "June" Woo
An-mei Hsu	Rose Hsu Jordan
Lindo Jong	Waverly Jong
Ying-ying St. Clair	Lena St. Clair

The Joy Luck Club

FEATHERS FROM A THOUSAND LI AWAY

*T*he old woman remembered a swan she had bought many years ago in Shanghai for a foolish sum. This bird, boasted the market vendor, was once a duck that stretched its neck in hopes of becoming a goose, and now look!—it is too beautiful to eat.

Then the woman and the swan sailed across an ocean many thousands of *li* wide, stretching their necks toward America. On her journey she cooed to the swan: "In America I will have a daughter just like me. But over there nobody will say her worth is measured by the loudness of her husband's belch. Over there nobody will look down on her, because I will make her speak only perfect American English. And over there she will always be too full to swallow any sorrow! She will know my meaning, because I will give her this swan—a creature that became more than what was hoped for."

But when she arrived in the new country, the immigration officials pulled her swan away from her, leaving the woman fluttering her arms and with only one swan feather for a memory. And then she had to fill out so many forms she forgot why she had come and what she had left behind.

Now the woman was old. And she had a daughter who grew up speaking only English and swallowing more Coca-Cola than sorrow. For a long time now the woman had wanted to give her daughter the single swan feather and tell her, "This feather may look worthless, but it comes from afar and carries with it all my good intentions." And she waited, year after year, for the day she could tell her daughter this in perfect American English.

JING-MEI WOO

The Joy Luck Club

My father has asked me to be the fourth corner at the Joy Luck Club. I am to replace my mother, whose seat at the mah jong table has been empty since she died two months ago. My father thinks she was killed by her own thoughts.

"She had a new idea inside her head," said my father. "But before it could come out of her mouth, the thought grew too big and burst. It must have been a very bad idea."

The doctor said she died of a cerebral aneurysm. And her friends at the Joy Luck Club said she died just like a rabbit: quickly and with unfinished business left behind. My mother was supposed to host the next meeting of the Joy Luck Club.

The week before she died, she called me, full of pride, full of life: "Auntie Lin cooked red bean soup for Joy Luck. I'm going to cook black sesame-seed soup."

"Don't show off," I said.

"It's not showoff." She said the two soups were almost the same, *chabudwo*. Or maybe she said *butong*, not the same thing at all. It was one of those Chinese expressions that means the better half of mixed intentions. I can never remember things I didn't understand in the first place.

My mother started the San Francisco version of the Joy Luck Club in 1949, two years before I was born. This was the year my mother and father left China with one stiff leather trunk filled only with fancy silk dresses. There was no time to pack anything else, my mother had explained to my father after they boarded the boat. Still his hands swam frantically between the slippery silks, looking for his cotton shirts and wool pants.

When they arrived in San Francisco, my father made her hide those shiny clothes. She wore the same brown-checked Chinese dress until the Refugee Welcome Society gave her two hand-me-down dresses, all too large in sizes for American women. The society was composed of a group of white-haired American missionary ladies from the First Chinese Baptist Church. And because of their gifts, my parents could not refuse their invitation to join the church. Nor could they ignore the old ladies' practical advice to improve their English through Bible study class on Wednesday nights and, later, through choir practice on Saturday mornings. This was how my parents met the Hsus, the Jongs, and the St. Clairs. My mother could sense that the women of these families also had unspeakable tragedies they had left behind in China and hopes they couldn't begin to express in their fragile English. Or at least, my mother recognized the numbness in these women's faces. And she saw how quickly their eyes moved when she told them her idea for the Joy Luck Club.

Joy Luck was an idea my mother remembered from the days of her first marriage in Kweilin, before the Japanese came. That's why I think of Joy Luck as her Kweilin story. It was the story she would always tell me when she was bored, when there was nothing to do, when every bowl had been washed and the Formica table had been wiped down twice, when my father sat reading the newspaper and smoking one Pall Mall cigarette after another, a warning not to disturb him. This is when my mother would take out a box of old ski sweaters sent to us by unseen relatives from Vancouver. She would snip the bottom of a sweater and pull out a kinky thread of yarn, anchoring it to a piece of cardboard. And as she began to roll with one sweeping rhythm, she would start her story. Over the years, she told me the same story, except for the ending, which grew darker, casting long shadows into her life, and eventually into mine.

"I dreamed about Kweilin before I ever saw it," my mother began, speaking Chinese. "I dreamed of jagged peaks lining a curving river, with magic moss greening the banks. At the tops of these peaks were white mists. And if you could float down this river and eat the moss for food, you would be strong enough to climb the peak. If you slipped, you would only fall into a bed of soft moss and laugh. And once you reached the top, you would be able to see everything and feel such happiness it would be enough to never have worries in your life ever again.

"In China, everybody dreamed about Kweilin. And when I arrived, I realized how shabby my dreams were, how poor my thoughts. When I saw the hills, I laughed and shuddered at the same time. The peaks looked like giant fried fish heads trying to jump out of a vat of oil. Behind each hill, I could see shadows of another fish, and then another and another. And then the clouds would move just a little and the hills would suddenly become monstrous elephants marching slowly toward me! Can you see this? And at the root of the hill were secret caves. Inside grew hanging rock gardens in the shapes and colors of cabbage, winter melons, turnips, and onions. These were things so strange and beautiful you can't ever imagine them.

"But I didn't come to Kweilin to see how beautiful it was. The man who was my husband brought me and our two babies to Kweilin because he thought we would be safe. He was an officer with the Kuomintang, and after he put us down in a small room in a two-story house, he went off to the northwest, to Chungking.

"We knew the Japanese were winning, even when the newspapers said they were not. Every day, every hour, thousands of people poured into the city, crowding the sidewalks, looking for places to live. They came from the East, West, North, and South. They were rich and poor, Shanghainese, Cantonese, northerners, and not just Chinese, but foreigners and missionaries of every religion. And there was, of course, the Kuomintang and their army officers who thought they were top level to everyone else.

"We were a city of leftovers mixed together. If it hadn't been for the Japanese, there would have been plenty of reason for fighting to break out among these different people. Can you see it? Shanghai people with north-water peasants, bankers with barbers, rickshaw pullers with Burma refugees. Everybody looked down on someone else. It didn't matter that everybody shared the same sidewalk to spit on and suffered the same fast-moving diarrhea. We all had the same stink, but everybody complained someone else smelled the worst. Me? Oh, I hated the American air force officers who said habba-habba sounds to make my face turn red. But the worst were the northern peasants who emptied their noses into their hands and pushed people around and gave everybody their dirty diseases.

"So you can see how quickly Kweilin lost its beauty for me. I no longer climbed the peaks to say, How lovely are these hills! I only wondered which hills the Japanese had reached. I sat in the dark corners of my house with a baby under each arm, waiting with nervous feet. When the sirens cried out to warn us of bombers, my neighbors and I jumped to our feet and scurried to the deep caves to hide like wild animals. But you can't stay in the dark for so long. Something inside of you starts to fade and you become like a starving person, crazy-hungry for light. Outside I could hear the bombing. Boom! Boom! And then the sound of raining rocks. And inside I was no longer hungry for the cabbage or the turnips of the hanging rock garden. I could only see the dripping bowels of an ancient hill that might collapse on top of me. Can you imagine how it is, to want to be neither inside nor outside, to want to be nowhere and disappear?

"So when the bombing sounds grew farther away, we would come back out like newborn kittens scratching our way back to the city. And always, I would be amazed to find the hills against the burning sky had not been torn apart.

"I thought up Joy Luck on a summer night that was so hot even the moths fainted to the ground, their wings were so heavy with the damp heat. Every place was so crowded there was no room for fresh air. Unbearable smells from the sewers rose up to my second-story window and the stink had nowhere else to go but into my nose. At all hours of the night and day, I heard screaming sounds. I didn't know if it was a peasant slitting the throat of a runaway pig or an officer beating a half-dead peasant for lying in his way on the sidewalk. I didn't go to the window to find out. What use would it have been? And that's when I thought I needed something to do to help me move.

"My idea was to have a gathering of four women, one for each corner of my mah jong table. I knew which women I wanted to ask. They were all young like me, with wishful faces. One was an army officer's wife, like myself. Another was a girl with very fine manners from a rich family in Shanghai. She had escaped with only a little money. And there was a girl from Nanking who had the blackest hair I have ever seen. She came from a low-class family, but she was pretty and pleasant and had married well, to an old man who died and left her with a better life.

"Each week one of us would host a party to raise money and to raise our spirits. The hostess had to serve special *dyansyin* foods to bring good fortune of all kinds—dumplings shaped like silver money ingots, long rice noodles for long life, boiled peanuts for conceiving sons, and of course, many good-luck oranges for a plentiful, sweet life.

"What fine food we treated ourselves to with our meager allowances! We didn't notice that the dumplings were stuffed mostly with stringy squash and that the oranges were spotted with wormy holes. We ate sparingly, not as if we didn't have enough, but to protest how we could not eat another bite, we had already bloated ourselves from earlier in the day. We knew we had luxuries few people could afford. We were the lucky ones.

"After filling our stomachs, we would then fill a bowl with

money and put it where everyone could see. Then we would sit down at the mah jong table. My table was from my family and was of a very fragrant red wood, not what you call rosewood, but *hong mu*, which is so fine there's no English word for it. The table had a very thick pad, so that when the mah jong *pai* were spilled onto the table the only sound was of ivory tiles washing against one another.

"Once we started to play, nobody could speak, except to say '*Pung!*' or '*Chr!*' when taking a tile. We had to play with seriousness and think of nothing else but adding to our happiness through winning. But after sixteen rounds, we would again feast, this time to celebrate our good fortune. And then we would talk into the night until the morning, saying stories about good times in the past and good times yet to come.

"Oh, what good stories! Stories spilling out all over the place! We almost laughed to death. A rooster that ran into the house screeching on top of dinner bowls, the same bowls that held him quietly in pieces the next day! And one about a girl who wrote love letters for two friends who loved the same man. And a silly foreign lady who fainted on a toilet when firecrackers went off next to her.

"People thought we were wrong to serve banquets every week while many people in the city were starving, eating rats and, later, the garbage that the poorest rats used to feed on. Others thought we were possessed by demons—to celebrate when even within our own families we had lost generations, had lost homes and fortunes, and were separated, husband from wife, brother from sister, daughter from mother. Hnnnh! How could we laugh, people asked.

"It's not that we had no heart or eyes for pain. We were all afraid. We all had our miseries. But to despair was to wish back for something already lost. Or to prolong what was already unbearable. How much can you wish for a favorite warm coat that hangs in the closet of a house that burned down with your mother and father inside of it? How long can you see in your mind arms and legs hanging from telephone wires and starving dogs running down the streets with half-chewed hands dangling from their jaws? What was worse, we asked among ourselves, to sit and wait for our own deaths with proper somber faces? Or to choose our own happiness?

"So we decided to hold parties and pretend each week had become the new year. Each week we could forget past wrongs done to us. We weren't allowed to think a bad thought. We feasted, we laughed, we played games, lost and won, we told the best stories. And each week, we could hope to be lucky. That hope was our only joy. And that's how we came to call our little parties Joy Luck."

My mother used to end the story on a happy note, bragging about her skill at the game. "I won many times and was so lucky the others teased that I had learned the trick of a clever thief," she said. "I won tens of thousands of *yuan*. But I wasn't rich. No. By then paper money had become worthless. Even toilet paper was worth more. And that made us laugh harder, to think a thousand-*yuan* note wasn't even good enough to rub on our bottoms."

I never thought my mother's Kweilin story was anything but a Chinese fairy tale. The endings always changed. Sometimes she said she used that worthless thousand-*yuan* note to buy a half-cup of rice. She turned that rice into a pot of porridge. She traded that gruel for two feet from a pig. Those two feet became six eggs, those eggs six chickens. The story always grew and grew.

And then one evening, after I had begged her to buy me a transistor radio, after she refused and I had sulked in silence for an hour, she said, "Why do you think you are missing something you never had?" And then she told me a completely different ending to the story.

"An army officer came to my house early one morning," she said, "and told me to go quickly to my husband in Chungking. And I knew he was telling me to run away from Kweilin. I knew what happened to officers and their families when the Japanese arrived. How could I go? There were no trains leaving Kweilin. My friend from Nanking, she was so good to me. She bribed a man to steal a wheelbarrow used to haul coal. She promised to warn our other friends.

"I packed my things and my two babies into this wheelbarrow and began pushing to Chungking four days before the Japanese marched into Kweilin. On the road I heard news of the slaughter from people running past me. It was terrible. Up to the last day, the Kuomintang insisted that Kweilin was safe, protected by the Chinese army. But later that day, the streets of Kweilin were strewn with newspapers reporting great Kuomintang victories, and on top of these papers, like fresh fish from a butcher, lay rows of people—men, women, and children who had never lost hope, but had lost their lives instead. When I heard this news, I walked faster and faster, asking myself at each step, Were they foolish? Were they brave?

"I pushed toward Chungking, until my wheel broke. I abandoned my beautiful mah jong table of *hong mu*. By then I didn't have enough feeling left in my body to cry. I tied scarves into slings and put a baby on each side of my shoulder. I carried a bag in each hand, one with clothes, the other with food. I carried these things until deep grooves grew in my hands. And I finally dropped one bag after the other when my hands began to bleed and became too slippery to hold onto anything.

"Along the way, I saw others had done the same, gradually given up hope. It was like a pathway inlaid with treasures that grew in value along the way. Bolts of fine fabric and books. Paintings of ancestors and carpenter tools. Until one could see cages of ducklings now quiet with thirst and, later still, silver urns lying in the road, where people had been too tired to carry them for any kind of future hope. By the time I arrived in Chungking I had lost everything except for three fancy silk dresses which I wore one on top of the other."

"What do you mean by 'everything'?" I gasped at the end. I was stunned to realize the story had been true all along. "What happened to the babies?"

She didn't even pause to think. She simply said in a way that made it clear there was no more to the story: "Your father is not my first husband. You are not those babies."

When I arrive at the Hsus' house, where the Joy Luck Club is meeting tonight, the first person I see is my father. "There she is! Never on time!" he announces. And it's true. Everybody's already here, seven family friends in their sixties and seventies. They look up and laugh at me, always tardy, a child still at thirty-six.

I'm shaking, trying to hold something inside. The last time I saw them, at the funeral, I had broken down and cried big gulping sobs. They must wonder now how someone like me can take my mother's place. A friend once told me that my mother and I were alike, that we had the same wispy hand gestures, the same girlish laugh and sideways look. When I shyly told my mother this, she seemed insulted and said, "You don't even know little percent of me! How can you be me?" And she's right. How can I be my mother at Joy Luck?

"Auntie, Uncle," I say repeatedly, nodding to each person there. I have always called these old family friends Auntie and Uncle. And then I walk over and stand next to my father.

He's looking at the Jongs' pictures from their recent China trip. "Look at that," he says politely, pointing to a photo of the Jongs' tour group standing on wide slab steps. There is nothing in this picture that shows it was taken in China rather than San Francisco, or any other city for that matter. But my father doesn't seem to be looking at the picture anyway. It's as though everything were the same to him, nothing stands out. He has always been politely indifferent. But what's the Chinese word that means indifferent because you can't *see* any differences? That's how troubled I think he is by my mother's death.

"Will you look at that," he says, pointing to another nondescript picture.

The Hsus' house feels heavy with greasy odors. Too many Chinese meals cooked in a too small kitchen, too many once fragrant smells compressed onto a thin layer of invisible grease. I remember how my mother used to go into other people's houses and restaurants and wrinkle her nose, then whisper very loudly: "I can see and feel the stickiness with my nose."

I have not been to the Hsus' house in many years, but the living room is exactly the same as I remember it. When Auntie An-mei and Uncle George moved to the Sunset district from Chinatown twenty-five years ago, they bought new furniture. It's all there, still looking mostly new under yellowed plastic. The same turquoise couch shaped in a semicircle of nubby tweed. The colonial end tables made out of heavy maple. A lamp of fake cracked porcelain. Only the scroll-length calendar, free from the Bank of Canton, changes every year.

I remember this stuff, because when we were children, Auntie An-mei didn't let us touch any of her new furniture except through the clear plastic coverings. On Joy Luck nights, my parents brought me to the Hsus'. Since I was the guest, I had to take care of all the younger children, so many children it seemed as if there were always one baby who was crying from having bumped its head on a table leg.

"You are responsible," said my mother, which meant I was in trouble if anything was spilled, burned, lost, broken, or dirty. I was responsible, no matter who did it. She and Auntie An-mei were dressed up in funny Chinese dresses with stiff stand-up collars and blooming branches of embroidered silk sewn over their breasts. These clothes were too fancy for real Chinese people, I thought, and too strange for American parties. In those days, before my mother told me her Kweilin story, I imagined Joy Luck was a shameful Chinese custom, like the secret gathering of the Ku Klux Klan or the tom-tom dances of TV Indians preparing for war.

But tonight, there's no mystery. The Joy Luck aunties are all wearing slacks, bright print blouses, and different versions of sturdy walking shoes. We are all seated around the dining room table under a lamp that looks like a Spanish candelabra. Uncle George puts on his bifocals and starts the meeting by reading the minutes:

"Our capital account is $24,825, or about $6,206 a couple,

$3,103 per person. We sold Subaru for a loss at six and three-quarters. We bought a hundred shares of Smith International at seven. Our thanks to Lindo and Tin Jong for the goodies. The red bean soup was especially delicious. The March meeting had to be canceled until further notice. We were sorry to have to bid a fond farewell to our dear friend Suyuan and extended our sympathy to the Canning Woo family. Respectfully submitted, George Hsu, president and secretary."

That's it. I keep thinking the others will start talking about my mother, the wonderful friendship they shared, and why I am here in her spirit, to be the fourth corner and carry on the idea my mother came up with on a hot day in Kweilin.

But everybody just nods to approve the minutes. Even my father's head bobs up and down routinely. And it seems to me my mother's life has been shelved for new business.

Auntie An-mei heaves herself up from the table and moves slowly to the kitchen to prepare the food. And Auntie Lin, my mother's best friend, moves to the turquoise sofa, crosses her arms, and watches the men still seated at the table. Auntie Ying, who seems to shrink even more every time I see her, reaches into her knitting bag and pulls out the start of a tiny blue sweater.

The Joy Luck uncles begin to talk about stocks they are interested in buying. Uncle Jack, who is Auntie Ying's younger brother, is very keen on a company that mines gold in Canada.

"It's a great hedge on inflation," he says with authority. He speaks the best English, almost accentless. I think my mother's English was the worst, but she always thought her Chinese was the best. She spoke Mandarin slightly blurred with a Shanghai dialect.

"Weren't we going to play mah jong tonight?" I whisper loudly to Auntie Ying, who's slightly deaf.

"Later," she says, "after midnight."

"Ladies, are you at this meeting or not?" says Uncle George.

After everybody votes unanimously for the Canada gold stock, I go into the kitchen to ask Auntie An-mei why the Joy Luck Club started investing in stocks.

"We used to play mah jong, winner take all. But the same

people were always winning, the same people always losing," she says. She is stuffing wonton, one chopstick jab of gingery meat dabbed onto a thin skin and then a single fluid turn with her hand that seals the skin into the shape of a tiny nurse's cap. "You can't have luck when someone else has skill. So long time ago, we decided to invest in the stock market. There's no skill in that. Even your mother agreed."

Auntie An-mei takes count of the tray in front of her. She's already made five rows of eight wonton each. "Forty wonton, eight people, ten each, five row more," she says aloud to herself, and then continues stuffing. "We got smart. Now we can all win and lose equally. We can have stock market luck. And we can play mah jong for fun, just for a few dollars, winner take all. Losers take home leftovers! So everyone can have some joy. Smart-hanh?"

I watch Auntie An-mei make more wonton. She has quick, expert fingers. She doesn't have to think about what she is doing. That's what my mother used to complain about, that Auntie An-mei never thought about what she was doing.

"She's not stupid," said my mother on one occasion, "but she has no spine. Last week, I had a good idea for her. I said to her, Let's go to the consulate and ask for papers for your brother. And she almost wanted to drop her things and go right then. But later she talked to someone. Who knows who? And that person told her she can get her brother in bad trouble in China. That person said FBI will put her on a list and give her trouble in the U.S. the rest of her life. That person said, You ask for a house loan and they say no loan, because your brother is a communist. I said, You already have a house! But still she was scared.

"Aunti An-mei runs this way and that," said my mother, "and she doesn't know why."

As I watch Auntie An-mei, I see a short bent woman in her seventies, with a heavy bosom and thin, shapeless legs. She has the flattened soft fingertips of an old woman. I wonder what Auntie An-mei did to inspire a lifelong stream of criticism from my mother. Then again, it seemed my mother was always displeased with all her friends, with me, and even with my father.

Something was always missing. Something always needed improving. Something was not in balance. This one or that had too much of one element, not enough of another.

The elements were from my mother's own version of organic chemistry. Each person is made of five elements, she told me.

Too much fire and you had a bad temper. That was like my father, whom my mother always criticized for his cigarette habit and who always shouted back that she should keep her thoughts to herself. I think he now feels guilty that he didn't let my mother speak her mind.

Too little wood and you bent too quickly to listen to other people's ideas, unable to stand on your own. This was like my Auntie An-mei.

Too much water and you flowed in too many directions, like myself, for having started half a degree in biology, then half a degree in art, and then finishing neither when I went off to work for a small ad agency as a secretary, later becoming a copywriter.

I used to dismiss her criticisms as just more of her Chinese superstitions, beliefs that conveniently fit the circumstances. In my twenties, while taking Introduction to Psychology, I tried to tell her why she shouldn't criticize so much, why it didn't lead to a healthy learning environment.

"There's a school of thought," I said, "that parents shouldn't criticize children. They should encourage instead. You know, people rise to other people's expectations. And when you criticize, it just means you're expecting failure."

"That's the trouble," my mother said. "You never rise. Lazy to get up. Lazy to rise to expectations."

"Time to eat," Auntie An-mei happily announces, bringing out a steaming pot of the wonton she was just wrapping. There are piles of food on the table, served buffet style, just like at the Kweilin feasts. My father is digging into the chow mein, which still sits in an oversize aluminum pan surrounded by little plastic packets of soy sauce. Auntie An-mei must have bought this on Clement Street. The wonton soup smells wonderful with delicate sprigs of cilantro floating on top. I'm drawn first to a large platter of *chaswei*, sweet barbecued pork cut into coin-sized slices, and then to a whole assortment of what I've always called finger goodies—thin-skinned pastries filled with chopped pork, beef, shrimp, and unknown stuffings that my mother used to describe as "nutritious things."

Eating is not a gracious event here. It's as though everybody had been starving. They push large forkfuls into their mouths, jab at more pieces of pork, one right after the other. They are not like the ladies of Kweilin, who I always imagined savored their food with a certain detached delicacy.

And then, almost as quickly as they started, the men get up and leave the table. As if on cue, the women peck at last morsels and then carry plates and bowls to the kitchen and dump them in the sink. The women take turns washing their hands, scrubbing them vigorously. Who started this ritual? I too put my plate in the sink and wash my hands. The women are talking about the Jongs' China trip, then they move toward a room in the back of the apartment. We pass another room, what used to be the bedroom shared by the four Hsu sons. The bunk beds with their scuffed, splintery ladders are still there. The Joy Luck uncles are already seated at the card table. Uncle George is dealing out cards, fast, as though he learned this technique in a casino. My father is passing out Pall Mall cigarettes, with one already dangling from his lips.

And then we get to the room in the back, which was once shared by the three Hsu girls. We were all childhood friends. And now they've all grown and married and I'm here to play in their room again. Except for the smell of camphor, it feels the same—as if Rose, Ruth, and Janice might soon walk in with their hair rolled up in big orange-juice cans and plop down on their identical narrow beds. The white chenille bedspreads are so worn they are almost translucent. Rose and I used to pluck the nubs out while talking about our boy problems. Everything is the same, except now a mahogany-colored mah jong table sits in the center. And next to it is a floor lamp, a long black pole with three oval spotlights attached like the broad leaves of a rubber plant.

Nobody says to me, "Sit here, this is where your mother used to sit." But I can tell even before everyone sits down. The chair closest to the door has an emptiness to it. But the feeling doesn't really have to do with the chair. It's her place on the table. Without having anyone tell me, I know her corner on the table was the East.

The East is where things begin, my mother once told me, the direction from which the sun rises, where the wind comes from.

Auntie An-mei, who is sitting on my left, spills the tiles onto the green felt tabletop and then says to me, "Now we wash tiles." We swirl them with our hands in a circular motion. They make a cool swishing sound as they bump into one another.

"Do you win like your mother?" asks Auntie Lin across from me. She is not smiling.

"I only played a little in college with some Jewish friends."

"Annh! Jewish mah jong," she says in disgusted tones. "Not the same thing." This is what my mother used to say, although she could never explain exactly why.

"Maybe I shouldn't play tonight. I'll just watch," I offer.

Auntie Lin looks exasperated, as though I were a simple child: "How can we play with just three people? Like a table with three legs, no balance. When Auntie Ying's husband died, she asked her brother to join. Your father asked you. So it's decided."

"What's the difference between Jewish and Chinese mah jong?" I once asked my mother. I couldn't tell by her answer if the games were different or just her attitude toward Chinese and Jewish people.

"Entirely different kind of playing," she said in her English explanation voice. "Jewish mah jong, they watch only for their own tile, play only with their eyes."

Then she switched to Chinese: "Chinese mah jong, you must play using your head, very tricky. You must watch what everybody else throws away and keep that in your head as well. And if nobody plays well, then the game becomes like Jewish mah jong. Why play? There's no strategy. You're just watching people make mistakes."

These kinds of explanations made me feel my mother and I

spoke two different languages, which we did. I talked to her in English, she answered back in Chinese.

"So what's the difference between Chinese and Jewish mah jong?" I ask Auntie Lin.

"Aii-ya," she exclaims in a mock scolding voice. "Your mother did not teach you anything?"

Auntie Ying pats my hand. "You a smart girl. You watch us, do the same. Help us stack the tiles and make four walls."

I follow Auntie Ying, but mostly I watch Auntie Lin. She is the fastest, which means I can almost keep up with the others by watching what she does first. Auntie Ying throws the dice and I'm told that Auntie Lin has become the East wind. I've become the North wind, the last hand to play. Auntie Ying is the South and Auntie An-mei is the West. And then we start taking tiles, throwing the dice, counting back on the wall to the right number of spots where our chosen tiles lie. I rearrange my tiles, sequences of bamboo and balls, doubles of colored number tiles, odd tiles that do not fit anywhere.

"Your mother was the best, like a pro," says Auntie An-mei while slowly sorting her tiles, considering each piece carefully.

Now we begin to play, looking at our hands, casting tiles, picking up others at an easy, comfortable pace. The Joy Luck aunties begin to make small talk, not really listening to each other. They speak in their special language, half in broken English, half in their own Chinese dialect. Auntie Ying mentions she bought yarn at half price, somewhere out in the avenues. Auntie An-mei brags about a sweater she made for her daughter Ruth's new baby. "She thought it was store-bought," she says proudly.

Auntie Lin explains how mad she got at a store clerk who refused to let her return a skirt with a broken zipper. "I was *chiszle*," she says, still fuming, "mad to death."

"But Lindo, you are still with us. You didn't die," teases Auntie Ying, and then as she laughs Auntie Lin says *'Pung!'* and *'Mah jong!'* and then spreads her tiles out, laughing back at Auntie Ying while counting up her points. We start washing tiles again and it grows quiet. I'm getting bored and sleepy.

"Oh, I have a story," says Auntie Ying loudly, startling everybody. Auntie Ying has always been the weird auntie, someone lost in her own world. My mother used to say, "Auntie Ying is not hard of hearing. She is hard of listening."

"Police arrested Mrs. Emerson's son last weekend," Auntie Ying says in a way that sounds as if she were proud to be the first with this big news. "Mrs. Chan told me at church. Too many TV set found in his car."

Auntie Lin quickly says, "Aii-ya, Mrs. Emerson good lady," meaning Mrs. Emerson didn't deserve such a terrible son. But now I see this is also said for the benefit of Auntie An-mei, whose own youngest son was arrested two years ago for selling stolen car stereos. Auntie An-mei is rubbing her tile carefully before discarding it. She looks pained.

"Everybody has TVs in China now," says Auntie Lin, changing the subject. "Our family there all has TV sets—not just black-and-white, but color and remote! They have everything. So when we asked them what we should buy them, they said nothing, it was enough that we would come to visit them. But we bought them different things anyway, VCR and Sony Walkman for the kids. They said, No, don't give it to us, but I think they liked it."

Poor Auntie An-mei rubs her tiles ever harder. I remember my mother telling me about the Hsus' trip to China three years ago. Auntie An-mei had saved two thousand dollars, all to spend on her brother's family. She had shown my mother the insides of her heavy suitcases. One was crammed with See's Nuts & Chews, M & M's, candy-coated cashews, instant hot chocolate with miniature marshmallows. My mother told me the other bag contained the most ridiculous clothes, all new: bright California-style beachwear, baseball caps, cotton pants with elastic waists, bomber jackets, Stanford sweatshirts, crew socks.

My mother had told her, "Who wants those useless things? They just want money." But Auntie An-mei said her brother was so poor and they were so rich by comparison. So she ignored my mother's advice and took the heavy bags and their two thousand dollars to China. And when their China tour finally arrived in Hangzhou, the whole family from Ningbo was there to meet them. It wasn't just Auntie An-mei's little brother, but also his wife's stepbrothers and stepsisters, and a distant cousin, and that cousin's husband and that husband's uncle. They had all brought their mothers-in-law and children, and even their village friends who were not lucky enough to have overseas Chinese relatives to show off.

As my mother told it, "Auntie An-mei had cried before she left for China, thinking she would make her brother very rich and happy by communist standards. But when she got home, she cried to me that everyone had a palm out and she was the only one who left with an empty hand."

My mother confirmed her suspicions. Nobody wanted the sweatshirts, those useless clothes. The M & M's were thrown in the air, gone. And when the suitcases were emptied, the relatives asked what else the Hsus had brought.

Auntie An-mei and Uncle George were shaken down, not just for two thousand dollars' worth of TVs and refrigerators but also for a night's lodging for twenty-six people in the Overlooking the Lake Hotel, for three banquet tables at a restaurant that catered to rich foreigners, for three special gifts for each relative, and finally, for a loan of five thousand *yuan* in foreign exchange to a cousin's so-called uncle who wanted to buy a motorcycle but who later disappeared for good along with the money. When the train pulled out of Hangzhou the next day, the Hsus found themselves depleted of some nine thousand dollars' worth of goodwill. Months later, after an inspiring Christmastime service at the First Chinese Baptist Church, Auntie An-mei tried to recoup her loss by saying it truly was more blessed to give than to receive, and my mother agreed, her longtime friend had blessings for at least several lifetimes.

Listening now to Auntie Lin bragging about the virtues of her family in China, I realize that Auntie Lin is oblivious to Auntie An-mei's pain. Is Auntie Lin being mean, or is it that my mother never told anybody but me the shameful story of Auntie An-mei's greedy family?

"So, Jing-mei, you go to school now?" says Auntie Lin.

"Her name is June. They all go by their American names," says Auntie Ying.

"That's okay," I say, and I really mean it. In fact, it's even becoming fashionable for American-born Chinese to use their Chinese names.

"I'm not in school anymore, though," I say. "That was more than ten years ago."

Auntie Lin's eyebrows arch. "Maybe I'm thinking of someone else daughter," she says, but I know right away she's lying. I know my mother probably told her I was going back to school to finish my degree, because somewhere back, maybe just six months ago, we were again having this argument about my being a failure, a "college drop-off," about my going back to finish.

Once again I had told my mother what she wanted to hear: "You're right. I'll look into it."

I had always assumed we had an unspoken understanding about these things: that she didn't really mean I was a failure, and I really meant I would try to respect her opinions more. But listening to Auntie Lin tonight reminds me once again: My mother and I never really understood one another. We translated each other's meanings and I seemed to hear less than what was said, while my mother heard more. No doubt she told Auntie Lin I was going back to school to get a doctorate.

Auntie Lin and my mother were both best friends and arch enemies who spent a lifetime comparing their children. I was one month older than Waverly Jong, Auntie Lin's prized daughter. From the time we were babies, our mothers compared the creases in our belly buttons, how shapely our earlobes were, how fast we healed when we scraped our knees, how thick and dark our hair, how many shoes we wore out in one year, and later, how smart Waverly was at playing chess, how many trophies she had won last month, how many newspapers had printed her name, how many cities she had visited.

I know my mother resented listening to Auntie Lin talk about Waverly when she had nothing to come back with. At first my mother tried to cultivate some hidden genius in me. She did housework for an old retired piano teacher down the hall who gave me lessons and free use of a piano to practice on in exchange. When I failed to become a concert pianist, or even an accompanist for the church youth choir, she finally explained that I was late-blooming, like Einstein, who everyone thought was retarded until he discovered a bomb.

Now it is Auntie Ying who wins this hand of mah jong, so we count points and begin again.

"Did you know Lena move to Woodside?" asks Auntie Ying with obvious pride, looking down at the tiles, talking to no one in particular. She quickly erases her smile and tries for some modesty. "Of course, it's not best house in neighborhood, not million-dollar house, not yet. But it's good investment. Better than paying rent. Better than somebody putting you under their thumb to rub you out."

So now I know Auntie Ying's daughter, Lena, told her about my being evicted from my apartment on lower Russian Hill. Even though Lena and I are still friends, we have grown naturally cautious about telling each other too much. Still, what little we say to one another often comes back in another guise. It's the same old game, everybody talking in circles.

"It's getting late," I say after we finish the round. I start to stand up, but Auntie Lin pushes me back down into the chair.

"Stay, stay. We talk awhile, get to know you again," she says. "Been a long time."

I know this is a polite gesture on the Joy Luck aunties' part— a protest when actually they are just as eager to see me go as I am to leave. "No, I really must go now, thank you, thank you," I say, glad I remembered how the pretense goes.

"But you must stay! We have something important to tell you, from your mother," Auntie Ying blurts out in her too-loud voice. The others look uncomfortable, as if this were not how they intended to break some sort of bad news to me.

I sit down. Auntie An-mei leaves the room quickly and returns with a bowl of peanuts, then quietly shuts the door. Everybody is quiet, as if nobody knew where to begin.

It is Auntie Ying who finally speaks. "I think your mother die with an important thought on her mind," she says in halting

English. And then she begins to speak in Chinese, calmly, softly.

"Your mother was a very strong woman, a good mother. She loved you very much, more than her own life. And that's why you can understand why a mother like this could never forget her other daughters. She knew they were alive, and before she died she wanted to find her daughters in China."

The babies in Kweilin, I think. I was not those babies. The babies in a sling on her shoulder. Her other daughters. And now I feel as if I were in Kweilin amidst the bombing and I can see these babies lying on the side of the road, their red thumbs popped out of their mouths, screaming to be reclaimed. Somebody took them away. They're safe. And now my mother's left me forever, gone back to China to get these babies. I can barely hear Auntie Ying's voice.

"She had searched for years, written letters back and forth," says Auntie Ying. "And last year she got an address. She was going to tell your father soon. Aii-ya, what a shame. A lifetime of waiting."

Auntie An-mei interrupts with an excited voice: "So your aunties and I, we wrote to this address," she says. "We say that a certain party, your mother, want to meet another certain party. And this party write back to us. They are your sisters, Jing-mei."

My sisters, I repeat to myself, saying these two words together for the first time.

Auntie An-mei is holding a sheet of paper as thin as wrapping tissue. In perfectly straight vertical rows I see Chinese characters written in blue fountain-pen ink. A word is smudged. A tear? I take the letter with shaking hands, marveling at how smart my sisters must be to be able to read and write Chinese.

The aunties are all smiling at me, as though I had been a dying person who has now miraculously recovered. Auntie Ying is handing me another envelope. Inside is a check made out to June Woo for $1,200. I can't believe it.

"My sisters are sending *me* money?" I ask.

"No, no," says Auntie Lin with her mock exasperated voice. "Every year we save our mah jong winnings for big banquet at fancy restaurant. Most times your mother win, so most is her money. We add just a little, so you can go Hong Kong, take a train to Shanghai, see your sisters. Besides, we all getting too rich, too fat." she pats her stomach for proof.

"See my sisters," I say numbly. I am awed by this prospect, trying to imagine what I would see. And I am embarrassed by the end-of-the-year-banquet lie my aunties have told to mask their generosity. I am crying now, sobbing and laughing at the same time, seeing but not understanding this loyalty to my mother.

"You must see your sisters and tell them about your mother's death," says Auntie Ying. "But most important, you must tell them about her life. The mother they did not know, they must now know."

"See my sisters, tell them about my mother," I say, nodding. "What will I say? What can I tell them about my mother? I don't know anything. She was my mother."

The aunties are looking at me as if I had become crazy right before their eyes.

"Not know your own mother?" cries Auntie An-mei with disbelief. "How can you say? Your mother is in your bones!"

"Tell them stories of your family here. How she became success," offers Auntie Lin.

"Tell them stories she told you, lessons she taught, what you know about her mind that has become your mind," says Auntie Ying. "You mother very smart lady."

I hear more choruses of "Tell them, tell them" as each Auntie frantically tries to think what should be passed on.

"Her kindness."

"Her smartness."

"Her dutiful nature to family."

"Her hopes, things that matter to her."

"The excellent dishes she cooked."

"Imagine, a daughter not knowing her own mother!"

And then it occurs to me. They are frightened. In me, they see their own daughters, just as ignorant, just as unmindful of all the truths and hopes they have brought to America. They see daughters who grow impatient when their mothers talk in Chinese, who think they are stupid when they explain things in fractured English. They see that joy and luck do not mean the same to their daughters, that to these closed American-born minds "joy luck" is not a word, it does not exist. They see daughters who will bear grandchildren born without any connecting hope passed from generation to generation.

"I will tell them everything," I say simply, and the aunties look at me with doubtful faces.

"I will remember everything about her and tell them," I say more firmly. And gradually, one by one, they smile and pat my hand. They still look troubled, as if something were out of balance. But they also look hopeful that what I say will become true. What more can they ask? What more can I promise?

They go back to eating their soft boiled peanuts, saying stories among themselves. They are young girls again, dreaming of good times in the past and good times yet to come. A brother from Ningbo who makes his sister cry with joy when he returns nine thousand dollars plus interest. A youngest son whose stereo and TV repair business is so good he sends leftovers to China. A daughter whose babies are able to swim like fish in a fancy pool in Woodside. Such good stories. The best. They are the lucky ones.

And I am sitting at my mother's place at the mah jong table, on the East, where things begin.

AN-MEI HSU

Scar

When I was a young girl in China, my grandmother told me my mother was a ghost. This did not mean my mother was dead. In those days, a ghost was anything we were forbidden to talk about. So I knew Popo wanted me to forget my mother on purpose, and this is how I came to remember nothing of her. The life that I knew began in the large house in Ningpo with the cold hallways and tall stairs. This was my uncle and auntie's family house, where I lived with Popo and my little brother.

But I often heard stories of a ghost who tried to take children away, especially strong-willed little girls who were disobedient. Many times Popo said aloud to all who could hear that my brother and I had fallen out of the bowels of a stupid goose, two eggs that nobody wanted, not even good enough to crack over rice porridge. She said this so that the ghosts would not steal us away. So you see, to Popo we were also very precious.

All my life, Popo scared me. I became even more scared when she grew sick. This was in 1923, when I was nine years old. Popo had swollen up like an overripe squash, so full her flesh had gone soft and rotten with a bad smell. She would call me into her room with the terrible stink and tell me stories. "An-mei," she said, calling me by my school name. "Listen carefully." She told me stories I could not understand.

One was about a greedy girl whose belly grew fatter and fatter.

This girl poisoned herself after refusing to say whose child she carried. When the monks cut open her body, they found inside a large white winter melon.

"If you are greedy, what is inside you is what makes you always hungry," said Popo.

Another time, Popo told me about a girl who refused to listen to her elders. One day this bad girl shook her head so vigorously to refuse her auntie's simple request that a little white ball fell from her ear and out poured all her brains, as clear as chicken broth.

"Your own thoughts are so busy swimming inside that everything else gets pushed out," Popo told me.

Right before Popo became so sick she could no longer speak, she pulled me close and talked to me about my mother. "Never say her name," she warned. "To say her name is to spit on your father's grave."

The only father I knew was a big painting that hung in the main hall. He was a large, unsmiling man, unhappy to be so still on the wall. His restless eyes followed me around the house. Even from my room at the end of the hall, I could see my father's watching eyes. Popo said he watched me for any signs of disrespect. So sometimes, when I had thrown pebbles at other children at school, or had lost a book through carelessness, I would quickly walk by my father with a know-nothing look and hide in a corner of my room where he could not see my face.

I felt our house was so unhappy, but my little brother did not seem to think so. He rode his bicycle through the courtyard, chasing chickens and other children, laughing over which ones shrieked the loudest. Inside the quiet house, he jumped up and down on Uncle and Auntie's best feather sofas when they were away visiting village friends.

But even my brother's happiness went away. One hot summer day when Popo was already very sick, we stood outside watching a village funeral procession marching by our courtyard. Just as it passed our gate, the heavy framed picture of the dead man toppled from its stand and fell to the dusty ground. An old lady screamed and fainted. My brother laughed and Auntie slapped him.

My auntie, who had a very bad temper with children, told him he had no *shou*, no respect for ancestors or family, just like our mother. Auntie had a tongue like hungry scissors eating silk cloth. So when my brother gave her a sour look, Auntie said our mother was so thoughtless she had fled north in a big hurry, without taking the dowry furniture from her marriage to my father, without bringing her ten pairs of silver chopsticks, without paying respect to my father's grave and those of our ancestors. When my brother accused Auntie of frightening our mother away, Auntie shouted that our mother had married a man named Wu Tsing who already had a wife, two concubines, and other bad children.

And when my brother shouted that Auntie was a talking chicken without a head, she pushed my brother against the gate and spat on his face.

"You throw strong words at me, but you are nothing," Auntie said. "You are the son of a mother who has so little respect she has become *ni*, a traitor to our ancestors. She is so beneath others that even the devil must look down to see her."

That is when I began to understand the stories Popo taught me, the lessons I had to learn for my mother. "When you lose your face, An-mei," Popo often said, "it is like dropping your necklace down a well. The only way you can get it back is to fall in after it."

Now I could imagine my mother, a thoughtless woman who laughed and shook her head, who dipped her chopsticks many times to eat another piece of sweet fruit, happy to be free of Popo, her unhappy husband on the wall, and her two disobedient children. I felt unlucky that she was my mother and unlucky that she had left us. These were the thoughts I had while hiding in the corner of my room where my father could not watch me.

I was sitting at the top of the stairs when she arrived. I knew it was my mother even though I had not seen her in all my memory. She stood just inside the doorway so that her face became a dark shadow. She was much taller than my auntie, almost as tall as my uncle. She looked strange, too, like the missionary ladies at our school who were insolent and bossy in their too-tall shoes, foreign clothes, and short hair.

My auntie quickly looked away and did not call her by name or offer her tea. An old servant hurried away with a displeased look. I tried to keep very still, but my heart felt like crickets scratching to get out of a cage. My mother must have heard, because she looked up. And when she did, I saw my own face looking back at me. Eyes that stayed wide open and saw too much.

In Popo's room my auntie protested, "Too late, too late," as my mother approached the bed. But this did not stop my mother.

"Come back, stay here," murmured my mother to Popo. "*Nuyer* is here. Your daughter is back." Popo's eyes were open, but now her mind ran in many different directions, not staying long enough to see anything. If Popo's mind had been clear she would have raised her two arms and flung my mother out of the room.

I watched my mother, seeing her for the first time, this pretty woman with her white skin and oval face, not too round like Auntie's or sharp like Popo's. I saw that she had a long white neck, just like the goose that had laid me. That she seemed to float back and forth like a ghost, dipping cool cloths to lay on Popo's bloated face. As she peered into Popo's eyes, she clucked soft worried sounds. I watched her carefully, yet it was her voice that confused me, a familiar sound from a forgotten dream.

When I returned to my room later that afternoon, she was there, standing tall. And because I remember Popo told me not to speak her name, I stood there, mute. She took my hand and led me to the settee. And then she also sat down as though we had done this every day.

My mother began to loosen my braids and brush my hair with long sweeping strokes.

"An-mei, you have been a good daughter?" she asked, smiling a secret look.

I looked at her with my know-nothing face, but inside I was trembling. I was the girl whose belly held a colorless winter melon.

"An-mei, you know who I am," she said with a small scold

45

in her voice. This time I did not look for fear my head would burst and my brains would dribble out of my ears.

She stopped brushing. And then I could feel her long smooth fingers rubbing and searching under my chin, finding the spot that was my smooth-neck scar. As she rubbed this spot, I became very still. It was as though she were rubbing the memory back into my skin. And then her hand dropped and she began to cry, wrapping her hands around her own neck. She cried with a wailing voice that was so sad. And then I remembered the dream with my mother's voice.

I was four years old. My chin was just above the dinner table, and I could see my baby brother sitting on Popo's lap, crying with an angry face. I could hear voices praising a steaming dark soup brought to the table, voices murmuring politely, *"Ching! Ching!"*—Please, eat!

And then the talking stopped. My uncle rose from his chair. Everyone turned to look at the door, where a tall woman stood. I was the only one who spoke.

"Ma," I had cried, rushing off my chair, but my auntie slapped my face and pushed me back down. Now everyone was standing up and shouting, and I heard my mother's voice crying, "An-mei! An-mei!" Above this noise, Popo's shrill voice spoke.

"Who is this ghost? Not an honored widow. Just a number-three concubine. If you take your daughter, she will become like you. No face. Never able to lift up her head."

Still my mother shouted for me to come. I remember her voice so clearly now. An-mei! An-mei! I could see my mother's face across the table. Between us stood the soup pot on its heavy chimney-pot stand—rocking slowly, back and forth. And then with one shout this dark boiling soup spilled forward and fell all over my neck. It was as though everyone's anger were pouring all over me.

This was the kind of pain so terrible that a little child should never remember it. But it is still in my skin's memory. I cried out loud only a little, because soon my flesh began to burst inside and out and cut off my breathing air.

I could not speak because of this terrible choking feeling. I could not see because of all the tears that poured out to wash away the pain. But I could hear my mother's crying voice. Popo and Auntie were shouting. And then my mother's voice went away.

Later that night Popo's voice came to me.

"An-mei, listen carefully." Her voice had the same scolding tone she used when I ran up and down the hallway. "An-mei, we have made your dying clothes and shoes for you. They are all white cotton."

I listened, scared.

"An-mei," she murmured, now more gently. "Your dying clothes are very plain. They are not fancy, because you are still a child. If you die, you will have a short life and you will still owe your family a debt. Your funeral will be very small. Our mourning time for you will be very short."

And then Popo said something that was worse than the burning on my neck.

"Even your mother has used up her tears and left. If you do not get well soon, she will forget you."

Popo was very smart. I came hurrying back from the other world to find my mother.

Every night I cried so that both my eyes and my neck burned. Next to my bed sat Popo. She would pour cool water over my neck from the hollowed cup of a large grapefruit. She would pour and pour until my breathing became soft and I could fall asleep. In the morning, Popo would use her sharp fingernails like tweezers and peel off the dead membranes.

In two years' time, my scar became pale and shiny and I had no memory of my mother. That is the way it is with a wound. The wound begins to close in on itself, to protect what is hurting so much. And once it is closed, you no longer see what is underneath, what started the pain.

I worshipped this mother from my dream. But the woman standing by Popo's bed was not the mother of my memory. Yet I came to love this mother as well. Not because she came to me and begged me to forgive her. She did not. She did not need to explain that Popo chased her out of the house when I was dying. This I knew. She did not need to tell me she married Wu Tsing to exchange one unhappiness for another. I knew this as well.

Here is how I came to love my mother. How I saw in her my own true nature. What was beneath my skin. Inside my bones.

It was late at night when I went to Popo's room. My auntie said it was Popo's dying time and I must show respect. I put on a clean dress and stood between my auntie and uncle at the foot of Popo's bed. I cried a little, not too loud.

I saw my mother on the other side of the room. Quiet and sad. She was cooking a soup, pouring herbs and medicines into the steaming pot. And then I saw her pull up her sleeve and pull out a sharp knife. She put this knife on the softest part of her arm. I tried to close my eyes, but could not.

And then my mother cut a piece of meat from her arm. Tears poured from her face and blood spilled to the floor.

My mother took her flesh and put it in the soup. She cooked magic in the ancient tradition to try to cure her mother this one last time. She opened Popo's mouth, already too tight from trying to keep her spirit in. She fed her this soup, but that night Popo flew away with her illness.

Even though I was young, I could see the pain of the flesh and the worth of the pain.

This is how a daughter honors her mother. It is *shou* so deep it is in your bones. The pain of the flesh is nothing. The pain you must forget. Because sometimes that is the only way to remember what is in your bones. You must peel off your skin, and that of your mother, and her mother before her. Until there is nothing. No scar, no skin, no flesh.

LINDO JONG

The Red Candle

I once sacrificed my life to keep my parents' promise. This means nothing to you, because to you promises mean nothing. A daughter can promise to come to dinner, but if she has a headache, if she has a traffic jam, if she wants to watch a favorite movie on TV, she no longer has a promise.

I watched this same movie when you did not come. The American soldier promises to come back and marry the girl. She is crying with a genuine feeling and he says, "Promise! Promise! Honey-sweetheart, my promise is as good as gold." Then he pushes her onto the bed. But he doesn't come back. His gold is like yours, it is only fourteen carats.

To Chinese people, fourteen carats isn't real gold. Feel my bracelets. They must be twenty-four carats, pure inside and out.

It's too late to change you, but I'm telling you this because I worry about your baby. I worry that someday she will say, "Thank you, Grandmother, for the gold bracelet. I'll never forget you." But later, she will forget her promise. She will forget she had a grandmother.

In this same war movie, the American soldier goes home and he falls to his knees asking another girl to marry him. And the girl's eyes run back and forth, so shy, as if she had never considered this before. And suddenly!—her eyes look straight down and she knows now she loves him, so much she wants to cry. "Yes," she says at last, and they marry forever.

This was not my case. Instead, the village matchmaker came to my family when I was just two years old. No, nobody told me this, I remember it all. It was summertime, very hot and dusty outside, and I could hear cicadas crying in the yard. We were under some trees in our orchard. The servants and my brothers were picking pears high above me. And I was sitting in my mother's hot sticky arms. I was waving my hand this way and that, because in front of me floated a small bird with horns and colorful paper-thin wings. And then the paper bird flew away and in front of me were two ladies. I remember them because one lady made watery "shrrhh, shrrhh" sounds. When I was older, I came to recognize this as a Peking accent, which sounds quite strange to Taiyuan people's ears.

The two ladies were looking at my face without talking. The lady with the watery voice had a painted face that was melting. The other lady had the dry face of an old tree trunk. She looked first at me, then at the painted lady.

Of course, now I know the tree-trunk lady was the old village matchmaker, and the other was Huang Taitai, the mother of the boy I would be forced to marry. No, it's not true what some Chinese say about girl babies being worthless. It depends on what kind of girl baby you are. In my case, people could see my value. I looked and smelled like a precious buncake, sweet with a good clean color.

The matchmaker bragged about me: "An earth horse for an earth sheep. This is the best marriage combination." She patted my arm and I pushed her hand away. Huang Taitai whispered in her shrrhh-shrrhh voice that perhaps I had an unusually bad *pichi*, a bad temper. But the matchmaker laughed and said, "Not so, not so. She is a strong horse. She will grow up to be a hard worker who serves you well in your old age."

And this is when Huang Taitai looked down at me with a cloudy face as though she could penetrate my thoughts and see my future intentions. I will never forget her look. Her eyes opened wide, she searched my face carefully and then she smiled. I could see a large gold tooth staring at me like the blinding sun and then the rest of her teeth opened wide as if she were going to swallow me down in one piece.

This is how I became betrothed to Huang Taitai's son, who I later discovered was just a baby, one year younger than I. His name was Tyan-yu—*tyan* for "sky," because he was so important, and *yu*, meaning "leftovers," because when he was born his father was very sick and his family thought he might die. Tyan-yu would be the leftover of his father's spirit. But his father lived and his grandmother was scared the ghosts would turn their attention to this baby boy and take him instead. So they watched him carefully, made all his decisions, and he became very spoiled.

But even if I had known I was getting such a bad husband, I had no choice, now or later. That was how backward families in the country were. We were always the last to give up stupid old-fashioned customs. In other cities already, a man could choose his own wife, with his parents' permission of course. But we were cut off from this type of new thought. You never heard if ideas were better in another city, only if they were worse. We were told stories of sons who were so influenced by bad wives that they threw their old, crying parents out into the street. So, Taiyuanese mothers continued to choose their daughters-in-law, ones who would raise proper sons, care for the old people, and faithfully sweep the family burial grounds long after the old ladies had gone to their graves.

Because I was promised to the Huangs' son for marriage, my own family began treating me as if I belonged to somebody else. My mother would say to me when the rice bowl went up to my face too many times, "Look how much Huang Taitai's daughter can eat."

My mother did not treat me this way because she didn't love me. She would say this biting back her tongue, so she wouldn't wish for something that was no longer hers.

I was actually a very obedient child, but sometimes I had a sour look on my face—only because I was hot or tired or very ill. This is when my mother would say, "Such an ugly face. The Huangs won't want you and our whole family will be disgraced." And I would cry more to make my face uglier.

"It's no use," my mother would say. "We have made a contract. It cannot be broken." And I would cry even harder.

I didn't see my future husband until I was eight or nine. The world that I knew was our family compound in the village outside of Taiyuan. My family lived in a modest two-story house with a smaller house in the same compound, which was really just two side-by-side rooms for our cook, an everyday servant, and their families. Our house sat on a little hill. We called this hill Three Steps to Heaven, but it was really just centuries of hardened layers of mud washed up by the Fen River. On the east wall of our compound was the river, which my father said liked to swallow little children. He said it had once swallowed the whole town of Taiyuan. The river ran brown in the summer. In the winter, the river was blue-green in the narrow fast-moving spots. In the wider places, it was frozen still, white with cold.

Oh, I can remember the new year when my family went to the river and caught many fish—giant slippery creatures plucked while they were still sleeping in their frozen riverbeds—so fresh that even after they were gutted they would dance on their tails when thrown into the hot pan.

That was also the year I first saw my husband as a little boy. When the firecrackers went off, he cried loud—wah!—with a big open mouth even though he was not a baby.

Later I would see him at red-egg ceremonies when one-month-old boy babies were given their real names. He would sit on his grandmother's old knees, almost cracking them with his weight. And he would refuse to eat everything offered to him, always turning his nose away as though someone were offering him a stinky pickle and not a sweet cake.

So I didn't have instant love for my future husband the way you see on television today. I thought of this boy more like a troublesome cousin. I learned to be polite to the Huangs and especially to Huang Taitai. My mother would push me toward Huang Taitai and say, "What do you say to your mother?" And

I would be confused, not knowing which mother she meant. So I would turn to my real mother and say, "Excuse me, Ma," and then I would turn to Huang Taitai and present her with a little goodie to eat, saying, "For you, Mother." I remember it was once a lump of *syaumei*, a little dumpling I loved to eat. My mother told Huang Taitai I had made this dumpling especially for her, even though I had only poked its steamy sides with my finger when the cook poured it onto the serving plate.

My life changed completely when I was twelve, the summer the heavy rains came. The Fen River which ran through the middle of my family's land flooded the plains. It destroyed all the wheat my family had planted that year and made the land useless for years to come. Even our house on top of the little hill became unlivable. When we came down from the second story, we saw the floors and furniture were covered with sticky mud. The courtyards were littered with uprooted trees, broken bits of walls, and dead chickens. We were so poor in all this mess.

You couldn't go to an insurance company back then and say, Somebody did this damage, pay me a million dollars. In those days, you were unlucky if you had exhausted your own possibilities. My father said we had no choice but to move the family to Wushi, to the south near Shanghai, where my mother's brother owned a small flour mill. My father explained that the whole family, except for me, would leave immediately. I was twelve years old, old enough to separate from my family and live with the Huangs.

The roads were so muddy and filled with giant potholes that no truck was willing to come to the house. All the heavy furniture and bedding had to be left behind, and these were promised to the Huangs as my dowry. In this way, my family was quite practical. The dowry was enough, more than enough, said my father. But he could not stop my mother from giving me her *chang*, a necklace made out of a tablet of red jade. When she put it around my neck, she acted very stern, so I knew she was very sad. "Obey your family. Do not disgrace us," she said. "Act happy when you arrive. Really, you're very lucky."

The Huangs' house also sat next to the river. While our house had been flooded, their house was untouched. This is because their house sat higher up in the valley. And this was the first time I realized the Huangs had a much better position than my family. They looked down on us, which made me understand why Huang Taitai and Tyan-yu had such long noses.

When I passed under the Huangs' stone-and-wood gateway arch, I saw a large courtyard with three or four rows of small, low buildings. Some were for storing supplies, others for servants and their families. Behind these modest buildings stood the main house.

I walked closer and stared at the house that would be my home for the rest of my life. The house had been in the family for many generations. It was not really so old or remarkable, but I could see it had grown up along with the family. There were four stories, one for each generation: great-grandparents, grand-parents, parents, and children. The house had a confused look. It had been hastily built and then rooms and floors and wings and decorations had been added on in every which manner, reflecting too many opinions. The first level was built of river rocks held together by straw-filled mud. The second and third levels were made of smooth bricks with an exposed walkway to give it the look of a palace tower. And the top level had gray slab walls topped with a red tile roof. To make the house seem important, there were two large round pillars holding up a ver-anda entrance to the front door. These pillars were painted red, as were the wooden window borders. Someone, probably Huang Taitai, had added imperial dragon heads at the corners of the roof.

Inside, the house held a different kind of pretense. The only nice room was a parlor on the first floor, which the Huangs used to receive guests. This room contained tables and chairs carved out of red lacquer, fine pillows embroidered with the Huang family name in the ancient style, and many precious things that gave the look of wealth and old prestige. The rest of the house was plain and uncomfortable and noisy with the complaints of twenty relatives. I think with each generation the house had grown smaller inside, more crowded. Each room had been cut in half to make two.

No big celebration was held when I arrived. Huang Taitai didn't have red banners greeting me in the fancy room on the first floor. Tyan-yu was not there to greet me. Instead, Huan Taitai hurried me upstairs to the second floor and into the kitchen, which was a place where family children didn't usually go. This was a place for cooks and servants. So I knew my standing.

That first day, I stood in my best padded dress at the low wooden table and began to chop vegetables. I could not keep my hands steady. I missed my family and my stomach felt bad, knowing I had finally arrived where my life said I belonged. But I was also determined to honor my parents' words, so Huang Taitai could never accuse my mother of losing face. She would not win that from our family.

As I was thinking this I saw an old servant woman stooping over the same low table gutting a fish, looking at me from the corner of her eye. I was crying and I was afraid she would tell Huang Taitai. So I gave a big smile and shouted, "What a lucky girl I am. I'm going to have the best life." And in this quick-thinking way I must have waved my knife too close to her nose because she cried angrily, "*Shemma bende ren!*"—What kind of fool are you? And I knew right away this was a warning, because when I shouted that declaration of happiness, I almost tricked myself into thinking it might come true.

I saw Tyan-yu at the evening meal. I was still a few inches taller than he, but he acted like a big warlord. I knew what kind of husband he would be, because he made special efforts to make me cry. He complained the soup was not hot enough and then spilled the bowl as if it were an accident. He waited until I had sat down to eat and then would demand another bowl of rice. He asked why I had such an unpleasant face when looking at him.

Over the next few years, Huang Taitai instructed the other

servants to teach me how to sew sharp corners on pillowcases and to embroider my future family's name. How can a wife keep her husband's household in order if she has never dirtied her own hands, Huang Taitai used to say as she introduced me to a new task. I don't think Huang Taitai ever soiled her hands, but she was very good at calling out orders and criticism.

"Teach her to wash rice properly so that the water runs clear. Her husband cannot eat muddy rice," she'd say to a cook servant.

Another time, she told a servant to show me how to clean a chamber pot: "Make her put her own nose to the barrel to make sure it's clean." That was how I learned to be an obedient wife. I learned to cook so well that I could smell if the meat stuffing was too salty before I even tasted it. I could sew such small stitches it looked as if the embroidery had been painted on. And even Huang Taitai complained in a pretend manner that she could scarcely throw a dirty blouse on the floor before it was cleaned and on her back once again, causing her to wear the same clothes every day.

After a while I didn't think it was a terrible life, no, not really. After a while, I hurt so much I didn't feel any difference. What was happier than seeing everybody gobble down the shiny mushrooms and bamboo shoots I had helped to prepare that day? What was more satisfying than having Huang Taitai nod and pat my head when I had finished combing her hair one hundred strokes? How much happier could I be after seeing Tyan-yu eat a whole bowl of noodles without once complaining about its taste or my looks? It's like those ladies you see on American TV these days, the ones who are so happy they have washed out a stain so the clothes look better than new.

Can you see how the Huangs almost washed their thinking into my skin? I came to think of Tyan-yu as a god, someone whose opinions were worth much more than my own life. I came to think of Huang Taitai as my real mother, someone I wanted to please, someone I should follow and obey without question.

When I turned sixteen on the lunar new year, Huang Taitai told me she was ready to welcome a grandson by next spring. Even if I had not wanted to marry, where would I go live instead?

Even though I was strong as a horse, how could I run away? The Japanese were in every corner of China.

"The Japanese showed up as uninvited guests," said Tyan-yu's grandmother, "and that's why nobody else came." Huang Taitai had made elaborate plans, but our wedding was very small.

She had asked the entire village and friends and family from other cities as well. In those days, you didn't do RSVP. It was not polite not to come. Huang Taitai didn't think the war would change people's good manners. So the cook and her helpers prepared hundreds of dishes. My family's old furniture had been shined up into an impressive dowry and placed in the front parlor. Huang Taitai had taken care to remove all the water and mud marks. She had even commissioned someone to write felicitous messages on red banners, as if my parents themselves had draped these decorations to congratulate me on my good luck. And she had arranged to rent a red palanquin to carry me from her neighbor's house to the wedding ceremony.

A lot of bad luck fell on our wedding day, even though the matchmaker had chosen a lucky day, the fifteenth day of the eighth moon, when the moon is perfectly round and bigger than any other time of the year. But the week before the moon arrived, the Japanese came. They invaded Shansi province, as well as the provinces bordering us. People were nervous. And the morning of the fifteenth, on the day of the wedding celebration, it began to rain, a very bad sign. When the thunder and lightning began, people confused it with Japanese bombs and would not leave their houses.

I heard later that poor Huang Taitai waited many hours for more people to come, and finally, when she could not wring any more guests out of her hands, she decided to start the ceremony. What could she do? She could not change the war.

I was at the neighbor's house. When they called me to come down and ride the red palanquin, I was sitting at a small dressing table by an open window. I began to cry and thought bitterly about my parents' promise. I wondered why my destiny had been decided, why I should have an unhappy life so someone else could have a happy one. From my seat by the window I could see the Fen River with its muddy brown waters. I thought about throwing my body into this river that had destroyed my family's happiness. A person has very strange thoughts when it seems that life is about to end.

It started to rain again, just a light rain. The people from downstairs called up to me once again to hurry. And my thoughts became more urgent, more strange.

I asked myself, What is true about a person? Would I change in the same way the river changes color but still be the same person? And then I saw the curtains blowing wildly, and outside rain was falling harder, causing everyone to scurry and shout. I smiled. And then I realized it was the first time I could see the power of the wind. I couldn't see the wind itself, but I could see it carried the water that filled the rivers and shaped the countryside. It caused men to yelp and dance.

I wiped my eyes and looked in the mirror. I was surprised at what I saw. I had on a beautiful red dress, but what I saw was even more valuable. I was strong. I was pure. I had genuine thoughts inside that no one could see, that no one could ever take away from me. I was like the wind.

I threw my head back and smiled proudly to myself. And then I draped the large embroidered red scarf over my face and covered these thoughts up. But underneath the scarf I still knew who I was. I made a promise to myself: I would always remember my parents' wishes, but I would never forget myself.

When I arrived at the wedding, I had the red scarf over my face and couldn't see anything in front of me. But when I bent my head forward, I could see out the sides. Very few people had come. I saw the Huangs, the same old complaining relatives now embarrassed by this poor showing, the entertainers with their violins and flutes. And there were a few village people who had been brave enough to come out for a free meal. I even saw servants and their children, who must have been added to make the party look bigger.

Someone took my hands and guided me down a path. I was

like a blind person walking to my fate. But I was no longer scared. I could see what was inside me.

A high official conducted the ceremony and he talked too long about philosophers and models of virtue. Then I heard the matchmaker speak about our birthdates and harmony and fertility. I tipped my veiled head forward and I could see her hands unfolding a red silk scarf and holding up a red candle for everyone to see.

The candle had two ends for lighting. One length had carved gold characters with Tyan-yu's name, the other with mine. The matchmaker lighted both ends and announced, "The marriage has begun." Tyan yanked the scarf off my face and smiled at his friends and family, never even looking at me. He reminded me of a young peacock I once saw that acted as if he had just claimed the entire courtyard by fanning his still-short tail.

I saw the matchmaker place the lighted red candle in a gold holder and then hand it to a nervous-looking servant. This servant was supposed to watch the candle during the banquet and all night to make sure neither end went out. In the morning the matchmaker was supposed to show the result, a little piece of black ash, and then declare, "This candle burned continuously at both ends without going out. This is a marriage that can never be broken."

I still can remember. That candle was a marriage bond that was worth more than a Catholic promise not to divorce. It meant I couldn't divorce and I couldn't ever remarry, even if Tyan-yu died. That red candle was supposed to seal me forever with my husband and his family, no excuses afterward.

And sure enough, the matchmaker made her declaration the next morning and showed she had done her job. But I know what really happened, because I stayed up all night crying about my marriage.

After the banquet, our small wedding party pushed us and half carried us up to the third floor to our small bedroom. People were shouting jokes and pulling boys from underneath the bed.

The matchmaker helped small children pull red eggs that had been hidden between the blankets. The boys who were about Tyan-yu's age made us sit on the bed side by side and everybody made us kiss so our faces would turn red with passion. Fire-crackers exploded on the walkway outside our open window and someone said this was a good excuse for me to jump into my husband's arms.

After everyone left, we sat there side by side without words for many minutes, still listening to the laughing outside. When it grew quiet, Tyan-yu said, "This is my bed. You sleep on the sofa." He threw a pillow and a thin blanket to me. I was so glad! I waited until he fell asleep and then I got up quietly and went outside, down the stairs and into the dark courtyard.

Outside it smelled as if it would soon rain again. I was crying, walking in my bare feet and feeling the wet heat still inside the bricks. Across the courtyard I could see the matchmaker's servant through a yellow-lit open window. She was sitting at a table, looking very sleepy as the red candle burned in its special gold holder. I sat down by a tree to watch my fate being decided for me.

I must have fallen asleep because I remember being startled awake by the sound of loud cracking thunder. That's when I saw the matchmaker's servant running from the room, scared as a chicken about to lose its head. Oh, she was asleep too, I thought, and now she thinks it's the Japanese. I laughed. The whole sky became light and then more thunder came, and she ran out of the courtyard and down the road, going so fast and hard I could see pebbles kicking up behind her. Where does she think she's running to, I wondered, still laughing. And then I saw the red candle flickering just a little with the breeze.

I was not thinking when my legs lifted me up and my feet ran me across the courtyard to the yellow-lit room. But I was hoping—I was praying to Buddha, the goddess of mercy, and the full moon—to make that candle go out. It fluttered a little and the flame bent down low, but still both ends burned strong. My throat filled with so much hope that it finally burst and blew out my husband's end of the candle.

I immediately shivered with fear. I thought a knife would

appear and cut me down dead. Or the sky would open up and blow me away. But nothing happened, and when my senses came back, I walked back to my room with fast guilty steps.

The next morning the matchmaker made her proud declaration in front of Tyan-yu, his parents, and myself. "My job is done," she announced, pouring the remaining black ash onto the red cloth. I saw her servant's shame-faced, mournful look.

I learned to love Tyan-yu, but it is not how you think. From the beginning, I would always become sick thinking he would someday climb on top of me and do his business. Every time I went into our bedroom, my hair would already be standing up. But during the first months, he never touched me. He slept in his bed, I slept on my sofa.

In front of his parents, I was an obedient wife, just as they taught me. I instructed the cook to kill a fresh young chicken every morning and cook it until pure juice came out. I would strain this juice myself into a bowl, never adding any water. I gave this to him for breakfast, murmuring good wishes about his health. And every night I would cook a special tonic soup called *tounau*, which was not only very delicious but has eight ingredients that guarantee long life for mothers. This pleased my mother-in-law very much.

But it was not enough to keep her happy. One morning, Huang Taitai and I were sitting in the same room, working on our embroidery. I was dreaming about my childhood, about a pet frog I once kept named Big Wind. Huang Taitai seemed restless, as if she had an itch in the bottom of her shoe. I heard her huffing and then all of a sudden she stood up from her chair, walked over to me, and slapped my face.

"Bad wife!" she cried. "If you refuse to sleep with my son, I refuse to feed you or clothe you." So that's how I knew what my husband had said to avoid his mother's anger. I was also boiling with anger, but I said nothing, remembering my promise to my parents to be an obedient wife.

That night I sat on Tyan-yu's bed and waited for him to touch me. But he didn't. I was relieved. The next night, I lay straight down on the bed next to him. And still he didn't touch me. So the next night, I took off my gown.

That's when I could see what was underneath Tyan-yu. He was scared and turned his face. He had no desire for me, but it was his fear that made me think he had no desire for any woman. He was like a little boy who had never grown up. After a while I was no longer afraid. I even began to think differently toward Tyan-yu. It was not like the way a wife loves a husband, but more like the way a sister protects a younger brother. I put my gown back on and lay down next to him and rubbed his back. I knew I no longer had to be afraid. I was sleeping with Tyan-yu. He would never touch me and I had a comfortable bed to sleep on.

After more months had passed and my stomach and breasts remained small and flat, Huang Taitai flew into another kind of rage. "My son says he's planted enough seeds for thousands of grandchildren. Where are they? It must be you are doing something wrong." And after that she confined me to the bed so that her grandchildren's seeds would not spill out so easily.

Oh, you think it is so much fun to lie in bed all day, never getting up. But I tell you it was worse than a prison. I think Huang Taitai became a little crazy.

She told the servants to take all sharp things out of the room, thinking scissors and knives were cutting off her next generation. She forbade me from sewing. She said I must concentrate and think of nothing but having babies. And four times a day, a very nice servant girl would come into my room, apologizing the whole time while making me drink a terrible-tasting medicine.

I envied this girl, the way she could walk out the door. Sometimes as I watched her from my window, I would imagine I was that girl, standing in the courtyard, bargaining with the traveling shoe mender, gossiping with other servant girls, scolding a handsome delivery man in her high teasing voice.

One day, after two months had gone by without any results, Huang Taitai called the old matchmaker to the house. The matchmaker examined me closely, looked up my birthdate and the hour of my birth, and then asked Huang Taitai about my nature. Finally, the matchmaker gave her conclusions: "It's clear what has happened. A woman can have sons only if she is deficient in one of the elements. Your daughter-in-law was born with enough wood, fire, water, and earth, and she was deficient in metal, which was a good sign. But when she was married, you loaded her down with gold bracelets and decorations and now she has all the elements, including metal. She's too balanced to have babies."

This turned out to be joyous news for Huang Taitai, for she liked nothing better than to reclaim all her gold and jewelry to help me become fertile. And it was good news for me too. Because after the gold was removed from my body, I felt lighter, more free. They say this is what happens if you lack metal. You begin to think as an independent person. That day I started to think about how I would escape this marriage without breaking my promise to my family.

It was really quite simple. I made the Huangs think it was their idea to get rid of me, that they would be the ones to say the marriage contract was not valid.

I thought about my plan for many days. I observed everyone around me, the thoughts they showed in their faces, and then I was ready. I chose an auspicious day, the third day of the third month. That's the day of the Festival of Pure Brightness. On this day, your thoughts must be clear as you prepare to think about your ancestors. That's the day when everyone goes to the family graves. They bring hoes to clear the weeds and brooms to sweep the stones and they offer dumplings and oranges as spiritual food. Oh, it's not a somber day, more like a picnic, but it has special meaning to someone looking for grandsons.

On the morning of that day, I woke up Tyan-yu and the entire house with my wailing. It took Huang Taitai a long time to come into my room. "What's wrong with her now," she cried from her room. "Go make her be quiet." But finally, after my wailing didn't stop, she rushed into my room, scolding me at the top of her voice.

I was clutching my mouth with one hand and my eyes with

another. My body was writhing as if I were seized by a terrible pain. I was quite convincing, because Huang Taitai drew back and grew small like a scared animal.

"What's wrong, little daughter? Tell me quickly," she cried.

"Oh, it's too terrible to think, too terrible to say," I said between gasps and more wailing.

After enough wailing, I said what was so unthinkable. "I had a dream," I reported. "Our ancestors came to me and said they wanted to see our wedding. So Tyan-yu and I held the same ceremony for our ancestors. We saw the matchmaker light the candle and give it to the servant to watch. Our ancestors were so pleased, so pleased. . . . "

Huang Taitai looked impatient as I began to cry softly again. "But then the servant left the room with our candle and a big wind came and blew the candle out. And our ancestors became very angry. They shouted that the marriage was doomed! They said that Tyan-yu's end of the candle had blown out! Our ancestors said Tyan-yu would die if he stayed in this marriage!"

Tyan-yu's face turned white. But Huang Taitai only frowned. "What a stupid girl to have such bad dreams!" And then she scolded everybody to go back to bed.

"Mother," I called to her in a hoarse whisper. "Please don't leave me! I am afraid! Our ancestors said if the matter is not settled, they would begin the cycle of destruction."

"What is this nonsense!" cried Huang Taitai, turning back toward me. Tyan-yu followed her, wearing his mother's same frowning face. And I knew they were almost caught, two ducks leaning into the pot.

"They knew you would not believe me," I said in a remorseful tone, "because they know I do not want to leave the comforts of my marriage. So our ancestors said they would plant the signs, to show our marriage is now rotting."

"What nonsense from your stupid head," said Huang Taitai, sighing. But she could not resist. "What signs?"

"In my dream, I saw a man with a long beard and a mole on his cheek."

"Tyan-yu's grandfather?" asked Huang Taitai. I nodded, remembering the painting I had observed on the wall.

"He said there are three signs. First, he has drawn a black spot on Tyan-yu's back, and this spot will grow and eat away Tyan-yu's flesh just as it ate away our ancestor's face before he died."

Huang Taitai quickly turned to Tyan-yu and pulled his shirt up. "Ai-ya!" she cried, because there it was, the same black mole, the size of a fingertip, just as I had always seen it these past five months of sleeping as sister and brother.

"And then our ancestor touched my mouth," and I patted my cheek as if it already hurt. "He said my teeth would start to fall out one by one, until I could no longer protest leaving this marriage."

Huang Taitai pried open my mouth and gasped upon seeing the open spot in the back of my mouth where a rotted tooth fell out four years ago.

"And finally, I saw him plant a seed in a servant girl's womb. He said this girl only pretends to come from a bad family. But she is really from imperial blood, and . . . "

I lay my head down on the pillow as if too tired to go on. Huang Taitai pushed my shoulder, "What does he say?"

"He said the servant girl is Tyan-yu's true spiritual wife. And the seed he has planted will grow into Tyan-yu's child."

By mid-morning they had dragged the matchmaker's servant over to our house and extracted her terrible confession.

And after much searching they found the servant girl I liked so much, the one I had watched from my window every day. I had seen her eyes grow bigger and her teasing voice become smaller whenever the handsome delivery man arrived. And later, I had watched her stomach grow rounder and her face become longer with fear and worry.

So you can imagine how happy she was when they forced her to tell the truth about her imperial ancestry. I heard later she was so struck with this miracle of marrying Tyan-yu she became a very religious person who ordered servants to sweep the ancestors' graves not just once a year, but once a day.

There's no more to the story. They didn't blame me so much. Huang Taitai got her grandson. I got my clothes, a rail ticket to Peking, and enough money to go to America. The Huangs asked only that I never tell anybody of any importance about the story of my doomed marriage.

It's a true story, how I kept my promise, how I sacrificed my life. See the gold metal I can now wear. I gave birth to your brothers and then your father gave me these two bracelets. Then I had you. And every few years, when I have a little extra money, I buy another bracelet. I know what I'm worth. They're always twenty-four carats, all genuine.

But I'll never forget. On the day of the Festival of Pure Brightness, I take off all my bracelets. I remember the day when I finally knew a genuine thought and could follow where it went. That was the day I was a young girl with my face under a red marriage scarf. I promised not to forget myself.

How nice it is to be that girl again, to take off my scarf, to see what is underneath and feel the lightness come back into my body!

YING-YING ST. CLAIR

The Moon Lady

For all these years I kept my mouth closed so selfish desires would not fall out. And because I remained quiet for so long now my daughter does not hear me. She sits by her fancy swimming pool and hears only her Sony Walkman, her cordless phone, her big, important husband asking her why they have charcoal and no lighter fluid.

All these years I kept my true nature hidden, running along like a small shadow so nobody could catch me. And because I moved so secretly now my daughter does not see me. She sees a list of things to buy, her checkbook out of balance, her ashtray sitting crooked on a straight table.

And I want to tell her this: We are lost, she and I, unseen and not seeing, unheard and not hearing, unknown by others.

I did not lose myself all at once. I rubbed out my face over the years washing away my pain, the same way carvings on stone are worn down by water.

Yet today I can remember a time when I ran and shouted, when I could not stand still. It is my earliest recollection: telling the Moon Lady my secret wish. And because I forgot what I wished for, that memory remained hidden from me all these many years.

But now I remember the wish, and I can recall the details of that entire day, as clearly as I see my daughter and the foolishness of her life.

In 1918, the year that I was four, the Moon Festival arrived during an autumn in Wushi that was unusually hot, terribly hot. When I awoke that morning, the fifteenth day of the eighth moon, the straw mat covering my bed was already sticky. Everything in the room smelled of wet grass simmering in the heat.

Earlier in the summer, the servants had covered all the windows with bamboo curtains to drive out the sun. Every bed was covered with a woven mat, our only bedding during the months of constant wet heat. And the hot bricks of the courtyard were crisscrossed with bamboo paths. Autumn had come, but without its cool mornings and evenings. And so the stale heat still remained in the shadows behind the curtains, heating up the acrid smells of my chamber pot, seeping into my pillow, chafing the back of my neck and puffing up my cheeks, so that I awoke that morning with a restless complaint.

There was another smell, outside, something burning, a pungent fragrance that was half sweet and half bitter. "What's that stinky smell?" I asked my amah, who always managed to appear next to my bed the instant I was awake. She slept on a cot in a little room next to mine.

"It is the same as I explained yesterday," she said, lifting me out of my bed and setting me on her knee. And my sleepy mind tried to remember what she had told me upon waking the morning before.

"We are burning the Five Evils," I said drowsily, then squirmed out of her warm lap. I climbed on top of a little stool and looked out the window into the courtyard below. I saw a green coil curled in the shape of a snake, with a tail that billowed yellow smoke. The other day, Amah had shown me that the snake had come out of a colorful box decorated with five evil creatures: a swimming snake, a jumping scorpion, a flying centipede, a dropping-down spider, and a springing lizard. The bite of any one of these creatures could kill a child, explained Amah. So I was relieved to think we had caught the Five Evils and were burning their corpses. I didn't know the green coil was merely incense used to chase away mosquitoes and small flies.

That day, instead of dressing me in a light cotton jacket and loose trousers, Amah brought out a heavy yellow silk jacket and skirt outlined with black bands.

"No time to play today," said Amah, opening the lined jacket. "Your mother has made you new tiger clothes for the Moon Festival. . . . " She lifted me into the pants. "Very important day, and now you are a big girl, so you can go to the ceremony."

"What is a ceremony?" I asked as Amah slipped the jacket over my cotton undergarments.

"It is a proper way to behave. You do this and that, so the gods do not punish you," said Amah as she fastened my frog clasps.

"What kind of punishment?" I asked boldly.

"Too many questions!" cried Amah. "You do not need to understand. Just behave, follow your mother's example. Light the incense, make an offering to the moon, bow your head. Do not shame me, Ying-ying."

I bowed my head with a pout. I noticed the black bands on my sleeves, the tiny embroidered peonies growing from curlicues of gold thread. I remembered watching my mother pushing a silver needle in and out, gently nudging flowers and leaves and vines to bloom on the cloth.

And then I heard voices in the courtyard. Standing on my stool, I strained to find them. Somebody was complaining about the heat: " . . . feel my arm, steamed soft clear to the bone." Many relatives from the north had arrived for the Moon Festival and were staying for the week.

Amah tried to pull a wide comb through my hair and I pretended to tumble off the stool as soon as she reached a knot.

"Stand still, Ying-ying!" she cried, her usual lament, while I giggled and wobbled on the stool. And then she yanked the full length of my hair like the reins of a horse and before I could fall off the stool again, she quickly twisted my hair into a single braid off to the side, weaving into it five strands of colorful silk. She wound my braid into a tight ball, then arranged and snipped the loose silk strands until they fell into a neat tassel.

She spun me around to inspect her handiwork. I was roasting in the lined silk jacket and pants obviously made with a cooler day in mind. My scalp was burning with the pain of Amah's attentions. What kind of day could be worth so much suffering?

"Pretty," pronounced Amah, even though I wore a scowl on my face.

"Who is coming today?" I asked.

"*Dajya*"—All the family—she said happily. "We are all going to Tai Lake. The family has rented a boat with a famous chef. And tonight at the ceremony you will see the Moon Lady."

"The Moon Lady! The Moon Lady!" I said, jumping up and down with great delight. And then, after I ceased to be amazed with the pleasant sounds of my voice saying new words, I tugged Amah's sleeve and asked: "Who is the Moon Lady?"

"Chang-o. She lives on the moon and today is the only day you can see her and have a secret wish fulfilled."

"What is a secret wish?"

"It is what you want but cannot ask," said Amah.

"Why can't I ask?"

"This is because . . . because if you ask it . . . it is no longer a wish but a selfish desire," said Amah. "Haven't I taught you— that it is wrong to think of your own needs? A girl can never ask, only listen."

"Then how will the Moon Lady know my wish?"

"Ai! You ask too much already! You can ask her because she is not an ordinary person."

Satisfied at last, I immediately said: "Then I will tell her I don't want to wear these clothes anymore."

"Ah! Did I not just explain?" said Amah. "Now that you have mentioned this to me, it is not a secret wish anymore."

During the morning meal nobody seemed in a hurry to go to the lake; this person and that always eating one more thing. And after breakfast everybody kept talking about things of little consequence. I grew more worried and unhappy by the minute.

" . . . Autumn moon warms. O! Geese shadows return." Baba was reciting a long poem he had deciphered from ancient stone inscriptions.

"The third word in the next line," explained Baba, "was worn off the slab, its meaning washed away by centuries of rain, almost lost to posterity forever."

"Ah, but fortunately," said my uncle, his eyes twinkling, "you are a dedicated scholar of ancient history and literature. You were able to solve it, I think."

My father responded with the line: "Mist flowers radiant. O! . . . "

Mama was telling my aunt and the old ladies how to mix various herbs and insects to produce a balm: "This you rub here, between these two spots. Rub it vigorously until your skin heats and the achiness is burned out."

"Ai! But how can I rub a swollen foot?" lamented the old lady. "Both inside and outside have a sour painful feeling. Too tender to even touch!"

"It is the heat," complained another old auntie. "Cooking all your flesh dry and brittle."

"And burning your eyes!" exclaimed my great-aunt.

I sighed over and over again every time they started a new topic. Amah finally noticed me and gave me a mooncake in the shape of a rabbit. She said I could sit in the courtyard and eat it with my two little half-sisters, Number Two and Number Three.

It is easy to forget about a boat when you have a rabbit mooncake in your hand. The three of us walked quickly out of the room, and as soon as we passed through the moongate that led to the inner courtyard, we tumbled and shrieked, running to see who could get to the stone bench first. I was the biggest, so I sat in the shady part, where the stone slab was cool. My half-sisters sat in the sun. I broke off a rabbit ear for each of them. The ears were just dough, no sweet filling or egg yolk inside, but my half-sisters were too little to know any better.

"Sister likes me better," said Number Two to Number Three.

"*Me* better," said Number Three to Number Two.

"Don't make trouble," I said to them both. I ate the rabbit's body, rolling my tongue over my lips to lick off the sticky bean paste.

We picked crumbs off one another, and after we finished our

treat it grew quiet and once again I became restless. Suddenly I saw a dragonfly with a large crimson body and transparent wings. I leapt off the bench and ran to chase it, and my half-sisters followed me, jumping and thrusting their hands upward as it flew away.

"Ying-ying!" I heard Amah call, and Number Two and Number Three ran off. Amah was standing in the courtyard and my mother and the other ladies were now coming through the moon-gate. Amah rushed over and bent down to smooth my yellow jacket. *"Syin yifu! Yidafadwo!"*—Your new clothes! Everything, all over the place!—she cried in a show of distress.

My mother smiled and walked over to me. She smoothed some of my wayward hairs back in place and tucked them into my coiled braid. "A boy can run and chase dragonflies, because that is his nature," she said. "But a girl should stand still. If you are still for a very long time, a dragonfly will no longer see you. Then it will come to you and hide in the comfort of your shadow." The old ladies clucked in agreement and then they all left me in the middle of the hot courtyard.

Standing perfectly still like that, I discovered my shadow. At first it was just a dark spot on the bamboo mats that covered the courtyard bricks. It had short legs and long arms, a dark coiled braid just like mine. When I shook my head, it shook its head. We flapped our arms. We raised one leg. I turned to walk away and it followed me. I turned back around quickly and it faced me. I lifted the bamboo mat to see if I could peel off my shadow, but it was under the mat, on the brick. I shrieked with delight at my shadow's own cleverness. I ran to the shade under the tree, watching my shadow chase me. It disappeared. I loved my shadow, this dark side of me that had my same restless nature.

And then I heard Amah calling me again. "Ying-ying! It is time. Are you ready to go to the lake?" I nodded my head and began to run toward her, my self running ahead. "Slowly, go slowly," admonished Amah.

Our entire family was already standing outside, chatting excitedly. Everybody was dressed in important-looking clothes. Baba was in a new brown-colored gown, which while plain was of an obviously fine-quality silk weave and workmanship. Mama had on a jacket and skirt with colors that were the reverse of mine: black silk with yellow bands. My half-sisters wore rose-colored tunics and so did their mothers, my father's concubines. My older brother had on a blue jacket embroidered with shapes resembling Buddha scepters for long life. Even the old ladies had put on their best clothes to celebrate: Mama's aunt, Baba's mother and her cousin, and Great-uncle's fat wife, who still plucked her forehead bald and always walked as if she were crossing a slippery stream, two tiny steps and then a scared look.

The servants had already packed and loaded a rickshaw with the day's basic provisions: a woven hamper filled with *zong zi*— the sticky rice wrapped in lotus leaves, some filled with roasted ham, some with sweet lotus seeds; a small stove for boiling water for hot tea; another hamper containing cups and bowls and chopsticks; a cotton sack of apples, pomegranates, and pears; sweaty earthen jars of preserved meats and vegetables; stacks of red boxes lined with four mooncakes each; and of course, sleeping mats for our afternoon nap.

Then everybody climbed into rickshaws, the younger children sitting next to their amahs. At the last moment, before we all set off, I wriggled out of Amah's grasp and jumped out of the rickshaw. I climbed into the rickshaw with my mother in it, which displeased Amah, because this was presumptuous behavior on my part and also because Amah loved me better than her own. She had given up her own child, a baby son, when her husband had died and she had come to our house to be my nursemaid. But I was very spoiled because of her; she had never taught me to think about her feelings. So I thought of Amah only as someone for my comfort, the way you might think of a fan in the summer or a heater in the winter, a blessing you appreciate and love only when it is no longer there.

When we arrived at the lake, I was disappointed to feel no cooling breezes. Our rickshaw pullers were soaked with sweat and their mouths were open and panting like horses. At the dock, I watched as the old ladies and men started climbing aboard a large boat our family had rented. The boat looked like a floating teahouse, with an open-air pavilion larger than the one in our courtyard. It had many red columns and a peaked tile roof, and behind that what looked like a garden house with round windows.

When it was our turn, Amah grasped my hand tightly and we bounced across the plank. But as soon as my feet touched the deck, I sprang free and, together with Number Two and Number Three, I pushed my way past people's legs enclosed in billows of dark and bright silk clothes—trying to see who would be the first to run the length of the boat.

I loved the unsteady feeling of almost falling one way then another. Red lanterns hanging from the roof and railings swayed, as if pushed by a breeze. My half-sisters and I ran our fingers over benches and small tables in the pavilion. We traced our fingers over the patterns of the ornamental wood railings and poked our faces through openings to see the water below. And then there were more things to find!

I opened a heavy door leading into the garden house and ran past a room that looked like a large sitting area. My sisters followed behind laughing. Through another door, I saw people in a kitchen. A man holding a big cleaver turned and saw us, then called to us, as we shyly smiled and backed away.

At the rear of the boat we saw poor-looking people: a man feeding sticks into a tall chimney stove, a woman chopping vegetables, and two rough-looking boys squatting close to the edge of the boat, holding what looked to be a piece of string attached to a wire-mesh cage lying just below the surface of the water. They gave us not even a glance.

We returned to the front of the boat, just in time to see the dock moving away from us. Mama and the other ladies were already seated on benches around the pavilion, fanning themselves furiously and slapping the sides of each other's heads when mosquitoes lighted. Baba and Uncle were leaning over a rail, talking in deep, serious voices. My brother and some of his boy cousins had found a long bamboo stick and were poking the water as if they could make the boat go faster. The servants were seated in a cluster at the front, heating water for tea, shelling roasted gingko nuts, and emptying out hampers of food for a noonday meal of cold dishes.

Even though Tai Lake is one of the largest in all of China, that day it seemed crowded with boats: rowboats, pedal boats, sailboats, fishing boats, and floating pavilions like ours. So we often passed other people leaning out to trail their hands in the cool water, some drifting by asleep beneath a cloth canopy or oil-coated umbrella.

Suddenly I heard people crying, "Ahh! Ahh! Ahh!" and I thought, At last, the day has begun! I raced to the pavilion and found aunts and uncles laughing as they used chopsticks to pick up dancing shrimp, still squirming in their shells, their tiny legs bristling. So this was what the mesh cage beneath the water had contained, freshwater shrimp, which my father was now dipping into a spicy bean-curd sauce and popping into his mouth with two bites and a swallow.

But the excitement soon waned, and the afternoon seemed to pass like any other at home. The same listlessness after the meal. A little drowsy gossip with hot tea. Amah telling me to lie down on my mat. The quiet as everyone slept through the hottest part of the day.

I sat up and saw Amah was still asleep, lying askew on her sleeping mat. I wandered to the back of the boat. The rough-looking boys were removing a large, squawking long-necked bird from a bamboo cage. The bird had a metal ring around its neck. One boy held onto the bird, wrapping his arms around the bird's wings. The other tied a thick rope to a loop on the metal neck ring. Then they released the bird and it swooped with a flurry of white wings, hovered over the edge of the boat, then sat on top of the shiny water. I walked over to the edge and looked at the bird. He looked back at me warily with one eye. Then the bird dove under the water and disappeared.

One of the boys threw a raft made of hollow reed flutes into the water and then dove in and emerged on top of the raft. In a few seconds, the bird also emerged, its head struggling to hold onto a large fish. The bird jumped onto the raft and then tried to swallow the fish, but of course, with the ring around its neck, it could not. In one motion, the boy on the raft snatched the fish from the bird's mouth and threw it to the other boy on the boat. I clapped my hands and the bird dove under water again.

For the next hour, while Amah and everybody else slept, I watched like a hungry cat waiting its turn, as fish after fish appeared in the bird's beak only to land in a wooden pail on the boat. Then the boy in the water cried to the other, "Enough!" and the boy on the boat shouted to someone high atop the part of the boat I could not see. And loud clanks and hissing sounds erupted as once again the boat began to move. Then the boy next to me dove into the water. Both boys got on the raft and crouched in the middle like two birds perched on a branch. I waved to them, envying their carefree ways, and soon they were far away, a little yellow spot bobbing on the water.

It would have been enough to see this one adventure. But I stayed, as if caught in a good dream. And sure enough, I turned around and a sullen woman was now squatting in front of the bucket of fish. I watched as she took out a sharp, thin knife and began to slice open the fish bellies, pulling out the red slippery insides and throwing them over her shoulder into the lake. I saw her scrape off the fish scales, which flew in the air like shards of glass. And then there were two chickens that no longer gurgled after their heads were chopped off. And a big snapping turtle that stretched out its neck to bite a stick, and—whuck!—off fell its head. And dark masses of thin freshwater eels, swimming furiously in a pot. Then the woman carried everything, without a word, into the kitchen. And there was nothing else to see.

It was not until then, too late, that I saw my new clothes—and the spots of bloods, flecks of fish scales, bits of feather and mud. What a strange mind I had! In my panic, in hearing waking voices toward the front of the boat, I quickly dipped my hands in the bowl of turtle's blood and smeared this on my sleeves, and on the front of my pants and jacket. And this is what I truly thought: that I could cover these spots by painting all my clothes crimson red, and that if I stood perfectly still no one would notice this change.

That is how Amah found me: an apparition covered with blood. I can still hear her voice, screaming in terror, running over to see what pieces of my body were missing, what leaky holes had appeared. And when she found nothing, after inspecting my ears and my nose and counting my fingers, she called me names, using words I had never heard before. But they sounded evil, the way she hurled and spat the words out. She yanked off my jacket, pulled off my pants. She said I smelled like "something evil this" and I looked like "something evil that." Her voice was trembling not so much with anger as with fear. "Your mother, now she will be glad to wash her hands of you," Amah said with great remorse. "She will banish us both to Kunming." And then I was truly frightened, because I had heard that Kunming was so far away nobody ever came to visit, and that it was a wild place surrounded by a stone forest ruled by monkeys. Amah left me crying on the back of the boat, standing in my white cotton undergarments and tiger slippers.

I had truly expected my mother to come soon. I imagined her seeing my soiled clothes, the little flowers she had worked so hard to make. I thought she would come to the back of the boat and scold me in her gentle way. But she did not come. Oh, once I heard some footsteps, but I saw only the faces of my half-sisters pressed to the door window. They looked at me wide-eyed, pointed to me, and then laughed and scampered off.

The water had turned a deep golden color, and then red, purple, and finally black. The sky had darkened and red lantern lights started to glow all over the lake. I could hear people talking and laughing, some voices from the front of our boat, some from other boats next to us. And then I heard the wooden kitchen door banging open and shut and the air filled with good rich smells. The voices from the pavilion cried in happy disbelief, "Ai! Look at this! And this!" I was hungry to be there.

I listened to their banquet while dangling my legs over the back. And although it was night, it was bright outside. I could see my reflection, my legs, my hands leaning on the edge, and my face. And above my head, I saw why it was so bright. In the dark water, I could see the full moon, a moon so warm and big it looked like the sun. And I turned around so I could find the Moon Lady and tell her my secret wish. But right at that moment, everybody else must have seen her too. Because firecrackers exploded, and I fell into the water not even hearing my own splash.

I was surprised by the cool comfort of the water, so that at first I was not frightened. It was like weightless sleep. And I expected Amah to come immediately and pick me up. But in the instant that I began to choke, I knew she would not come. I thrashed my arms and legs under the water. The sharp water had swum up my nose, into my throat and eyes, and this made me thrash even harder. "Amah!" I tried to cry and I was so angry at her for abandoning me, for making me wait and suffer unnecessarily. And then a dark shape brushed by me and I knew it was one of the Five Evils, a swimming snake.

It wrapped around me and squeezed my body like a sponge, then tossed me into the choking air—and I fell headlong into a rope net filled with writhing fish. Water gushed out of my throat, so that now I was choking and wailing.

When I turned my head, I saw four shadows, with the moon in back of them. A dripping figure was climbing into the boat. "Is it too small? Should we throw it back? Or is it worth some money?" said the dripping man, panting. And the others laughed. I became quiet. I knew who these people were. When Amah and I passed people like these in the streets, she would put her hands over my eyes and ears.

"Stop now," scolded the woman in the boat, "you've frightened her. She thinks we're brigands who are going to sell her for a slave." And then she said in a gentle voice, "Where are you from, little sister?"

The dripping man bent down and looked at me. "Oh, a little girl. Not a fish!"

"Not a fish! Not a fish!" murmured the others, chuckling.

I began to shiver, too scared to cry. The air smelled dangerous, the sharp odors of gunpowder and fish.

"Do not pay any attention to them," said the woman. "Are you from another fishing boat? Which one? Do not be afraid. Point."

Out on the water I saw rowboats and pedal boats and sailboats, and fishing boats like this one, with a long bow and small house in the middle. I looked hard, my heart beating fast.

"There!" I said, and pointed to a floating pavilion filled with laughing people and lanterns. "There! There!" And I began to cry, desperate to reach my family and be comforted. The fishing boat glided swiftly over, toward the good cooking smells.

"*E!*" called the woman up to the boat. "Have you lost a little girl, a girl who fell in the water?"

There were some shouts from the floating pavilion, and I strained to see faces of Amah, Baba, Mama. People were crowded on one side of the pavilion, leaning over, pointing, looking into our boat. All strangers, laughing red faces, loud voices. Where was Amah? Why did my mother not come? A little girl pushed her way through some legs.

"That's not me!" she cried. "I'm here. I didn't fall in the water." The people in the boat roared with laughter and turned away.

"Little sister, you were mistaken," said the woman as the fishing boat glided away. I said nothing. I began to shiver again. I had seen nobody who cared that I was missing. I looked out over the water at the hundreds of dancing lanterns. Firecrackers were exploding and I could hear more people laughing. The farther we glided, the bigger the world became. And I now felt I was lost forever.

The woman continued to stare at me. My braid was unfurled. My undergarments were wet and gray. I had lost my slippers and was barefoot.

"What shall we do?" said one of the men quietly. "Nobody to claim her."

"Maybe she is a beggar girl," said one of the men. "Look at her clothes. She is one of those children who ride the flimsy rafts to beg for money."

I was filled with terror. Maybe this was true. I had turned into a beggar girl, lost without my family.

"Anh! Don't you have eyes?" said the woman crossly. "Look at her skin, too pale. And her feet, the bottoms are soft."

"Put her on the shore, then," said the man. "If she truly has a family, they will look for her there."

"Such a night!" sighed another man. "Always someone falling in on holiday nights. Drunken poets and little children. Lucky she didn't drown." They chatted like this, back and forth, moving slowly toward shore. One man pushed the boat with a long bamboo pole and we glided between other boats. When we reached the dock, the man who had fished me out of the water lifted me out of the boat with his fishy-smelling hands.

"Be careful next time, little sister," called the woman as their boat glided away.

On the dock, with the bright moon behind me, I once again saw my shadow. It was shorter this time, shrunken and wild-looking. We ran together over to some bushes along a walkway and hid. In this hiding place I could hear people talking as they walked by. I could hear frogs and crickets. And then—flutes and tinkling cymbals, a sounding gong and drums!

I looked through the branches of the bushes and in front I could see a crowd of people and, above them, a stage holding up the moon. A young man burst out from the side of a stage and told the crowd, "And now the Moon Lady will come and tell her sad tale to you, in a shadow play, classically sung."

The Moon Lady! I thought, and the very sound of those magic words made me forget my troubles. I heard more cymbals and gongs and then a shadow of a woman appeared against the moon. Her hair was undone and she was combing it. She began to speak. Such a sweet, wailing voice!

"My fate and my penance," she began to lament, pulling her long fingers through her hair, "to live here on the moon, while my husband lives on the sun. So that each day and each night, we pass each other, never seeing one another, except this one evening, the night of the mid-autumn moon."

The crowd moved closer. The Moon Lady plucked her lute and began her singing tale.

On the other side of the moon I saw the silhouette of a man appear. The Moon Lady held her arms out to embrace him— "O! Hou Yi, my husband, Master Archer of the Skies!" she sang. But her husband did not seem to notice her. He was gazing at the sky. And as the sky grew brighter, his mouth began to open wide—in horror or delight, I could not tell.

The Moon Lady clutched her throat and fell into a heap,

crying, "The drought of ten suns in the eastern sky!" And just as she sang this, the Master Archer pointed his magic arrows and shot down nine suns which burst open with blood. "Sinking into a simmering sea!" she sang happily, and I could hear these suns sizzling and crackling in death.

And now a fairy—the Queen Mother of the Western Skies!— was flying toward the Master Archer. She opened a box and held up a glowing ball—no, not a baby sun but a magic peach, the peach of everlasting life! I could see the Moon Lady pretending to be busy with her embroidery, but she was watching her husband. She saw him hide the peach in a box. And then the Master Archer raised his bow and vowed to fast for one year to show he had the patience to live forever. And after he ran off, the Moon Lady wasted not one moment to find the peach and eat it!

As soon as she tasted it, she began to rise, then fly—not like the Queen Mother—but like a dragonfly with broken wings. "Flung from this earth by my own wantonness!" she cried just as her husband dashed back home, shouting, "Thief! Life-stealing wife!" He picked up his bow, aimed an arrow at his wife and—with the rumblings of a gong, the sky went black.

Wyah! Wyah! The sad lute music began again as the sky on the stage lightened. And there stood the poor lady against a moon as bright as the sun. Her hair was now so long it swept the floor, wiping up her tears. An eternity had passed since she last saw her husband, for this was her fate: to stay lost on the moon, forever seeking her own selfish wishes.

"For woman is yin," she cried sadly, "the darkness within, where untempered passions lie. And man is yang, bright truth lighting our minds."

At the end of her singing tale, I was crying, shaking with despair. Even though I did not understand her entire story, I understood her grief. In one small moment, we had both lost the world, and there was no way to get it back.

A gong sounded, and the Moon Lady bowed her head and looked serenely to the side. The crowd clapped vigorously. And now the same young man as before came out on the stage and announced, "Wait, everybody! The Moon Lady has consented to grant one secret wish to each person here. . . . " The crowd stirred with excitement, people murmuring in high voices. "For a small monetary donation . . . "continued the young man. And the crowd laughed and groaned, then began to disperse. The young man shouted, "A once-a-year opportunity!" But nobody was listening to him, except my shadow and me in the bushes.

"I have a wish! I have one!" I shouted as I ran forward in my bare feet. But the young man paid no attention to me and walked off the stage. I kept running toward the moon to tell the Moon Lady what I wanted, because now I knew what my wish was. I darted fast as a lizard behind the stage, to the other side of the moon.

I saw her, standing still for just a moment. She was beautiful, ablaze with the light from a dozen kerosene lamps. And then she shook her long shadowy tresses and began to walk down the steps.

"I have a wish," I said in a whisper, and still she did not hear me. So I walked closer yet, until I could see the face of the Moon Lady: shrunken cheeks, a broad oily nose, large glaring teeth, and red-stained eyes. A face so tired that she wearily pulled off her hair, her long gown fell from her shoulders. And as the secret wish fell from my lips, the Moon Lady looked at me and became a man.

For many years, I could not remember what I wanted that night from the Moon Lady, or how it was that I was found again by my family. Both of these things seemed an illusion to me, a wish granted that could not be trusted. And so even though I was found—later that night after Amah, Baba, Uncle, and the others shouted for me along the waterway—I never believed my family found the same girl.

And then, over the years, I forgot the rest of what happened that day: the pitiful story the Moon Lady sang, the pavilion boat, the bird with the ring on its neck, the tiny flowers blooming on my sleeve, the burning of the Five Evils.

But now that I am old, moving every year closer to the end of my life, I also feel closer to the beginning. And I remember everything that happened that day because it has happened many times in my life. The same innocence, trust, and restlessness, the wonder, fear, and loneliness. How I lost myself.

I remember all these things. And tonight, on the fifteenth day of the eighth moon, I also remember what I asked the Moon Lady so long ago. I wished to be found.

THE
TWENTY-SIX
MALIGNANT
GATES

"*Do not ride your bicycle around the corner,*" the mother had told the daughter when she was seven.

"*Why not!*" protested the girl.

"*Because then I cannot see you and you will fall down and cry and I will not hear you.*"

"*How do you know I'll fall?*" whined the girl.

"*It is in a book,* The Twenty-Six Malignant Gates, *all the bad things that can happen to you outside the protection of this house.*"

"*I don't believe you. Let me see the book.*"

"*It is written in Chinese. You cannot understand it. That is why you must listen to me.*"

"*What are they, then?*" the girl demanded. "*Tell me the twenty-six bad things.*"

But the mother sat knitting in silence.

"*What twenty-six!*" shouted the girl.

The mother still did not answer her.

"*You can't tell me because you don't know! You don't know anything!*" And the girl ran outside, jumped on her bicycle, and in her hurry to get away, she fell before she even reached the corner.

WAVERLY JONG

Rules of the Game

I was six when my mother taught me the art of invisible strength. It was a strategy for winning arguments, respect from others, and eventually, though neither of us knew it at the time, chess games.

"Bite back your tongue," scolded my mother when I cried loudly, yanking her hand toward the store that sold bags of salted plums. At home, she said, "Wise guy, he not go against wind. In Chinese we say, Come from South, blow with wind—poom!— North will follow. Strongest wind cannot be seen."

The next week I bit back my tongue as we entered the store with the forbidden candies. When my mother finished her shopping, she quietly plucked a small bag of plums from the rack and put it on the counter with the rest of the items.

My mother imparted her daily truths so she could help my older brothers and me rise above our circumstances. We lived in San Francisco's Chinatown. Like most of the other Chinese children who played in the back alleys of restaurants and curio shops, I didn't think we were poor. My bowl was always full, three five-course meals every day, beginning with a soup full of mysterious things I didn't want to know the names of.

We lived on Waverly Place, in a warm, clean, two-bedroom

flat that sat above a small Chinese bakery specializing in steamed pastries and dim sum. In the early morning, when the alley was still quiet, I could smell fragrant red beans as they were cooked down to a pasty sweetness. By daybreak, our flat was heavy with the odor of fried sesame balls and sweet curried chicken crescents. From my bed, I would listen as my father got ready for work, then locked the door behind him, one-two-three clicks.

At the end of our two-block alley was a small sandlot playground with swings and slides well-shined down the middle with use. The play area was bordered by wood-slat benches where old-country people sat cracking roasted watermelon seeds with their golden teeth and scattering the husks to an impatient gathering of gurgling pigeons. The best playground, however, was the dark alley itself. It was crammed with daily mysteries and adventures. My brothers and I would peer into the medicinal herb shop, watching old Li dole out onto a stiff sheet of white paper the right amount of insect shells, saffron-colored seeds, and pungent leaves for his ailing customers. It was said that he once cured a woman dying of an ancestral curse that had eluded the best of American doctors. Next to the pharmacy was a printer who specialized in gold-embossed wedding invitations and festive red banners.

Farther down the street was Ping Yuen Fish Market. The front window displayed a tank crowded with doomed fish and turtles struggling to gain footing on the slimy green-tiled sides. A hand-written sign informed tourists, "Within this store, is all for food, not for pet." Inside, the butchers with their bloodstained white smocks deftly gutted the fish while customers cried out their orders and shouted, "Give me your freshest," to which the butchers always protested, "All are freshest." On less crowded market days, we would inspect the crates of live frogs and crabs which we were warned not to poke, boxes of dried cuttlefish, and row upon row of iced prawns, squid, and slippery fish. The sanddabs made me shiver each time; their eyes lay on one flattened side and reminded me of my mother's story of a careless girl who ran into a crowded street and was crushed by a cab. "Was smash flat," reported my mother.

At the corner of the alley was Hong Sing's, a four-table café with a recessed stairwell in front that led to a door marked "Tradesmen." My brothers and I believed the bad people emerged from this door at night. Tourists never went to Hong Sing's, since the menu was printed only in Chinese. A Caucasian man with a big camera once posed me and my playmates in front of the restaurant. He had us move to the side of the picture window so the photo would capture the roasted duck with its head dangling from a juice-covered rope. After he took the picture, I told him he should go into Hong Sing's and eat dinner. When he smiled and asked me what they served, I shouted, "Guts and duck's feet and octopus gizzards!" Then I ran off with my friends, shrieking with laughter as we scampered across the alley and hid in the entryway grotto of the China Gem Company, my heart pounding with hope that he would chase us.

My mother named me after the street that we lived on: Waverly Place Jong, my official name for important American documents. But my family called me Meimei, "Little Sister." I was the youngest, the only daughter. Each morning before school, my mother would twist and yank on my thick black hair until she had formed two tightly wound pigtails. One day, as she struggled to weave a hard-toothed comb through my disobedient hair, I had a sly thought.

I asked her, "Ma, what is Chinese torture?" My mother shook her head. A bobby pin was wedged between her lips. She wetted her palm and smoothed the hair above my ear, then pushed the pin in so that it nicked sharply against my scalp.

"Who say this word?" she asked without a trace of knowing how wicked I was being. I shrugged my shoulders and said, "Some boy in my class said Chinese people do Chinese torture."

"Chinese people do many things," she said simply. "Chinese people do business, do medicine, do painting. Not lazy like American people. We do torture. Best torture."

My older brother Vincent was the one who actually got the chess set. We had gone to the annual Christmas party held at the First Chinese Baptist Church at the end of the alley. The missionary ladies had put together a Santa bag of gifts donated by members of another church. None of the gifts had names on them. There were separate sacks for boys and girls of different ages.

One of the Chinese parishioners had donned a Santa Claus costume and a stiff paper beard with cotton balls glued to it. I think the only children who thought he was the real thing were too young to know that Santa Claus was not Chinese. When my turn came up, the Santa man asked me how old I was. I thought it was a trick question; I was seven according to the American formula and eight by the Chinese calendar. I said I was born on March 17, 1951. That seemed to satisfy him. He then solemnly asked if I had been a very, very good girl this year and did I believe in Jesus Christ and obey my parents. I knew the only answer to that. I nodded back with equal solemnity.

Having watched the other children opening their gifts, I already knew that the big gifts were not necessarily the nicest ones. One girl my age got a large coloring book of biblical characters, while a less greedy girl who selected a smaller box received a glass vial of lavender toilet water. The sound of the box was also important. A ten-year-old boy had chosen a box that jangled when he shook it. It was a tin globe of the world with a slit for inserting money. He must have thought it was full of dimes and nickels, because when he saw that it had just ten pennies, his face fell with such undisguised disappointment that his mother slapped the side of his head and led him out of the church hall, apologizing to the crowd for her son who had such bad manners he couldn't appreciate such a fine gift.

As I peered into the sack, I quickly fingered the remaining presents, testing their weight, imagining what they contained. I chose a heavy, compact one that was wrapped in shiny silver foil and a red satin ribbon. It was a twelve-pack of Life Savers and I spent the rest of the party arranging and rearranging the candy tubes in the order of my favorites. My brother Winston chose wisely as well. His present turned out to be a box of intricate plastic parts; the instructions on the box proclaimed that when they were properly assembled he would have an authentic miniature replica of a World War II submarine.

Vincent got the chess set, which would have been a very decent present to get at a church Christmas party, except it was obviously used and, as we discovered later, it was missing a black pawn and a white knight. My mother graciously thanked the unknown benefactor, saying, "Too good. Cost too much." At which point, an old lady with fine white, wispy hair nodded toward our family and said with a whistling whisper, "Merry, merry Christmas."

When we got home, my mother told Vincent to throw the chess set away. "She not want it. We not want it," she said, tossing her head stiffly to the side with a tight, proud smile. My brothers had deaf ears. They were already lining up the chess pieces and reading from the dog-eared instruction book.

I watched Vincent and Winston play during Christmas week. The chess board seemed to hold elaborate secrets waiting to be untangled. The chessmen were more powerful than Old Li's magic herbs that cured ancestral curses. And my brothers wore such serious faces that I was sure something was at stake that was greater than avoiding the tradesmen's door to Hong Sing's.

"Let me! Let me!" I begged between games when one brother or the other would sit back with a deep sigh of relief and victory, the other annoyed, unable to let go of the outcome. Vincent at first refused to let me play, but when I offered my Life Savers as replacements for the buttons that filled in for the missing pieces, he relented. He chose the flavors: wild cherry for the black pawn and peppermint for the white knight. Winner could eat both.

As our mother sprinkled flour and rolled out small doughy circles for the steamed dumplings that would be our dinner that night, Vincent explained the rules, pointing to each piece. "You have sixteen pieces and so do I. One king and queen, two bishops, two knights, two castles, and eight pawns. The pawns can only move forward one step, except on the first move. Then they can move two. But they can only take men by moving crossways like this, except in the beginning, when you can move ahead and take another pawn."

"Why?" I asked as I moved my pawn. "Why can't they move more steps?"

"Because they're pawns," he said.

"But why do they go crossways to take other men. Why aren't there any women and children?"

"Why is the sky blue? Why must you always ask stupid questions?" asked Vincent. "This is a game. These are the rules. I didn't make them up. See. Here. In the book." He jabbed a page with a pawn in his hand. "Pawn. P-A-W-N. Pawn. Read it yourself."

My mother patted the flour off her hands. "Let me see book," she said quietly. She scanned the pages quickly, not reading the foreign English symbols, seeming to search deliberately for nothing in particular.

"This American rules," she concluded at last. "Every time people come out from foreign country, must know rules. You not know, judge say, Too bad, go back. They not telling you why so you can use their way go forward. They say, Don't know why, you find out yourself. But they knowing all the time. Better you take it, find out why yourself." She tossed her head back with a satisfied smile.

I found out about all the whys later. I read the rules and looked up all the big words in a dictionary. I borrowed books from the Chinatown library. I studied each chess piece, trying to absorb the power each contained.

I learned about opening moves and why it's important to control the center early on; the shortest distance between two points is straight down the middle. I learned about the middle game and why tactics between two adversaries are like clashing ideas; the one who plays better has the clearest plans for both attacking and getting out of traps. I learned why it is essential in the endgame to have foresight, a mathematical understanding of all possible moves, and patience; all weaknesses and advantages become evident to a strong adversary and are obscured to a tiring opponent. I discovered that for the whole game one must gather invisible strengths and see the endgame before the game begins.

I also found out why I should never reveal "why" to others.

A little knowledge withheld is a great advantage one should store for future use. That is the power of chess. It is a game of secrets in which one must show and never tell.

I loved the secrets I found within the sixty-four black and white squares. I carefully drew a handmade chessboard and pinned it to the wall next to my bed, where at night I would stare for hours at imaginary battles. Soon I no longer lost any games or Life Savers, but I lost my adversaries. Winston and Vincent decided they were more interested in roaming the streets after school in their Hopalong Cassidy cowboy hats.

On a cold spring afternoon, while walking home from school, I detoured through the playground at the end of our alley. I saw a group of old men, two seated across a folding table playing a game of chess, others smoking pipes, eating peanuts, and watching. I ran home and grabbed Vincent's chess set, which was bound in a cardboard box with rubber bands. I also carefully selected two prized rolls of Life Savers. I came back to the park and approached a man who was observing the game.

"Want to play?" I asked him. His face widened with surprise and he grinned as he looked at the box under my arm.

"Little sister, been a long time since I play with dolls," he said, smiling benevolently. I quickly put the box down next to him on the bench and displayed my retort.

Lau Po, as he allowed me to call him, turned out to be a much better player than my brothers. I lost many games and many Life Savers. But over the weeks, with each diminishing roll of candies, I added new secrets. Lau Po gave me the names. The Double Attack from the East and West Shores. Throwing Stones on the Drowning Man. The Sudden Meeting of the Clan. The Surprise from the Sleeping Guard. The Humble Servant Who Kills the King. Sand in the Eyes of Advancing Forces. A Double Killing Without Blood.

There were also the fine points of chess etiquette. Keep captured men in neat rows, as well-tended prisoners. Never announce "Check" with vanity, lest someone with an unseen sword slit your throat. Never hurl pieces into the sandbox after you have lost a game, because then you must find them again, by yourself, after apologizing to all around you. By the end of the summer, Lau Po had taught me all he knew, and I had become a better chess player.

A small weekend crowd of Chinese people and tourists would gather as I played and defeated my opponents one by one. My mother would join the crowds during these outdoor exhibition games. She sat proudly on the bench, telling my admirers with proper Chinese humility, "Is luck."

A man who watched me play in the park suggested that my mother allow me to play in local chess tournaments. My mother smiled graciously, an answer that meant nothing. I desperately wanted to go, but I bit back my tongue. I knew she would not let me play among strangers. So as we walked home I said in a small voice that I didn't want to play in the local tournament. They would have American rules. If I lost, I would bring shame on my family.

"Is shame you fall down nobody push you," said my mother.

During my first tournament, my mother sat with me in the front row as I waited for my turn. I frequently bounced my legs to unstick them from the cold metal seat of the folding chair. When my name was called, I leapt up. My mother unwrapped something in her lap. It was her *chang,* a small tablet of red jade which held the sun's fire. "Is luck," she whispered, and tucked it into my dress pocket. I turned to my opponent, a fifteen-year-old boy from Oakland. He looked at me, wrinkling his nose.

As I began to play, the boy disappeared, the color ran out of the room, and I saw only my white pieces and his black ones waiting on the other side. A light wind began blowing past my ears. It whispered secrets only I could hear.

"Blow from the South," it murmured. "The wind leaves no trail." I saw a clear path, the traps to avoid. The crowd rustled. "Shhh! Shhh!" said the corners of the room. The wind blew stronger. "Throw sand from the East to distract him." The knight came forward ready for the sacrifice. The wind hissed, louder and louder. "Blow, blow, blow. He cannot see. He is blind now. Make him lean away from the wind so he is easier to knock down."

"Check," I said, as the wind roared with laughter. The wind died down to little puffs, my own breath.

My mother placed my first trophy next to a new plastic chess set that the neighborhood Tao society had given to me. As she wiped each piece with a soft cloth, she said, "Next time win more, lose less."

"Ma, it's not how many pieces you lose," I said. "Sometimes you need to lose pieces to get ahead."

"Better to lose less, see if you really need."

At the next tournament, I won again, but it was my mother who wore the triumphant grin.

"Lost eight piece this time. Last time was eleven. What I tell you? Better off lose less!" I was annoyed, but I couldn't say anything.

I attended more tournaments, each one farther away from home. I won all games, in all divisions. The Chinese bakery downstairs from our flat displayed my growing collection of trophies in its window, amidst the dust-covered cakes that were never picked up. The day after I won an important regional tournament, the window encased a fresh sheet cake with whipped-cream frosting and red script saying, "Congratulations, Waverly Jong, Chinatown Chess Champion." Soon after that, a flower shop, headstone engraver, and funeral parlor offered to sponsor me in national tournaments. That's when my mother decided I no longer had to do the dishes. Winston and Vincent had to do my chores.

"Why does she get to play and we do all the work," complained Vincent.

"Is new American rules," said my mother. "Meimei play, squeeze all her brains out for win chess. You play, worth squeeze towel."

By my ninth birthday, I was a national chess champion. I was still some 429 points away from grand-master status, but I was touted as the Great American Hope, a child prodigy and a girl to boot. They ran a photo of me in *Life* magazine next to a quote in which Bobby Fischer said, "There will never be a woman grand master." "Your move, Bobby," said the caption.

The day they took the magazine picture I wore neatly plaited braids clipped with plastic barrettes trimmed with rhinestones. I was playing in a large high school auditorium that echoed with phlegmy coughs and the squeaky rubber knobs of chair legs sliding across freshly waxed wooden floors. Seated across from me was an American man, about the same age as Lau Po, maybe fifty. I remember that his sweaty brow seemed to weep at my every move. He wore a dark, malodorous suit. One of his pockets was stuffed with a great white kerchief on which he wiped his palm before sweeping his hand over the chosen chess piece with great flourish.

In my crisp pink-and-white dress with scratchy lace at the neck, one of two my mother had sewn for these special occasions, I would clasp my hands under my chin, the delicate points of my elbows poised lightly on the table in the manner my mother had shown me for posing for the press. I would swing my patent leather shoes back and forth like an impatient child riding on a school bus. Then I would pause, suck in my lips, twirl my chosen piece in midair as if undecided, and then firmly plant it in its new threatening place, with a triumphant smile thrown back at my opponent for good measure.

I no longer played in the alley of Waverly Place. I never visited the playground where the pigeons and old men gathered. I went to school, then directly home to learn new chess secrets, cleverly concealed advantages, more escape routes.

But I found it difficult to concentrate at home. My mother had a habit of standing over me while I plotted out my games. I think she thought of herself as my protective ally. Her lips would be sealed tight, and after each move I made, a soft "Hmmmmph" would escape from her nose.

"Ma, I can't practice when you stand there like that," I said one day. She retreated to the kitchen and made loud noises with the pots and pans. When the crashing stopped, I could see out of the corner of my eye that she was standing in the doorway. "Hmmmph!" Only this one came out of her tight throat.

My parents made many concessions to allow me to practice.

One time I complained that the bedroom I shared was so noisy that I couldn't think. Thereafter, my brothers slept in a bed in the living room facing the street. I said I couldn't finish my rice; my head didn't work right when my stomach was too full. I left the table with half-finished bowls and nobody complained. But there was one duty I couldn't avoid. I had to accompany my mother on Saturday market days when I had no tournament to play. My mother would proudly walk with me, visiting many shops, buying very little. "This my daughter Wave-ly Jong," she said to whoever looked her way.

One day, after we left a shop I said under my breath, "I wish you wouldn't do that, telling everybody I'm your daughter." My mother stopped walking. Crowds of people with heavy bags pushed past us on the sidewalk, bumping into first one shoulder, then another.

"Aiii-ya. So shame be with mother?" She grasped my hand even tighter as she glared at me.

I looked down. "It's not that, it's just so obvious. It's just so embarrassing."

"Embarrass you be my daughter?" Her voice was cracking with anger.

"That's not what I meant. That's not what I said."

"What you say?"

I knew it was a mistake to say anything more, but I heard my voice speaking. "Why do you have to use me to show off? If you want to show off, then why don't you learn to play chess."

My mother's eyes turned into dangerous black slits. She had no words for me, just sharp silence.

I felt the wind rushing around my hot ears. I jerked my hand out of my mother's tight grasp and spun around, knocking into an old woman. Her bag of groceries spilled to the ground.

"Aii-ya! Stupid girl!" my mother and the woman cried. Oranges and tin cans careened down the sidewalk. As my mother stooped to help the old woman pick up the escaping food, I took off.

I raced down the street, dashing between people, not looking back as my mother screamed shrilly, "Meimei! Meimei!" I fled down an alley, past dark curtained shops and merchants washing the grime off their windows. I sped into the sunlight, into a large street crowded with tourists examining trinkets and souvenirs. I ducked into another dark alley, down another street, up another alley. I ran until it hurt and I realized I had nowhere to go, that I was not running from anything. The alleys contained no escape routes.

My breath came out like angry smoke. It was cold. I sat down on an upturned plastic pail next to a stack of empty boxes, cupping my chin with my hands, thinking hard. I imagined my mother, first walking briskly down one street or another looking for me, then giving up and returning home to await my arrival. After two hours, I stood up on creaking legs and slowly walked home.

The alley was quiet and I could see the yellow lights shining from our flat like two tiger's eyes in the night. I climbed the sixteen steps to the door, advancing quietly up each so as not to make any warning sounds. I turned the knob; the door was locked. I heard a chair moving, quick steps, the locks turning— click! click! click!—and then the door opened.

"About time you got home," said Vincent. "Boy, are you in trouble."

He slid back to the dinner table. On a platter were the remains of a large fish, its fleshy head still connected to bones swimming upstream in vain escape. Standing there waiting for my punishment, I heard my mother speak in a dry voice.

"We not concerning this girl. This girl not have concerning for us."

Nobody looked at me. Bone chopsticks clinked against the insides of bowls being emptied into hungry mouths.

I walked into my room, closed the door, and lay down on my bed. The room was dark, the ceiling filled with shadows from the dinnertime lights of neighboring flats.

In my head, I saw a chessboard with sixty-four black and white squares. Opposite me was my opponent, two angry black slits. She wore a triumphant smile. "Strongest wind cannot be seen," she said.

Her black men advanced across the plane, slowly marching to each successive level as a single unit. My white pieces screamed as they scurried and fell off the board one by one. As her men drew closer to my edge, I felt myself growing light. I rose up into the air and flew out the window. Higher and higher, above the alley, over the tops of tiled roofs, where I was gathered up by the wind and pushed up toward the night sky until everything below me disappeared and I was alone.

I closed my eyes and pondered my next move.

LENA ST. CLAIR

The Voice from
the Wall

When I was little, my mother told me my great-grandfather had sentenced a beggar to die in the worst possible way, and that later the dead man came back and killed my great-grandfather. Either that, or he died of influenza one week later.

I used to play out the beggar's last moments over and over again in my head. In my mind, I saw the executioner strip off the man's shirt and lead him into the open yard. "This traitor," read the executioner, "is sentenced to die the death of a thousand cuts." But before he could even raise the sharp sword to whittle his life away, they found the beggar's mind had already broken into a thousand pieces. A few days later, my great-grandfather looked up from his books and saw this same man looking like a smashed vase hastily put back together. "As the sword was cutting me down," said the ghost, "I thought this was the worst I would ever have to endure. But I was wrong. The worst is on the other side." And the dead man embraced my great-grandfather with the jagged pieces of his arm and pulled him through the wall, to show him what he meant.

I once asked my mother how he really died. She said, "In bed, very quickly, after being sick for only two days."

"No, no, I mean the other man. How was he killed? Did they slice off his skin first? Did they use a cleaver to chop up his bones? Did he scream and feel all one thousand cuts?"

"Annh! Why do you Americans have only these morbid thoughts in your mind?" cried my mother in Chinese. "That man has been dead for almost seventy years. What does it matter how he died?"

I always thought it mattered, to know what is the worst possible thing that can happen to you, to know how you can avoid it, to not be drawn by the magic of the unspeakable. Because, even as a young child, I could sense the unspoken terrors that surrounded our house, the ones that chased my mother until she hid in a secret dark corner of her mind. And still they found her. I watched, over the years, as they devoured her, piece by piece, until she disappeared and became a ghost.

As I remember it, the dark side of my mother sprang from the basement in our old house in Oakland. I was five and my mother tried to hide it from me. She barricaded the door with a wooden chair, secured it with a chain and two types of key locks. And it became so mysterious that I spent all my energies unraveling this door, until the day I was finally able to pry it open with my small fingers, only to immediately fall headlong into the dark chasm. And it was only after I stopped screaming— I had seen the blood of my nose on my mother's shoulder— only then did my mother tell me about the bad man who lived in the basement and why I should never open the door again. He had lived there for thousands of years, she said, and was so evil and hungry that had my mother not rescued me so quickly, this bad man would have planted five babies in me and then eaten us all in a six-course meal, tossing our bones on the dirty floor.

And after that I began to see terrible things. I saw these things with my Chinese eyes, the part of me I got from my mother. I saw devils dancing feverishly beneath a hole I had dug in the sandbox. I saw that lightning had eyes and searched to strike down little children. I saw a beetle wearing the face of a child, which I promptly squashed with the wheel of my tricycle. And when I became older, I could see things that Causasian girls at school did not. Monkey rings that would split in two and send a swinging child hurtling through space. Tether balls that could splash a girl's head all over the playground in front of laughing friends.

I didn't tell anyone about the things I saw, not even my mother. Most people didn't know I was half Chinese, maybe because my last name is St. Clair. When people first saw me, they thought I looked like my father, English-Irish, big-boned and delicate at the same time. But if they looked really close, if they knew that they were there, they could see the Chinese parts. Instead of having cheeks like my father's sharp-edged points, mine were smooth as beach pebbles. I didn't have his straw-yellow hair or his white skin, yet my coloring looked too pale, like something that was once darker and had faded in the sun.

And my eyes, my mother gave me my eyes, no eyelids, as if they were carved on a jack-o'-lantern with two swift cuts of a short knife. I used to push my eyes in on the sides to make them rounder. Or I'd open them very wide until I could see the white parts. But when I walked around the house like that, my father asked me why I looked so scared.

I have a photo of my mother with this same scared look. My father said the picture was taken when Ma was first released from Angel Island Immigration Station. She stayed there for three weeks, until they could process her papers and determine whether she was a War Bride, a Displaced Person, a Student, or the wife of a Chinese-American citizen. My father said they didn't have rules for dealing with the Chinese wife of a Caucasian citizen. Somehow, in the end, they declared her a Displaced Person, lost in a sea of immigration categories.

My mother never talked about her life in China, but my father said he saved her from a terrible life there, some tragedy she could not speak about. My father proudly named her in her immigration papers: Betty St. Clair, crossing out her given name of Gu Ying-ying. And then he put down the wrong birthyear, 1916 instead of 1914. So, with the sweep of a pen, my mother lost her name and became a Dragon instead of a Tiger.

In this picture you can see why my mother looks displaced. She is clutching a large clam-shaped bag, as though someone might steal this from her as well if she is less watchful. She has on an ankle-length Chinese dress with modest vents at the side. And on top she is wearing a Westernized suit jacket, awkwardly stylish on my mother's small body, with its padded shoulders, wide lapels, and oversize cloth buttons. This was my mother's wedding dress, a gift from my father. In this outfit she looks as if she were neither coming from nor going to someplace. Her chin is bent down and you can see the precise part in her hair, a neat white line drawn from above her left brow then over the black horizon of her head.

And even though her head is bowed, humble in defeat, her eyes are staring up past the camera, wide open.

"Why does she look scared?" I asked my father.

And my father explained: It was only because he said "Cheese," and my mother was struggling to keep her eyes open until the flash went off, ten seconds later.

My mother often looked this way, waiting for something to happen, wearing this scared look. Only later she lost the struggle to keep her eyes open.

"Don't look at her," said my mother as we walked through Chinatown in Oakland. She had grabbed my hand and pulled me close to her body. And of course I looked. I saw a woman sitting on the sidewalk, leaning against a building. She was old and young at the same time, with dull eyes as though she had not slept for many years. And her feet and her hands—the tips were as black as if she had dipped them in India ink. But I knew they were rotted.

"What did she do to herself?" I whispered to my mother.

"She met a bad man," said my mother. "She had a baby she didn't want."

And I knew that was not true. I knew my mother made up anything to warn me, to help me avoid some unknown danger. My mother saw danger in everything, even in other Chinese people. Where we lived and shopped, everyone spoke Cantonese or English. My mother was from Wushi, near Shanghai. So she spoke Mandarin and a little bit of English. My father, who spoke only a few canned Chinese expressions, insisted my mother learn English. So with him, she spoke in moods and gestures, looks and silences, and sometimes a combination of English punctuated by hesitations and Chinese frustration: *"Shwo buchulai"*— Words cannot come out. So my father would put words in her mouth.

"I think Mom is trying to say she's tired," he would whisper when my mother became moody.

"I think she's saying we're the best dam family in the country!" he'd exclaim when she had cooked a wonderfully fragrant meal.

But with me, when we were alone, my mother would speak in Chinese, saying things my father could not possibly imagine. I could understand the words perfectly, but not the meanings. One thought led to another without connection.

"You must not walk in any direction but to school and back home," warned my mother when she decided I was old enough to walk by myself.

"Why?" I asked.

"You can't understand these things," she said.

"Why not?"

"Because I haven't put it in your mind yet."

"Why not?"

"Aii-ya! Such questions! Because it is too terrible to consider. A man can grab you off the streets, sell you to someone else, make you have a baby. Then you'll kill the baby. And when they find this baby in a garbage can, then what can be done? You'll go to jail, die there."

I knew this was not a true answer. But I also made up lies to prevent bad things from happening in the future. I often lied when I had to translate for her, the endless forms, instructions, notices from school, telephone calls. *"Shemma yisz?"*—What meaning?—she asked me when a man at a grocery store yelled at her for opening up jars to smell the insides. I was so embarrassed I told her that Chinese people were not allowed to shop there. When the school sent a notice home about a polio vaccination, I told her the time and place, and added that all students were now required to use metal lunch boxes, since they had discovered old paper bags can carry polio germs.

"We're moving up in the world," my father proudly announced, this being the occasion of his promotion to sales supervisor of a clothing manufacturer. "Your mother is thrilled."

And we did move up, across the bay to San Francisco and up a hill in North Beach, to an Italian neighborhood, where the sidewalk was so steep I had to lean into the slant to get home from school each day. I was ten and I was hopeful that we might be able to leave all the old fears behind in Oakland.

The apartment building was three stories high, two apartments per floor. It had a renovated façade, a recent layer of white stucco topped with connected rows of metal fire-escape ladders. But inside it was old. The front door with its narrow glass panes opened into a musty lobby that smelled of everybody's life mixed together. Everybody meant the names on the front door next to their little buzzers: Anderson, Giordino, Hayman, Ricci, Sorci, and our name, St. Clair. We lived on the middle floor, stuck between cooking smells that floated up and feet sounds that drifted down. My bedroom faced the street, and at night, in the dark, I could see in my mind another life. Cars struggling to climb the steep, fog-shrouded hill, gunning their deep engines and spinning their wheels. Loud, happy people, laughing, puffing, gasping: "Are we almost there?" A beagle scrambling to his feet to start his yipping yowl, answered a few seconds later by fire truck sirens and an angry woman hissing, "Sammy! Bad dog! Hush now!" And with all this soothing predictability, I would soon fall asleep.

My mother was not happy with the apartment, but I didn't see that at first. When we moved in, she busied herself with getting settled, arranging the furniture, unpacking dishes, hanging pictures on the wall. It took her about one week. And soon after that, when she and I were walking to the bus stop, she met a man who threw her off balance.

He was a red-faced Chinese man, wobbling down the sidewalk

as if he were lost. His runny eyes saw us and he quickly stood up straight and threw out his arms, shouting, "I found you! Suzie Wong, girl of my dreams! Hah!" And with his arms and mouth wide open, he started rushing toward us. My mother dropped my hand and covered her body with her arms as if she were naked, unable to do anything else. In that moment as she let go, I started to scream, seeing this dangerous man lunging closer. I was still screaming after two laughing men grabbed this man and, shaking him, said, "Joe, stop it, for Chrissake. You're scaring that poor little girl and her maid."

The rest of the day—while riding on the bus, walking in and out of stores, shopping for our dinner—my mother trembled. She clutched my hand so tightly it hurt. And once when she let go of my hand to take her wallet out of her purse at the cash register, I started to slip away to look at the candy. She grabbed my hand back so fast I knew at that instant how sorry she was that she had not protected me better.

As soon as we got home from grocery shopping, she began to put the cans and vegetables away. And then, as if something were not quite right, she removed the cans from one shelf and switched them with the cans on another. Next she walked briskly into the living room and moved a large round mirror from the wall facing the front door to a wall by the sofa.

"What are you doing?" I asked.

She whispered something in Chinese about "things not being balanced," and I thought she meant how things looked, not how things felt. And then she started to move the larger pieces: the sofa, chairs, end tables, a Chinese scroll of goldfish.

"What's going on here?" asked my father when he came home from work.

"She's making it look better," I said.

And the next day, when I came home from school, I saw she had again rearranged everything. Everything was in a different place. I could see that some terrible danger lay ahead.

"Why are you doing this?" I asked her, afraid she would give me a true answer.

But she whispered some Chinese nonsense instead: "When something goes against your nature, you are not in balance. This house was built too steep, and a bad wind from the top blows all your strength back down the hill. So you can never get ahead. You are always rolling backward."

And then she started pointing to the walls and doors of the apartment. "See how narrow this doorway is, like a neck that has been strangled. And the kitchen faces this toilet room, so all your worth is flushed away."

"But what does it mean? What's going to happen if it's not balanced?" I asked my mother.

My father explained it to me later. "Your mother is just practicing her nesting instincts," he said. "All mothers get it. You'll see when you're older."

I wondered why my father never worried. Was he blind? Why did my mother and I see something more?

And then a few days later, I found out that my father had been right all along. I came home from school, walked into my bedroom, and saw it. My mother had rearranged my room. My bed was no longer by the window but against a wall. And where my bed once was—now there stood a used crib. So the secret danger was a ballooning stomach, the source of my mother's imbalance. My mother was going to have a baby.

"See," said my father as we both looked at the crib. "Nesting instincts. Here's the nest. And here's where the baby goes." He was so pleased with this imaginary baby in the crib. He didn't see what I later saw. My mother began to bump into things, into table edges as if she forgot her stomach contained a baby, as if she were headed for trouble instead. She did not speak of the joys of having a new baby; she talked about a heaviness around her, about things being out of balance, not in harmony with one another. So I worried about that baby, that it was stuck somewhere between my mother's stomach and this crib in my room.

With my bed against the wall, the nighttime life of my imagination changed. Instead of street sounds, I began to hear voices coming from the wall, from the apartment next door. The front-door buzzer said a family called the Sorcis lived there.

That first night I heard the muffled sound of someone shouting. A woman? A girl? I flattened my ear against the wall and heard a woman's angry voice, then another, the higher voice of a girl shouting back. And now, the voices turned toward me, like fire sirens turning onto our street, and I could hear the accusations fading in and out: *Who am I to say!* . . . *Why do you keep buggin' me?* . . . *Then get out and stay out!* . . . *rather die rather be dead!* . . . *Why doncha then!*

Then I heard scraping sounds, slamming, pushing and shouts and then *whack! whack! whack!* Someone was killing. Someone was being killed. Screams and shouts, a mother had a sword high above a girl's head and was starting to slice her life away, first a braid, then her scalp, an eyebrow, a toe, a thumb, the point of her cheek, the slant of her nose, until there was nothing left, no sounds.

I lay back against my pillow, my heart pounding at what I had just witnessed with my ears and my imagination. A girl had just been killed. I hadn't been able to stop myself from listening. I wasn't able to stop what happened. The horror of it all.

But the next night, the girl came back to life with more screams, more beating, her life once more in peril. And so it continued, night after night, a voice pressing against my wall telling me that this was the worst possible thing that could happen: the terror of not knowing when it would ever stop.

Sometimes I heard this loud family across the hallway that separated our two apartment doors. Their apartment was by the stairs going up to the third floor. Ours was by the stairs going down to the lobby.

"You break your legs sliding down that banister, I'm gonna break your neck," a woman shouted. Her warnings were followed by the sounds of feet stomping on the stairs. "And don't forget to pick up Pop's suits!"

I knew their terrible life so intimately that I was startled by the immediacy of seeing her in person for the first time. I was pulling the front door shut while balancing an armload of books. And when I turned around, I saw her coming toward me just a few feet away and I shrieked and dropped everything. She snickered and I knew who she was, this tall girl whom I guessed to be about twelve, two years older than I was. Then she bolted down the stairs and I quickly gathered up my books and followed her, careful to walk on the other side of the street.

She didn't seem like a girl who had been killed a hundred times. I saw no traces of blood-stained clothes; she wore a crisp white blouse, a blue cardigan sweater, and a blue-green pleated skirt. In fact, as I watched her, she seemed quite happy, her two brown braids bouncing jauntily in rhythm to her walk. And then, as if she knew that I was thinking about her, she turned her head. She gave me a scowl and quickly ducked down a side street and walked out of my sight.

Every time I saw her after that, I would pretend to look down, busy rearranging my books or the buttons on my sweater, guilty that I knew everything about her.

My parents' friends Auntie Su and Uncle Canning picked me up at school one day and took me to the hospital to see my mother. I knew this was serious because everything they said was unnecessary but spoken with solemn importance.

"It is now four o'clock," said Uncle Canning, looking at his watch.

"The bus is never on time," said Auntie Su.

When I visited my mother in the hospital, she seemed half asleep, tossing back and forth. And then her eyes popped open, staring at the ceiling.

"My fault, my fault. I knew this before it happened," she babbled. "I did nothing to prevent it."

"Betty darling, Betty darling," said my father frantically. But my mother kept shouting these accusations to herself. She grabbed my hand and I realized her whole body was shaking. And then she looked at me, in a strange way, as if she were begging me for her life, as if I could pardon her. She was mumbling in Chinese.

"Lena, what's she saying?" cried my father. For once, he had no words to put in my mother's mouth.

And for once, I had no ready answer. It struck me that the worst possible thing had happened. That what she had been fearing had come true. They were no longer warnings. And so I listened.

"When the baby was ready to be born," she murmured, "I could already hear him screaming inside my womb. His little fingers, they were clinging to stay inside. But the nurses, the doctor, they said to push him out, make him come. And when his head popped out, the nurses cried, His eyes are wide open! He sees everything! Then his body slipped out and he lay on the table, steaming with life.

"When I looked at him, I saw right away. His tiny legs, his small arms, his thin neck, and then a large head so terrible I could not stop looking at it. This baby's eyes were open and his head—it was open too! I could see all the way back, to where his thoughts were supposed to be, and there was nothing there. No brain, the doctor shouted! His head is just an empty eggshell!

"And then this baby, maybe he heard us, his large head seemed to fill with hot air and rise up from the table. The head turned to one side, then to the other. It looked right through me. I knew he could see everything inside me. How I had given no thought to killing my other son! How I had given no thought to having this baby!"

I could not tell my father what she had said. He was so sad already with this empty crib in his mind. How could I tell him she was crazy?

So this is what I translated for him: "She says we must all think very hard about having another baby. She says she hopes this baby is very happy on the other side. And she thinks we should leave now and go have dinner."

After the baby died, my mother fell apart, not all at once, but piece by piece, like plates falling off a shelf one by one. I never knew when it would happen, so I became nervous all the time, waiting.

Sometimes she would start to make dinner, but would stop halfway, the water running full steam in the sink, her knife poised in the air over half-chopped vegetables, silent, tears flowing. And sometimes we'd be eating and we would have to stop and put our forks down because she had dropped her face into her hands and was saying, *"Mei gwansyi"*—It doesn't matter. My father would just sit there, trying to figure out what it was that didn't matter this much. And I would leave the table, knowing it would happen again, always a next time.

My father seemed to fall apart in a different way. He tried to make things better. But it was as if he were running to catch things before they fell, only he would fall before he could catch anything.

"She's just tired," he explained to me when we were eating dinner at the Gold Spike, just the two of us, because my mother was lying like a statue on her bed. I knew he was thinking about her because he had this worried face, staring at his dinner plate as if it were filled with worms instead of spaghetti.

At home, my mother looked at everything around her with empty eyes. My father would come home from work, patting my head, saying, "How's my big girl," but always looking past me, toward my mother. I had such fears inside, not in my head but in my stomach. I could no longer see what was so scary, but I could feel it. I could feel every little movement in our silent house. And at night, I could feel the crashing loud fights on the other side of my bedroom wall, this girl being beaten to death. In bed, with the blanket edge lying across my neck, I used to wonder which was worse, our side or theirs? And after thinking about this for a while, after feeling sorry for myself, it comforted me somewhat to think that this girl next door had a more unhappy life.

But one night after dinner our doorbell rang. This was curious, because usually people rang the buzzer downstairs first.

"Lena, could you see who it is?" called my father from the kitchen. He was doing the dishes. My mother was lying in bed. My mother was now always "resting" and it was as if she had died and become a living ghost.

I opened the door cautiously, then swung it wide open with surprise. It was the girl from next door. I stared at her with undisguised amazement. She was smiling back at me, and she looked ruffled, as if she had fallen out of bed with her clothes on.

"Who is it?" called my father.

"It's next door!" I shouted to my father. "It's . . ."

"Teresa," she offered quickly.

"It's Teresa!" I yelled back to my father.

"Invite her in," my father said at almost the same moment that Teresa squeezed past me and into our apartment. Without being invited, she started walking toward my bedroom. I closed the front door and followed her two brown braids that were bouncing like whips beating the back of a horse.

She walked right over to my window and began to open it. "What are you doing?" I cried. She sat on the window ledge, looked out on the street. And then she looked at me and started to giggle. I sat down on my bed watching her, waiting for her to stop, feeling the cold air blow in from the dark opening.

"What's so funny?" I finally said. It occurred to me that perhaps she was laughing at me, at my life. Maybe she had listened through the wall and heard nothing, the stagnant silence of our unhappy house.

"Why are you laughing?" I demanded.

"My mother kicked me out," she finally said. She talked with a swagger, seeming to be proud of this fact. And then she snickered a little and said, "We had this fight and she pushed me out the door and locked it. So now she thinks I'm going to wait outside the door until I'm sorry enough to apologize. But I'm not going to."

"Then what are you going to do?" I asked breathlessly, certain that her mother would kill her for good this time.

"I'm going to use your fire escape to climb back into my bedroom," she whispered back. "And she's going to wait. And when she gets worried, she'll open the front door. Only I won't be there! I'll be in my bedroom, in bed." She giggled again.

"Won't she be mad when she finds you?"

"Nah, she'll just be glad I'm not dead or something. Oh, she'll pretend to be mad, sort of. We do this kind of stuff all the time." And then she slipped through my window and soundlessly made her way back home.

I stared at the open window for a long time, wondering about her. How could she go back? Didn't she see how terrible her life was? Didn't she recognize it would never stop?

I lay down on my bed waiting to hear the screams and shouts. And late at night I was still awake when I heard the loud voices next door. Mrs. Sorci was shouting and crying, *You stupida girl. You almost gave me a heart attack.* And Teresa was yelling back, *I coulda been killed. I almost fell and broke my neck.* And then I heard them laughing and crying, crying and laughing, shouting with love.

I was stunned. I could almost see them hugging and kissing one another. I was crying for joy with them, because I had been wrong.

And in my memory I can still feel the hope that beat in me that night. I clung to this hope, day after day, night after night, year after year. I would watch my mother lying in her bed, babbling to herself as she sat on the sofa. And yet I knew that this, the worst possible thing, would one day stop. I still saw bad things in my mind, but now I found ways to change them. I still heard Mrs. Sorci and Teresa having terrible fights, but I saw something else.

I saw a girl complaining that the pain of not being seen was unbearable. I saw the mother lying in bed in her long flowing robes. Then the girl pulled out a sharp sword and told her mother, "Then you must die the death of a thousand cuts. It is the only way to save you."

The mother accepted this and closed her eyes. The sword came down and sliced back and forth, up and down, *whish! whish! whish!* And the mother screamed and shouted, cried out in terror and pain. But when she opened her eyes, she saw no blood, no shredded flesh.

The girl said, "Do you see now?"

The mother nodded: "Now I have perfect understanding. I have already experienced the worst. After this, there is no worst possible thing."

And the daughter said, "Now you must come back, to the other side. Then you can see why you were wrong."

And the girl grabbed her mother's hand and pulled her through the wall.

ROSE HSU JORDAN

Half and Half

As proof of her faith, my mother used to carry a small leatherette Bible when she went to the First Chinese Baptist Church every Sunday. But later, after my mother lost her faith in God, that leatherette Bible wound up wedged under a too-short table leg, a way for her to correct the imbalances of life. It's been there for over twenty years.

My mother pretends that Bible isn't there. Whenever anyone asks her what it's doing there, she says, a little too loudly, "Oh, this? I forgot." But I know she sees it. My mother is not the best housekeeper in the world, and after all these years that Bible is still clean white.

Tonight I'm watching my mother sweep under the same kitchen table, something she does every night after dinner. She gently pokes her broom around the table leg propped up by the Bible. I watch her, sweep after sweep, waiting for the right moment to tell her about Ted and me, that we're getting divorced. When I tell her, I know she's going to say, "This cannot be."

And when I say that it is certainly true, that our marriage is over, I know what else she will say: "Then you must save it."

And even though I know it's hopeless—there's absolutely

nothing left to save—I'm afraid if I tell her that, she'll still persuade me to try.

I think it's ironic that my mother wants me to fight the divorce. Seventeen years ago she was chagrined when I started dating Ted. My older sisters had dated only Chinese boys from church before getting married.

Ted and I met in a politics of ecology class when he leaned over and offered to pay me two dollars for the last week's notes. I refused the money and accepted a cup of coffee instead. This was during my second semester at UC Berkeley, where I had enrolled as a liberal arts major and later changed to fine arts. Ted was in his third year in pre-med, his choice, he told me, ever since he dissected a fetal pig in the sixth grade.

I have to admit that what I initially found attractive in Ted were precisely the things that made him different from my brothers and the Chinese boys I had dated: his brashness; the assuredness in which he asked for things and expected to get them; his opinionated manner; his angular face and lanky body; the thickness of his arms; the fact that his parents immigrated from Tarrytown, New York, not Tientsin, China.

My mother must have noticed these same differences after Ted picked me up one evening at my parents' house. When I returned home, my mother was still up, watching television.

"He is American," warned my mother, as if I had been too blind to notice. A *waigoren*."

"I'm American too," I said. "And it's not as if I'm going to marry him or something."

Mrs. Jordan also had a few words to say. Ted had casually invited me to a family picnic, the annual clan reunion held by the polo fields in Golden Gate Park. Although we had dated only a few times in the last month—and certainly had never slept together, since both of us lived at home—Ted introduced me to all his relatives as his girlfriend, which, until then, I didn't know I was.

Later, when Ted and his father went off to play volleyball with the others, his mother took my hand, and we started walking along the grass, away from the crowd. She squeezed my palm warmly but never seemed to look at me.

"I'm so glad to meet you *finally*," Mrs. Jordan said. I wanted to tell her I wasn't really Ted's girlfriend, but she went on. "I think it's nice that you and Ted are having such a lot of fun together. So I hope you won't misunderstand what I have to say."

And then she spoke quietly about Ted's future, his need to concentrate on his medical studies, why it would be years before he could even think about marriage. She assured me she had nothing whatsoever against minorities; she and her husband, who owned a chain of office-supply stores, personally knew many fine people who were Oriental, Spanish, and even black. But Ted was going to be in one of those professions where he would be judged by a different standard, by patients and other doctors who might not be as understanding as the Jordans were. She said it was so unfortunate the way the rest of the world was, how unpopular the Vietnam War was.

"Mrs. Jordan, I am not Vietnamese," I said softly, even though I was on the verge of shouting. "And I have no intention of marrying your son."

When Ted drove me home that day, I told him I couldn't see him anymore. When he asked me why, I shrugged. When he pressed me, I told him what his mother had said, verbatim, without comment.

"And you're just going to sit there! Let my mother decide what's right?" he shouted, as if I were a co-conspirator who had turned traitor. I was touched that Ted was so upset.

"What should we do?" I asked, and I had a pained feeling I thought was the beginning of love.

In those early months, we clung to each other with a rather silly desperation, because, in spite of anything my mother or Mrs. Jordan could say, there was nothing that really prevented us from seeing one another. With imagined tragedy hovering over us, we became inseparable, two halves creating the whole: yin and yang. I was victim to his hero. I was always in danger and he was always rescuing me. I would fall and he would lift me up. It was exhilarating and draining. The emotional effect of saving and being saved was addicting to both of us. And that, as much as anything we ever did in bed, was how we made love to each other: conjoined where my weaknesses needed protection.

"What should we do?" I continued to ask him. And within a year of our first meeting we were living together. The month before Ted started medical school at UCSF we were married in the Episcopal church, and Mrs. Jordan sat in the front pew, crying as was expected of the groom's mother. When Ted finished his residency in dermatology, we bought a run-down three-story Victorian with a large garden in Ashbury Heights. Ted helped me set up a studio downstairs so I could take in work as a free-lance production assistant for graphic artists.

Over the years, Ted decided where we went on vacation. He decided what new furniture we should buy. He decided we should wait until we moved into a better neighborhood before having children. We used to discuss some of these matters, but we both knew the question would boil down to my saying, "Ted, you decide." After a while, there were no more discussions. Ted simply decided. And I never thought of objecting. I preferred to ignore the world around me, obsessing only over what was in front of me: my T-square, my X-acto knife, my blue pencil.

But last year Ted's feelings about what he called "decision and responsibility" changed. A new patient had come to him asking what she could do about the spidery veins on her cheeks. And when he told her he could suck the red veins out and make her beautiful again, she believed him. But instead, he accidentally sucked a nerve out, and the left side of her smile fell down and she sued him.

After he lost the malpractice lawsuit—his first, and a big shock to him I now realize—he started pushing me to make decisons. Did I think we should buy an American car or a Japanese car? Should we change from whole-life to term insurance? What did I think about that candidate who supported the contras? What about a family?

I thought about things, the pros and the cons. But in the end

I would be so confused, because I never believed there was ever any one right answer, yet there were many wrong ones. So whenever I said, "You decide," or "I don't care," or "Either way is fine with me," Ted would say in his impatient voice, "No, *you* decide. You can't have it both ways, none of the responsibility, none of the blame."

I could feel things changing between us. A protective veil had been lifted and Ted now started pushing me about everything. He asked me to decide on the most trivial matters, as if he were baiting me. Italian food or Thai. One appetizer or two. Which appetizer. Credit card or cash. Visa or MasterCard.

Last month, when he was leaving for a two-day dermatology course in Los Angeles, he asked if I wanted to come along and then quickly, before I could say anything, he added, "Never mind, I'd rather go alone."

"More time to study," I agreed.

"No, because you can never make up your mind about anything," he said.

And I protested, "But it's only with things that aren't important."

"Nothing is important to you, then," he said in a tone of disgust.

"Ted, if you want me to go, I'll go."

And it was as if something snapped in him. "How the hell did we ever get married? Did you just say 'I do' because the minister said 'repeat after me'? What would you have done with your life if I had never married you? Did it ever occur to you?"

This was such a big leap in logic, between what I said and what he said, that I thought we were like two people standing apart on separate mountain peaks, recklessly leaning forward to throw stones at one another, unaware of the dangerous chasm that separated us.

But now I realize Ted knew what he was saying all along. He wanted to show me the rift. Because later that evening he called from Los Angeles and said he wanted a divorce.

Ever since Ted's been gone, I've been thinking, Even if I had expected it, even if I had known what I was going to do with my life, it still would have knocked the wind out of me.

When something that violent hits you, you can't help but lose your balance and fall. And after you pick yourself up, you realize you can't trust anybody to save you—not your husband, not your mother, not God. So what can you do to stop yourself from tilting and falling all over again?

My mother believed in God's will for many years. It was as if she had turned on a celestial faucet and goodness kept pouring out. She said it was faith that kept all these good things coming our way, only I thought she said "fate," because she couldn't pronounce that "th" sound in "faith."

And later, I discovered that maybe it was fate all along, that faith was just an illusion that somehow you're in control. I found out the most *I* could have was hope, and with that I was not denying any possibility, good or bad. I was just saying, If there is a choice, dear God or whatever you are, here's where the odds should be placed.

I remember the day I started thinking this, it was such a revelation to me. It was the day my mother lost her faith in God. She found that things of unquestioned certainty could never be trusted again.

We had gone to the beach, to a secluded spot south of the city near Devil's Slide. My father had read in *Sunset* magazine that this was a good place to catch ocean perch. And although my father was not a fisherman but a pharmacist's assistant who had once been a doctor in China, he believed in his *nengkan*, his ability to do anything he put his mind to. My mother believed she had *nengkan* to cook anything my father had a mind to catch. It was this belief in their *nengkan* that had brought my parents to America. It had enabled them to have seven children and buy a house in the Sunset district with very little money. It had given them the confidence to believe their luck would never run out, that God was on their side, that the house gods had only benevolent things to report and our ancestors were pleased, that lifetime warranties meant our lucky streak would never break, that all the elements were in balance, the right amount of wind and water.

So there we were, the nine of us: my father, my mother, my two sisters, four brothers, and myself, so confident as we walked along our first beach. We marched in single file across the cool gray sand, from oldest to youngest. I was in the middle, fourteen years old. We would have made quite a sight, if anyone else had been watching, nine pairs of bare feet trudging, nine pairs of shoes in hand, nine black-haired heads turned toward the water to watch the waves tumbling in.

The wind was whipping the cotton trousers around my legs and I looked for some place where the sand wouldn't kick into my eyes. I saw we were standing in the hollow of a cove. It was like a giant bowl, cracked in half, the other half washed out to sea. My mother walked toward the right, where the beach was clean, and we all followed. On this side, the wall of the cove curved around and protected the beach from both the rough surf and the wind. And along this wall, in its shadow, was a reef ledge that started at the edge of the beach and continued out past the cove where the waters became rough. It seemed as though a person could walk out to sea on this reef, although it looked very rocky and slippery. On the other side of the cove, the wall was more jagged, eaten away by the water. It was pitted with crevices, so when the waves crashed against the wall, the water spewed out of these holes like white gulleys.

Thinking back, I remember that this beach cove was a terrible place, full of wet shadows that chilled us and invisible specks that flew into our eyes and made it hard for us to see the dangers. We were all blind with the newness of this experience: a Chinese family trying to act like a typical American family at the beach.

My mother spread out an old striped bedspread, which flapped in the wind until nine pairs of shoes weighed it down. My father assembled his long bamboo fishing pole, a pole he had made with his own two hands, remembering its design from his childhood in China. And we children sat huddled shoulder to shoulder on the blanket, reaching into the grocery sack full of bologna sandwiches, which we hungrily ate salted with sand from our fingers.

Then my father stood up and admired his fishing pole, its grace, its strength. Satisfied, he picked up his shoes and walked to the edge of the beach and then onto the reef to the point just before it was wet. My two older sisters, Janice and Ruth, jumped up from the blanket and slapped their thighs to get the sand off. Then they slapped each other's back and raced off down the beach shrieking. I was about to get up and chase them, but my mother nodded toward my four brothers and reminded me: *"Dangsying tamende shenti,"* which means "Take care of them," or literally, "Watch out for their bodies." These bodies were the anchors of my life: Matthew, Mark, Luke, and Bing. I fell back onto the sand, groaning as my throat grew tight, as I made the same lament: "Why?" Why did *I* have to care for them?

And she gave me the same answer: *"Yiding."*

I must. Because they were my brothers. My sisters had once taken care of me. How else could I learn responsibility? How else could I appreciate what my parents had done for me?

Matthew, Mark, and Luke were twelve, ten, and nine, old enough to keep themselves loudly amused. They had already buried Luke in a shallow grave of sand so that only his head stuck out. Now they were starting to pat together the outlines of a sand-castle wall on top of him.

But Bing was only four, easily excitable and easily bored and irritable. He didn't want to play with the other brothers because they had pushed him off to the side, admonishing him, "No, Bing, you'll just wreck it."

So Bing wandered down the beach, walking stiffly like an ousted emperor, picking up shards of rock and chunks of driftwood and flinging them with all his might into the surf. I trailed behind, imagining tidal waves and wondering what I would do if one appeared. I called to Bing every now and then, "Don't go too close to the water. You'll get your feet wet." And I thought how much I seemed like my mother, always worried beyond reason inside, but at the same time talking about the danger as if it were less than it really was. The worry surrounded me, like

123

the wall of the cove, and it made me feel everything had been considered and was now safe.

My mother had a superstition, in fact, that children were predisposed to certain dangers on certain days, all depending on their Chinese birthdate. It was explained in a little Chinese book called *The Twenty-Six Malignant Gates*. There, on each page, was an illustration of some terrible danger that awaited young innocent children. In the corners was a description written in Chinese, and since I couldn't read the characters, I could only see what the picture meant.

The same little boy appeared in each picture: climbing a broken tree limb, standing by a falling gate, slipping in a wooden tub, being carried away by a snapping dog, fleeing from a bolt of lightning. And in each of these pictures stood a man who looked as if he were wearing a lizard costume. He had a big crease in his forehead, or maybe it was actually that he had two round horns. In one picture, the lizard man was standing on a curved bridge, laughing as he watched the little boy falling forward over the bridge rail, his slippered feet already in the air.

It would have been enough to think that even one of these dangers could befall a child. And even though the birthdates corresponded to only one danger, my mother worried about them all. This was because she couldn't figure out how the Chinese dates, based on the lunar calendar, translated into American dates. So by taking them all into account, she had absolute faith she could prevent every one of them.

The sun had shifted and moved over the other side of the cove wall. Everything had settled into place. My mother was busy keeping sand from blowing onto the blanket, then shaking sand out of shoes, and tacking corners of blankets back down again with the now clean shoes. My father was still standing at the end of the reef, patiently casting out, waiting for *nengkan* to manifest itself as a fish. I could see small figures farther down on the beach, and I could tell they were my sisters by their two dark heads and yellow pants. My brothers' shrieks were mixed with those of seagulls. Bing had found an empty soda bottle and was using this to dig sand next to the dark cove wall. And I sat on the sand, just where the shadows ended and the sunny part began.

Bing was pounding the soda bottle against the rock, so I called to him, "Don't dig so hard. You'll bust a hole in the wall and fall all the way to China." And I laughed when he looked at me as though he thought what I said was true. He stood up and started walking toward the water. He put one foot tentatively on the reef, and I warned him, "Bing."

"I'm gonna see Daddy," he protested.

"Stay close to the wall, then, away from the water," I said. "Stay away from the mean fish."

And I watched as he inched his way along the reef, his back hugging the bumpy cove wall. I still see him, so clearly that I almost feel I can make him stay there forever.

I see him standing by the wall, safe, calling to my father, who looks over his shoulder toward Bing. How glad I am that my father is going to watch him for a while! Bing starts to walk over and then something tugs on my father's line and he's reeling as fast as he can.

Shouts erupt. Someone has thrown sand in Luke's face and he's jumped out of his sand grave and thrown himself on top of Mark, thrashing and kicking. My mother shouts for me to stop them. And right after I pull Luke off Mark, I look up and see Bing walking alone to the edge of the reef. In the confusion of the fight, nobody notices. I am the only one who sees what Bing is doing.

Bing walks one, two, three steps. His little body is moving so quickly, as if he spotted something wonderful by the water's edge. And I think, *He's going to fall in.* I'm expecting it. And just as I think this, his feet are already in the air, in a moment of balance, before he splashes into the sea and disappears without leaving so much as a ripple in the water.

I sank to my knees watching that spot where he disappeared, not moving, not saying anything. I couldn't make sense of it. I was thinking, Should I run to the water and try to pull him out? Should I shout to my father? Can I rise on my legs fast enough? Can I take it all back and forbid Bing from joining my father on the ledge?

And then my sisters were back, and one of them said, "Where's Bing?" There was silence for a few seconds and then shouts and sand flying as everyone rushed past me toward the water's edge. I stood there unable to move as my sisters looked by the cove wall, as my brothers scrambled to see what lay behind pieces of driftwood. My mother and father were trying to part the waves with their hands.

We were there for many hours. I remember the search boats and the sunset when dusk came. I had never seen a sunset like that: a bright orange flame touching the water's edge and then fanning out, warming the sea. When it became dark, the boats turned their yellow orbs on and bounced up and down on the dark shiny water.

As I look back, it seems unnatural to think about the colors of the sunset and boats at a time like that. But we all had strange thoughts. My father was calculating minutes, estimating the temperature of the water, readjusting his estimate of when Bing fell. My sisters were calling, "Bing! Bing!" as if he were hiding in some bushes high above the beach cliffs. My brothers sat in the car, quietly reading comic books. And when the boats turned off their yellow orbs, my mother went for a swim. She had never swum a stroke in her life, but her faith in her own *nengkan* convinced her that what these Americans couldn't do, she could. She could find Bing.

And when the rescue people finally pulled her out of the water, she still had her *nengkan* intact. Her hair, her clothes, they were all heavy with the cold water, but she stood quietly, calm and regal as a mermaid queen who had just arrived out of the sea. The police called off the search, put us all in our car, and sent us home to grieve.

I had expected to be beaten to death, by my father, by my mother, by my sisters and brothers. I knew it was my fault. I hadn't watched him closely enough, and yet I saw him. But as we sat in the dark living room, I heard them, one by one whispering their regrets.

"I was selfish to want to go fishing," said my father.

"We shouldn't have gone for a walk," said Janice, while Ruth blew her nose yet another time.

"Why'd you have to throw sand in my face?" moaned Luke. "Why'd you have to make me start a fight?"

And my mother quietly admitted to me, "I told you to stop their fight. I told you to take your eyes off him."

If I had had any time at all to feel a sense of relief, it would have quickly evaporated, because my mother also said, "So now I am telling you, we must go and find him, quickly, tomorrow morning." And everybody's eyes looked down. But I saw it as my punishment: to go out with my mother, back to the beach, to help her find Bing's body.

Nothing prepared me for what my mother did the next day. When I woke up, it was still dark and she was already dressed. On the kitchen table was a thermos, a teacup, the white leatherette Bible, and the car keys.

"Is Daddy ready?" I asked.

"Daddy's not coming," she said.

"Then how will we get there? Who will drive us?"

She picked up the keys and I followed her out the door to the car. I wondered the whole time as we drove to the beach how she had learned to drive overnight. She used no map. She drove smoothly ahead, turning down Geary, then the Great Highway, signaling at all the right times, getting on the Coast Highway and easily winding the car around the sharp curves that often led inexperienced drivers off and over the cliffs.

When we arrived at the beach, she walked immediately down the dirt path and over to the end of the reef ledge, where I had seen Bing disappear. She held in her hand the white Bible. And looking out over the water, she called to God, her small voice carried up by the gulls to heaven. It began with "Dear God" and ended with "Amen," and in between she spoke in Chinese.

"I have always believed in your blessings," she praised God in that same tone she used for exaggerated Chinese compliments. "We knew they would come. We did not question them. Your decisions were our decisions. You rewarded us for our faith.

"In return we have always tried to show our deepest respect. We went to your house. We brought you money. We sang your songs. You gave us more blessings. And now we have misplaced one of them. We were careless. This is true. We had so many good things, we couldn't keep them in our mind all the time.

"So maybe you hid him from us to teach us a lesson, to be more careful with your gifts in the future. I have learned this. I have put it in my memory. And now I have come to take Bing back."

I listened quietly as my mother said these words, horrified. And I began to cry when she added, "Forgive us for his bad manners. My daughter, this one standing here, will be sure to teach him better lessons of obedience before he visits you again."

After her prayer, her faith was so great that she saw him, three times, waving to her from just beyond the first wave. *"Nale!"*— There! And she would stand straight as a sentinel, until three times her eyesight failed her and Bing turned into a dark spot of churning seaweed.

My mother did not let her chin fall down. She walked back to the beach and put the Bible down. She picked up the thermos and teacup and walked to the water's edge. Then she told me that the night before she had reached back into her life, back when she was a girl in China, and this is what she had found.

"I remember a boy who lost his hand in a firecracker accident," she said. "I saw the shreds of this boy's arm, his tears, and then I heard his mother's claim that he would grow back another hand, better than the last. This mother said she would pay back an ancestral debt ten times over. She would use a water treatment to soothe the wrath of Chu Jung, the three-eyed god of fire. And true enough, the next week this boy was riding a bicycle, both hands steering a straight course past my astonished eyes!"

And then my mother became very quiet. She spoke again in a thoughtful, respectful manner.

"An ancestor of ours once stole water from a sacred well. Now the water is trying to steal back. We must sweeten the temper of the Coiling Dragon who lives in the sea. And then we must make him loosen his coils from Bing by giving him another treasure he can hide."

My mother poured out tea sweetened with sugar into the teacup, and threw this into the sea. And then she opened her fist. In her palm was a ring of watery blue sapphire, a gift from her mother, who had died many years before. This ring, she told me, drew coveting stares from women and made them inattentive to the children they guarded so jealously. This would make the Coiling Dragon forgetful of Bing. She threw the ring into the water.

But even with this, Bing did not appear right away. For an hour or so, all we saw was seaweed drifting by. And then I saw her clasp her hands to her chest, and she said in a wondrous voice, "See, it's because we were watching the wrong direction." And I too saw Bing trudging wearily at the far end of the beach, his shoes hanging in his hand, his dark head bent over in exhaustion. I could feel what my mother felt. The hunger in our hearts was instantly filled. And then the two of us, before we could even get to our feet, saw him light a cigarette, grow tall, and become a stranger.

"Ma, let's go," I said as softly as possible.

"He's there," she said firmly. She pointed to the jagged wall across the water. "I see him. He is in a cave, sitting on a little step above the water. He is hungry and a little cold, but he has learned now not to complain too much."

And then she stood up and started walking across the sandy beach as though it were a solid paved path, and I was trying to follow behind, struggling and stumbling in the soft mounds. She marched up the steep path to where the car was parked, and she wasn't even breathing hard as she pulled a large inner tube from the trunk. To this lifesaver, she tied the fishing line from my father's bamboo pole. She walked back and threw the tube into the sea, holding onto the pole.

"This will go where Bing is. I will bring him back," she said fiercely. I had never heard so much *nengkan* in my mother's voice.

The tube followed her mind. It drifted out, toward the other side of the cove where it was caught by stronger waves. The line became taut and she strained to hold on tight. But the line snapped and then spiraled into the water.

We both climbed toward the end of the reef to watch. The tube had now reached the other side of the cove. A big wave smashed it into the wall. The bloated tube leapt up and then it was sucked in, under the wall and into a cavern. It popped out. Over and over again, it disappeared, emerged, glistening black, faithfully reporting it had seen Bing and was going back to try to pluck him from the cave. Over and over again, it dove and popped back up again, empty but still hopeful. And then, after a dozen or so times, it was sucked into the dark recess, and when it came out, it was torn and lifeless.

At that moment, and not until that moment, did she give up. My mother had a look on her face that I'll never forget. It was one of complete despair and horror, for losing Bing, for being so foolish as to think she could use faith to change fate. And it made me angry—so blindingly angry—that everything had failed us.

I know now that I had never expected to find Bing, just as I know now I will never find a way to save my marriage. My mother tells me, though, that I should still try.

"What's the point?" I say. "There's no hope. There's no reason to keep trying."

"Because you must," she says. "This is not hope. Not reason. This is your fate. This is your life, what you must do."

"So what can I do?"

And my mother says, "You must think for yourself, what you must do. If someone tells you, then you are not trying." And then she walks out of the kitchen to let me think about this.

I think about Bing, how I knew he was in danger, how I let it happen. I think about my marriage, how I had seen the signs, really I had. But I just let it happen. And I think now that fate is shaped half by expectation, half by inattention. But somehow, when you lose something you love, faith takes over. You have to pay attention to what you lost. You have to undo the expectation.

My mother, she still pays attention to it. That Bible under the table, I know she sees it. I remember seeing her write in it before she wedged it under.

I lift the table and slide the Bible out. I put the Bible on the table, flipping quickly through the pages, because I know it's there. On the page before the New Testament begins, there's a section called "Deaths," and that's where she wrote "Bing Hsu" lightly, in erasable pencil.

JING-MEI WOO

Two Kinds

My mother believed you could be anything you wanted to be in America. You could open a restaurant. You could work for the government and get good retirement. You could buy a house with almost no money down. You could become rich. You could become instantly famous.

"Of course you can be prodigy, too," my mother told me when I was nine. "You can be best anything. What does Auntie Lindo know? Her daughter, she is only best tricky."

America was where all my mother's hopes lay. She had come here in 1949 after losing everything in China: her mother and father, her family home, her first husband, and two daughters, twin baby girls. But she never looked back with regret. There were so many ways for things to get better.

We didn't immediately pick the right kind of prodigy. At first my mother thought I could be a Chinese Shirley Temple. We'd watch Shirley's old movies on TV as though they were training films. My mother would poke my arm and say, "*Ni kan*"—You watch. And I would see Shirley tapping her feet, or singing a sailor song, or pursing her lips into a very round O while saying, "Oh my goodness."

"*Ni kan*," said my mother as Shirley's eyes flooded with tears. "You already know how. Don't need talent for crying!"

Soon after my mother got this idea about Shirley Temple, she took me to a beauty training school in the Mission district and put me in the hands of a student who could barely hold the scissors without shaking. Instead of getting big fat curls, I emerged with an uneven mass of crinkly black fuzz. My mother dragged me off to the bathroom and tried to wet down my hair.

"You look like Negro Chinese," she lamented, as if I had done this on purpose.

The instructor of the beauty training school had to lop off these soggy clumps to make my hair even again. "Peter Pan is very popular these days," the instructor assured my mother. I now had hair the length of a boy's, with straight-across bangs that hung at a slant two inches above my eyebrows. I liked the haircut and it made me actually look forward to my future fame.

In fact, in the beginning, I was just as excited as my mother, maybe even more so. I pictured this prodigy part of me as many different images, trying each one on for size. I was a dainty ballerina girl standing by the curtains, waiting to hear the right music that would send me floating on my tiptoes. I was like the Christ child lifted out of the straw manger, crying with holy indignity. I was Cinderella stepping from her pumpkin carriage with sparkly cartoon music filling the air.

In all of my imaginings, I was filled with a sense that I would soon become *perfect*. My mother and father would adore me. I would be beyond reproach. I would never feel the need to sulk for anything.

But sometimes the prodigy in me became impatient. "If you don't hurry up and get me out of here, I'm disappearing for good," it warned. "And then you'll always be nothing."

Every night after dinner, my mother and I would sit at the Formica kitchen table. She would present new tests, taking her examples from stories of amazing children she had read in *Ripley's Believe It or Not*, or *Good Housekeeping*, *Reader's Digest*, and a dozen other magazines she kept in a pile in our bathroom. My mother got these magazines from people whose houses she cleaned. And since she cleaned many houses each week, we had a great assortment. She would look through them all, searching for stories about remarkable children.

The first night she brought out a story about a three-year-old boy who knew the capitals of all the states and even most of the European countries. A teacher was quoted as saying the little boy could also pronounce the names of the foreign cities correctly.

"What's the capital of Finland?" my mother asked me, looking at the magazine story.

All I knew was the capital of California, because Sacramento was the name of the street we lived on in Chinatown. "Nairobi!" I guessed, saying the most foreign word I could think of. She checked to see if that was possibly one way to pronounce "Helsinki" before showing me the answer.

The tests got harder—multiplying numbers in my head, finding the queen of hearts in a deck of cards, trying to stand on my head without using my hands, predicting the daily temperatures in Los Angeles, New York, and London.

One night I had to look at a page from the Bible for three minutes and then report everything I could remember. "Now Jehoshaphat had riches and honor in abundance and . . . that's all I remember, Ma," I said.

And after seeing my mother's disappointed face once again, something inside of me began to die. I hated the tests, the raised hopes and failed expectations. Before going to bed that night, I looked in the mirror above the bathroom sink and when I saw only my face staring back—and that it would always be this ordinary face—I began to cry. Such a sad, ugly girl! I made high-pitched noises like a crazed animal, trying to scratch out the face in the mirror.

And then I saw what seemed to be the prodigy side of me—because I had never seen that face before. I looked at my reflection, blinking so I could see more clearly. The girl staring back at me was angry, powerful. This girl and I were the same. I had new thoughts, willful thoughts, or rather thoughts filled with lots of won'ts. I won't let her change me, I promised myself. I won't be what I'm not.

So now on nights when my mother presented her tests, I performed listlessly, my head propped on one arm. I pretended to be bored. And I was. I got so bored I started counting the bellows of the foghorns out on the bay while my mother drilled me in other areas. The sound was comforting and reminded me of the cow jumping over the moon. And the next day, I played a game with myself, seeing if my mother would give up on me before eight bellows. After a while I usually counted only one, maybe two bellows at most. At last she was beginning to give up hope.

Two or three months had gone by without any mention of my being a prodigy again. And then one day my mother was watching *The Ed Sullivan Show* on TV. The TV was old and the sound kept shorting out. Every time my mother got halfway up from the sofa to adjust the set, the sound would go back on and Ed would be talking. As soon as she sat down, Ed would go silent again. She got up, the TV broke into loud piano music. She sat down. Silence. Up and down, back and forth, quiet and loud. It was like a stiff embraceless dance between her and the TV set. Finally she stood by the set with her hand on the sound dial.

She seemed entranced by the music, a little frenzied piano piece with this mesmerizing quality, sort of quick passages and then teasing lilting ones before it returned to the quick playful parts.

"*Ni kan*," my mother said, calling me over with hurried hand gestures, "Look here."

I could see why my mother was fascinated by the music. It was being pounded out by a little Chinese girl, about nine years old, with a Peter Pan haircut. The girl had the sauciness of a Shirley Temple. She was proudly modest like a proper Chinese child. And she also did this fancy sweep of a curtsy, so that the fluffy skirt of her white dress cascaded slowly to the floor like the petals of a large carnation.

In spite of these warning signs, I wasn't worried. Our family had no piano and we couldn't afford to buy one, let alone reams of sheet music and piano lessons. So I could be generous in my comments when my mother bad-mouthed the little girl on TV.

"Play note right, but doesn't sound good! No singing sound," complained my mother.

"What are you picking on her for?" I said carelessly. "She's pretty good. Maybe she's not the best, but she's trying hard." I knew almost immediately I would be sorry I said that.

"Just like you," she said. "Not the best. Because you not trying." She gave a little huff as she let go of the sound dial and sat down on the sofa.

The little Chinese girl sat down also to play an encore of "Anitra's Dance" by Grieg. I remember the song, because later on I had to learn how to play it.

Three days after watching *The Ed Sullivan Show*, my mother told me what my schedule would be for piano lessons and piano practice. She had talked to Mr. Chong, who lived on the first floor of our apartment building. Mr. Chong was a retired piano teacher and my mother had traded housecleaning services for weekly lessons and a piano for me to practice on every day, two hours a day, from four until six.

When my mother told me this, I felt as though I had been sent to hell. I whined and then kicked my foot a little when I couldn't stand it anymore.

"Why don't you like me the way I am? I'm *not* a genius! I can't play the piano. And even if I could, I wouldn't go on TV if you paid me a million dollars!" I cried.

My mother slapped me. "Who ask you be genius?" she shouted. "Only ask you be your best. For you sake. You think I want you be genius? Hnnh! What for! Who ask you!"

"So ungrateful," I heard her mutter in Chinese. "If she had as much talent as she has temper, she would be famous now."

Mr. Chong, whom I secretly nicknamed Old Chong, was very strange, always tapping his fingers to the silent music of an invisible orchestra. He looked ancient in my eyes. He had lost most of the hair on top of his head and he wore thick glasses and had eyes that always looked tired and sleepy. But he must have been younger than I thought, since he lived with his mother and was not yet married.

I met Old Lady Chong once and that was enough. She had this peculiar smell like a baby that had done something in its pants. And her fingers felt like a dead person's, like an old peach I once found in the back of the refrigerator; the skin just slid off the meat when I picked it up.

I soon found out why Old Chong had retired from teaching piano. He was deaf. "Like Beethoven!" he shouted to me. "We're both listening only in our head!" And he would start to conduct his frantic silent sonatas.

Our lessons went like this. He would open the book and point to different things, explaining their purpose: "Key! Treble! Bass! No sharps or flats! So this is C major! Listen now and play after me!"

And then he would play the C scale a few times, a simple chord, and then, as if inspired by an old, unreachable itch, he gradually added more notes and running trills and a pounding bass until the music was really something quite grand.

I would play after him, the simple scale, the simple chord, and then I just played some nonsense that sounded like a cat running up and down on top of garbage cans. Old Chong smiled and applauded and then said, "Very good! But now you must learn to keep time!"

So that's how I discovered that Old Chong's eyes were too slow to keep up with the wrong notes I was playing. He went through the motions in half-time. To help me keep rhythm, he stood behind me, pushing down on my right shoulder for every beat. He balanced pennies on top of my wrists so I would keep them still as I slowly played scales and arpeggios. He had me curve my hand around an apple and keep that shape when playing chords. He marched stiffly to show me how to make each finger dance up and down, staccato like an obedient little soldier.

He taught me all these things, and that was how I also learned I could be lazy and get away with mistakes, lots of mistakes. If I hit the wrong notes because I hadn't practiced enough, I never corrected myself. I just kept playing in rhythm. And Old Chong kept conducting his own private reverie.

So maybe I never really gave myself a fair chance. I did pick up the basics pretty quickly, and I might have become a good pianist at that young age. But I was so determined not to try, not to be anybody different that I learned to play only the most ear-splitting preludes, the most discordant hymns.

Over the next year, I practiced like this, dutifully in my own way. And then one day I heard my mother and her friend Lindo Jong both talking in a loud bragging tone of voice so others could hear. It was after church, and I was leaning against the brick wall wearing a dress with stiff white petticoats. Auntie Lindo's daughter, Waverly, who was about my age, was standing farther down the wall about five feet away. We had grown up together and shared all the closeness of two sisters squabbling over crayons and dolls. In other words, for the most part, we hated each other. I thought she was snotty. Waverly Jong had gained a certain amount of fame as "Chinatown's Littlest Chinese Chess Champion."

"She bring home too many trophy," lamented Auntie Lindo that Sunday. "All day she play chess. All day I have no time do nothing but dust off her winnings." She threw a scolding look at Waverly, who pretended not to see her.

"You lucky you don't have this problem," said Auntie Lindo with a sigh to my mother.

And my mother squared her shoulders and bragged: "Our problem worser than yours. If we ask Jing-mei wash dish, she hear nothing but music. It's like you can't stop this natural talent."

And right then, I was determined to put a stop to her foolish pride.

A few weeks later, Old Chong and my mother conspired to have me play in a talent show which would be held in the church hall. By then, my parents had saved up enough to buy me a secondhand piano, a black Wurlitzer spinet with a scarred bench. It was the showpiece of our living room.

For the talent show, I was to play a piece called "Pleading Child" from Schumann's *Scenes from Childhood*. It was a simple, moody piece that sounded more difficult than it was. I was supposed to memorize the whole thing, playing the repeat parts twice to make the piece sound longer. But I dawdled over it, playing a few bars and then cheating, looking up to see what notes followed. I never really listened to what I was playing. I daydreamed about being somewhere else, about being someone else.

The part I liked to practice best was the fancy curtsy: right foot out, touch the rose on the carpet with a pointed foot, sweep to the side, left leg bends, look up and smile.

My parents invited all the couples from the Joy Luck Club to witness my debut. Auntie Lindo and Uncle Tin were there. Waverly and her two older brothers had also come. The first two rows were filled with children both younger and older than I was. The littlest ones got to go first. They recited simple nursery rhymes, squawked out tunes on miniature violins, twirled Hula Hoops, pranced in pink ballet tutus, and when they bowed or curtsied, the audience would sigh in unison, "Awww," and then clap enthusiastically.

When my turn came, I was very confident. I remember my childish excitement. It was as if I knew, without a doubt, that the prodigy side of me really did exist. I had no fear whatsoever, no nervousness. I remember thinking to myself, This is it! This is it! I looked out over the audience, at my mother's blank face, my father's yawn, Auntie Lindo's stiff-lipped smile, Waverly's sulky expression. I had on a white dress layered with sheets of lace, and a pink bow in my Peter Pan haircut. As I sat down I envisioned people jumping to their feet and Ed Sullivan rushing up to introduce me to everyone on TV.

And I started to play. It was so beautiful. I was so caught up in how lovely I looked that at first I didn't worry how I would sound. So it was a surprise to me when I hit the first wrong note and I realized something didn't sound quite right. And then I hit another and another followed that. A chill started at the top of my head and began to trickle down. Yet I couldn't stop playing, as though my hands were bewitched. I kept thinking my fingers would adjust themselves back, like a train switching to the right track. I played this strange jumble through two repeats, the sour notes staying with me all the way to the end.

When I stood up, I discovered my legs were shaking. Maybe I had just been nervous and the audience, like Old Chong, had seen me go through the right motions and had not heard anything wrong at all. I swept my right foot out, went down on my knee, looked up and smiled. The room was quiet, except for Old Chong, who was beaming and shouting, "Bravo! Bravo! Well done!" But then I saw my mother's face, her stricken face. The audience clapped weakly, and as I walked back to my chair, with my whole face quivering as I tried not to cry, I heard a little boy whisper loudly to his mother, "That was awful," and the mother whispered back, "Well, she certainly tried."

And now I realized how many people were in the audience, the whole world it seemed. I was aware of eyes burning into my back. I felt the shame of my mother and father as they sat stiffly throughout the rest of the show.

We could have escaped during intermission. Pride and some strange sense of honor must have anchored my parents to their chairs. And so we watched it all: the eighteen-year-old boy with a fake mustache who did a magic show and juggled flaming hoops while riding a unicycle. The breasted girl with white makeup who sang from *Madama Butterfly* and got honorable mention. And the eleven-year-old boy who won first prize playing a tricky violin song that sounded like a busy bee.

After the show, the Hsus, the Jongs, and the St. Clairs from the Joy Luck Club came up to my mother and father.

"Lots of talented kids," Auntie Lindo said vaguely, smiling broadly.

"That was somethin' else," said my father, and I wondered if he was referring to me in a humorous way, or whether he even remembered what I had done.

Waverly looked at me and shrugged her shoulders. "You aren't a genius like me," she said matter-of-factly. And if I hadn't felt so bad, I would have pulled her braids and punched her stomach.

But my mother's expression was what devastated me: a quiet, blank look that said she had lost everything. I felt the same way, and it seemed as if everybody were now coming up, like gawkers at the scene of an accident, to see what parts were actually missing. When we got on the bus to go home, my father was humming the busy-bee tune and my mother was silent. I kept thinking she wanted to wait until we got home before shouting at me. But when my father unlocked the door to our apartment, my mother walked in and then went to the back, into the bedroom. No accusations. No blame. And in a way, I felt disappointed. I had been waiting for her to start shouting, so I could shout back and cry and blame her for all my misery.

I assumed my talent-show fiasco meant I never had to play the piano again. But two days later, after school, my mother came out of the kitchen and saw me watching TV.

"Four clock," she reminded me as if it were any other day. I was stunned, as though she were asking me to go through the talent-show torture again. I wedged myself more tightly in front of the TV.

"Turn off TV," she called from the kitchen five minutes later.

I didn't budge. And then I decided. I didn't have to do what my mother said anymore. I wasn't her slave. This wasn't China. I had listened to her before and look what happened. She was the stupid one.

She came out from the kitchen and stood in the arched entryway of the living room. "Four clock," she said once again, louder.

"I'm not going to play anymore," I said nonchalantly. "Why should I? I'm not a genius."

She walked over and stood in front of the TV. I saw her chest was heaving up and down in an angry way.

"No!" I said, and I now felt stronger, as if my true self had finally emerged. So this was what had been inside me all along.

"No! I won't!" I screamed.

She yanked me by the arm, pulled me off the floor, snapped off the TV. She was frighteningly strong, half pulling, half carrying me toward the piano as I kicked the throw rugs under my feet. She lifted me up and onto the hard bench. I was sobbing by now, looking at her bitterly. Her chest was heaving even more and her mouth was open, smiling crazily as if she were pleased I was crying.

"You want me to be someone that I'm not!" I sobbed. "I'll never be the kind of daughter you want me to be!"

"Only two kinds of daughters," she shouted in Chinese. "Those who are obedient and those who follow their own mind! Only one kind of daughter can live in this house. Obedient daughter!"

"Then I wish I wasn't your daughter. I wish you weren't my mother," I shouted. As I said these things I got scared. It felt like worms and toads and slimy things crawling out of my chest, but it also felt good, as if this awful side of me had surfaced, at last.

"Too late change this," said my mother shrilly.

And I could sense her anger rising to its breaking point. I wanted to see it spill over. And that's when I remembered the babies she had lost in China, the ones we never talked about. "Then I wish I'd never been born!" I shouted. "I wish I were dead! Like them."

It was as if I had said the magic words. Alakazam!—and her face went blank, her mouth closed, her arms went slack, and she backed out of the room, stunned, as if she were blowing away like a small brown leaf, thin, brittle, lifeless.

It was not the only disappointment my mother felt in me. In the years that followed, I failed her so many times, each time asserting my own will, my right to fall short of expectations. I didn't get straight As. I didn't become class president. I didn't get into Stanford. I dropped out of college.

For unlike my mother, I did not believe I could be anything I wanted to be. I could only be me.

And for all those years, we never talked about the disaster at the recital or my terrible accusations afterward at the piano bench. All that remained unchecked, like a betrayal that was now unspeakable. So I never found a way to ask her why she had hoped for something so large that failure was inevitable.

And even worse, I never asked her what frightened me the most: Why had she given up hope?

For after our struggle at the piano, she never mentioned my playing again. The lessons stopped. The lid to the piano was closed, shutting out the dust, my misery, and her dreams.

So she surprised me. A few years ago, she offered to give me the piano, for my thirtieth birthday. I had not played in all those years. I saw the offer as a sign of forgiveness, a tremendous burden removed.

"Are you sure?" I asked shyly. "I mean, won't you and Dad miss it?"

"No, this your piano," she said firmly. "Always your piano. You only one can play."

"Well, I probably can't play anymore," I said. "It's been years."

"You pick up fast," said my mother, as if she knew this was certain. "You have natural talent. You could been genius if you want to."

"No I couldn't."

"You just not trying," said my mother. And she was neither angry nor sad. She said it as if to announce a fact that could never be disproved. "Take it," she said.

But I didn't at first. It was enough that she had offered it to me. And after that, every time I saw it in my parents' living room, standing in front of the bay windows, it made me feel proud, as if it were a shiny trophy I had won back.

Last week I sent a tuner over to my parents' apartment and had the piano reconditioned, for purely sentimental reasons. My mother had died a few months before and I had been getting things in order for my father, a little bit at a time. I put the jewelry in special silk pouches. The sweaters she had knitted in yellow, pink, bright orange—all the colors I hated—I put those in moth-proof boxes. I found some old Chinese silk dresses, the kind with little slits up the sides. I rubbed the old silk against my skin, then wrapped them in tissue and decided to take them home with me.

After I had the piano tuned, I opened the lid and touched the keys. It sounded even richer than I remembered. Really, it was a very good piano. Inside the bench were the same exercise notes with handwritten scales, the same secondhand music books with their covers held together with yellow tape.

I opened up the Schumann book to the dark little piece I had played at the recital. It was on the left-hand side of the page, "Pleading Child." It looked more difficult than I remembered. I played a few bars, surprised at how easily the notes came back to me.

And for the first time, or so it seemed, I noticed the piece on the right-hand side. It was called "Perfectly Contented." I tried to play this one as well. It had a lighter melody but the same flowing rhythm and turned out to be quite easy. "Pleading Child" was shorter but slower; "Perfectly Contented" was longer, but faster. And after I played them both a few times, I realized they were two halves of the same song.

AMERICAN TRANSLATION

"*Wah!*" cried the mother upon seeing the mirrored armoire in the master suite of her daughter's new condominium. "You cannot put mirrors at the foot of the bed. All your marriage happiness will bounce back and turn the opposite way."

"Well, that's the only place it fits, so that's where it stays," said the daughter, irritated that her mother saw bad omens in everything. She had heard these warnings all her life.

The mother frowned, reaching into her twice-used Macy's bag. "Hunh, lucky I can fix it for you, then." And she pulled out the gilt-edged mirror she had bought at the Price Club last week. It was her housewarming present. She leaned it against the headboard, on top of the two pillows.

"You hang it here," said the mother, pointing to the wall above. "This mirror sees that mirror—haule!—multiply your peach-blossom luck."

"What is peach-blossom luck?"

The mother smiled, mischief in her eyes. "It is in here," she said, pointing to the mirror. "Look inside. Tell me, am I not right? In this mirror is my future grandchild, already sitting on my lap next spring."

And the daughter looked—and haule! There it was: her own reflection looking back at her.

LENA ST. CLAIR

Rice Husband

To this day, I believe my mother has the mysterious ability to see things before they happen. She has a Chinese saying for what she knows. *Chunwang chihan:* If the lips are gone, the teeth will be cold. Which means, I suppose, one thing is always the result of another.

But she does not predict when earthquakes will come, or how the stock market will do. She sees only bad things that affect our family. And she knows what causes them. But now she laments that she never did anything to stop them.

One time when I was growing up in San Francisco, she looked at the way our new apartment sat too steeply on the hill. She said the new baby in her womb would fall out dead, and it did.

When a plumbing and bathroom fixtures store opened up across the street from our bank, my mother said the bank would soon have all its money drained away. And one month later, an officer of the bank was arrested for embezzlement.

And just after my father died last year, she said she knew this would happen. Because a philodendron plant my father had given her had withered and died, despite the fact that she watered it faithfully. She said the plant had damaged its roots and no water could get to it. The autopsy report she later received showed my father had had ninety-percent blockage of the arteries before he died of a heart attack at the age of seventy-four. My father was not Chinese like my mother, but English-Irish American, who enjoyed his five slices of bacon and three eggs sunny-side up every morning.

I remember this ability of my mother's, because now she is visiting my husband and me in the house we just bought in Woodside. And I wonder what she will see.

Harold and I were lucky to find this place, which is near the summit of Highway 9, then a left-right-left down three forks of unmarked dirt roads, unmarked because the residents always tear down the signs to keep out salesmen, developers, and city inspectors. We are only a forty-minute drive to my mother's apartment in San Francisco. This became a sixty-minute ordeal coming back from San Francisco, when my mother was with us in the car. After we got to the two-lane winding road to the summit, she touched her hand gently to Harold's shoulder and softly said, "Ai, tire squealing." And then a little later, "Too much tear and wear on car."

Harold had smiled and slowed down, but I could see his hands were clenched on the steering wheel of the Jaguar, as he glanced nervously in his rearview mirror at the line of impatient cars that was growing by the minute. And I was secretly glad to watch his discomfort. He was always the one who tailgated old ladies in their Buicks, honking his horn and revving the engine as if he would run them over unless they pulled over.

And at the same time, I hated myself for being mean-spirited, for thinking Harold deserved this torment. Yet I couldn't help myself. I was mad at Harold and he was exasperated with me. That morning, before we picked my mother up, he had said, "You should pay for the exterminators, because Mirugai is your cat and so they're *your* fleas. It's only fair."

None of our friends could ever believe we fight over something as stupid as fleas, but they would also never believe that our problems are much, much deeper than that, so deep I don't even know where bottom is.

And now that my mother is here—she is staying for a week,

or until the electricians are done rewiring her building in San Francisco—we have to pretend nothing is the matter.

Meanwhile she asks over and over again why we had to pay so much for a renovated barn and a mildew-lined pool on four acres of land, two of which are covered with redwood trees and poison oak. Actually she doesn't really ask, she just says, "Aii, so much money, so much," as we show her different parts of the house and land. And her laments always compel Harold to explain to my mother in simple terms: "Well, you see, it's the details that cost so much. Like this wood floor. It's hand-bleached. And the walls here, this marbleized effect, it's hand-sponged. It's really worth it."

And my mother nods and agrees: "Bleach and sponge cost so much."

During our brief tour of the house, she's already found the flaws. She says the slant of the floor makes her feel as if she is "running down." She thinks the guest room where she will be staying—which is really a former hayloft shaped by a sloped roof—has "two lopsides." She sees spiders in high corners and even fleas jumping up in the air—pah! pah! pah!—like little spatters of hot oil. My mothers knows, underneath all the fancy details that cost so much, this house is still a barn.

She can see all this. And it annoys me that all she sees are the bad parts. But then I look around and everything she's said is true. And this convinces me she can see what else is going on, between Harold and me. She knows what's going to happen to us. Because I remember something else she saw when I was eight years old.

My mother had looked in my rice bowl and told me I would marry a bad man.

"Aii, Lena," she had said after that dinner so many years ago, "your future husband have one pock mark for every rice you not finish."

She put my bowl down. "I once know a pock-mark man. Mean man, bad man."

And I thought of a mean neighbor boy who had tiny pits in

his cheeks, and it was true, those marks were the size of rice grains. This boy was about twelve and his name was Arnold.

Arnold would shoot rubber bands at my legs whenever I walked past his building on my way home from school, and one time he ran over my doll with his bicycle, crushing her legs below the knees. I didn't want this cruel boy to be my future husband. So I picked up that cold bowl of rice and scraped the last few grains into my mouth, then smiled at my mother, confident my future husband would be not Arnold but someone whose face was as smooth as the porcelain in my now clean bowl.

But my mother sighed. "Yesterday, you not finish rice either." I thought of those unfinished mouthfuls of rice, and then the grains that lined my bowl the day before, and the day before that. By the minute, my eight-year-old heart grew more and more terror-stricken over the growing possibility that my future husband was fated to be this mean boy Arnold. And thanks to my poor eating habits, his hideous face would eventually resemble the craters of the moon.

This would have been a funny incident to remember from my childhood, but it is actually a memory I recall from time to time with a mixture of nausea and remorse. My loathing for Arnold had grown to such a point that I eventually found a way to make him die. I let one thing result from another. Of course, all of it could have been just loosely connected coincidences. And whether that's true or not, I know the *intention* was there. Because when I want something to happen—or not happen—I begin to look at all events and all things as relevant, an opportunity to take or avoid.

I found the opportunity. The same week my mother told me about the rice bowl and my future husband, I saw a shocking film at Sunday school. I remember the teacher had dimmed the lights so that all we could see were silhouettes of one another. Then the teacher looked at us, a roomful of squirmy, well-fed Chinese-American children, and she said, "This film will show you why you should give tithings to God, to do God's work."

She said, "I want you to think about a nickel's worth of candy money, or however much you eat each week—your Good and

Plentys, your Necco wafers, your jujubes—and compare that to what you are about to see. And I also want you to think about what your true blessings in life really are."

And then she set the film projector clattering away. The film showed missionaries in Africa and India. These good souls worked with people whose legs were swollen to the size of tree trunks, whose numb limbs had become as twisted as jungle vines. But the most terrible of the afflictions were men and women with leprosy. Their faces were covered with every kind of misery I could imagine: pits and pustules, cracks and bumps, and fissures that I was sure erupted with the same vehemence as snails writhing in a bed of salt. If my mother had been in the room, she would have told me these poor people were victims of future husbands and wives who had failed to eat *platefuls* of food.

After seeing this film, I did a terrible thing. I saw what I had to do so I would not have to marry Arnold. I began to leave more rice in my bowl. And then I extended my prodigal ways beyond Chinese food. I did not finish my creamed corn, broccoli, Rice Krispies, or peanut butter sandwiches. And once, when I bit into a candy bar and saw how lumpy it was, how full of secret dark spots and creamy goo, I sacrificed that as well.

I considered that probably nothing would happen to Arnold, that he might not get leprosy, move to Africa and die. And this somehow balanced the dark possibility that he might.

He didn't die right away. In fact, it was some five years later, by which time I had become quite thin. I had stopped eating, not because of Arnold, whom I had long forgotten, but to be fashionably anorexic like all the other thirteen-year-old girls who were dieting and finding other ways to suffer as teenagers. I was sitting at the breakfast table, waiting for my mother to finish packing a sack lunch which I always promptly threw away as soon as I rounded the corner. My father was eating with his fingers, dabbing the ends of his bacon into the egg yolks with one hand, while holding the newspaper with the other.

"Oh my, listen to this," he said, still dabbing. And that's when he announced that Arnold Reisman, a boy who lived in our old neighborhood in Oakland, had died of complications from measles. He had just been accepted to Cal State Hayward and was planning to become a podiatrist.

" 'Doctors were at first baffled by the disease, which they report is extremely rare and generally attacks children between the ages of ten and twenty, months to years after they have contracted the measles virus,' " read my father. " 'The boy had had a mild case of the measles when he was twelve, reported his mother. Problems this year were first noticed when the boy developed motor coordination problems and mental lethargy which increased until he fell into a coma. The boy, age seventeen, never regained consciousness.'

"Didn't you know that boy?" asked my father, and I stood there mute.

"This is shame," said my mother, looking at me. "This is terrible shame."

And I thought she could see through me and that she knew I was the one who had caused Arnold to die. I was terrified.

That night, in my room, I gorged myself. I had stolen a half-gallon of strawberry ice cream from the freezer, and I forced spoonful after spoonful down my throat. And later, for several hours after that, I sat hunched on the fire escape landing outside my bedroom, retching back into the ice cream container. And I remember wondering why it was that eating something good could make me feel so terrible, while vomiting something terrible could make me feel so good.

The thought that I could have caused Arnold's death is not so ridiculous. Perhaps he *was* destined to be my husband. Because I think to myself, even today, how can the world in all its chaos come up with so many coincidences, so many similarities and exact opposites? Why did Arnold single me out for his rubber-band torture? How is it that he contracted measles the same year I began consciously to hate him? And why did I think of Arnold in the first place—when my mother looked in my rice bowl—and then come to hate him so much? Isn't hate merely the result of wounded love?

And even when I can finally dismiss all of this as ridiculous,

I still feel that somehow, for the most part, we deserve what we get. I didn't get Arnold. I got Harold.

Harold and I work at the same architectural firm, Livotny & Associates. Only Harold Livotny is a partner and I am an associate. We met eight years ago, before he started Livotny & Associates. I was twenty-eight, a project assistant, and he was thirty-four. We both worked in the restaurant design and development division of Harned Kelley & Davis.

We started seeing each other for working lunches, to talk about the projects, and we would always split the tab right in half, even though I usually ordered only a salad because I have this tendency to gain weight easily. Later, when we started meeting secretly for dinner, we still divided the bill.

And we just continued that way, everything right down the middle. If anything, I encouraged it. Sometimes I insisted on paying for the whole thing: meal, drinks, and tip. And it really didn't bother me.

"Lena, you're really extraordinary," Harold said after six months of dinners, five months of post-prandial lovemaking, and one week of timid and silly love confessions. We were lying in bed, between new purple sheets I had just bought for him. His old set of white sheets was stained in revealing places, not very romantic.

And he nuzzled my neck and whispered, "I don't think I've ever met another woman, who's so together . . ."—and I remember feeling a hiccup of fear upon hearing the words "another woman," because I could imagine dozens, hundreds of adoring women eager to buy Harold breakfast, lunch, and dinner to feel the pleasure of his breath on their skin.

Then he bit my neck and said in a rush, "Nor anyone who's as soft and squishy and lovable as you are."

And with that, I swooned inside, caught off balance by this latest revelation of love, wondering how such a remarkable person as Harold could think I was extraordinary.

Now that I'm angry at Harold, it's hard to remember what was so remarkable about him. And I know they're there, the good qualities, because I wasn't that stupid to fall in love with him, to marry him. All I can remember is how awfully lucky I felt, and consequently how worried I was that all this undeserved good fortune would someday slip away. When I fantasized about moving in with him, I also dredged up my deepest fears: that he would tell me I smelled bad, that I had terrible bathroom habits, that my taste in music and television was appalling. I worried that Harold would someday get a new prescription for his glasses and he'd put them on one morning, look me up and down, and say, "Why, gosh, you aren't the girl I thought you were, are you?"

And I think that feeling of fear never left me, that I would be caught someday, exposed as a sham of a woman. But recently, a friend of mine, Rose, who's in therapy now because her marriage has already fallen apart, told me those kinds of thoughts are commonplace in women like us.

"At first I thought it was because I was raised with all this Chinese humility," Rose said. "Or that maybe it was because when you're Chinese you're supposed to accept everything, flow with the Tao and not make waves. But my therapist said, Why do you blame your culture, your ethnicity? And I remembered reading an article about baby boomers, how we expect the best and when we get it we worry that maybe we should have expected more, because it's all diminishing returns after a certain age."

And after my talk with Rose, I felt better about myself and I thought, Of course, Harold and I are equals, in many respects. He's not exactly handsome in the classic sense, although clear-skinned and certainly attractive in that wiry intellectual way. And I may not be a raving beauty, but a lot of women in my aerobics class tell me I'm "exotic" in an unusual way, and they're jealous that my breasts don't sag, now that small breasts are in. Plus, one of my clients said I have incredible vitality and exuberance.

So I think I deserve someone like Harold, and I mean in the good sense and not like bad karma. We're equals. I'm also smart. I have common sense. And I'm intuitive, highly so. I was the one who told Harold he was good enough to start his own firm.

When we were still working at Harned Kelley & Davis, I said, "Harold, this firm knows just what a good deal it has with you. You're the goose who lays the golden egg. If you started your own business today, you'd walk away with more than half of the restaurant clients."

And he said, laughing, "Half? Boy, that's love."

And I shouted back, laughing with him, "More than half! You're that good. You're the best there is in restaurant design and development. You know it and I know it, and so do a lot of restaurant developers."

That was the night he decided to "go for it," as he put it, which is a phrase I have personally detested ever since a bank I used to work for adopted the slogan for its employee productivity contest.

But still, I said to Harold, "Harold, I want to help you go for it, too. I mean, you're going to need money to start this business."

He wouldn't hear of taking any money from me, not as a favor, not as a loan, not as an investment, or even as the down payment on a partnership. He said he valued our relationship too much. He didn't want to contaminate it with money. He explained, "I wouldn't want a handout any more than you'd want one. As long as we keep the money thing separate, we'll always be sure of our love for each other."

I wanted to protest. I wanted to say, "No! I'm not really this way about money, the way we've been doing it. I'm really into giving freely. I want . . ." But I didn't know where to begin. I wanted to ask him who, what woman, had hurt him this way, that made him so scared about accepting love in all its wonderful forms. But then I heard him saying what I'd been waiting to hear for a long, long time.

"Actually, you could help me out if you moved in with me. I mean, that way I could use the five hundred dollars' rent you paid to me . . ."

"That's a wonderful idea," I said immediately, knowing how embarrassed he was to have to ask me that way. I was so deliriously happy that it didn't matter that the rent on my studio was really only four hundred thirty-five. Besides, Harold's place was much nicer, a two-bedroom flat with a two-hundred-forty-degree view of the bay. It was worth the extra money, no matter whom I shared the place with.

So within the year, Harold and I quit Harned Kelley & Davis and he started Livotny & Associates, and I went to work there as a project coordinator. And no, he didn't get half the restaurant clients of Harned Kelley & Davis. In fact, Harned Kelley & Davis threatened to sue if he walked away with even one client over the next year. So I gave him pep talks in the evening when he was discouraged. I told him how he should do more avant-garde thematic restaurant design, to differentiate himself from the other firms.

"Who needs another brass and oakwood bar and grill?" I said. "Who wants another pasta place in sleek Italian moderno? How many places can you go to with police cars lurching out of the walls? This town is chockablock with restaurants that are just clones of the same old themes. You can find a niche. Do something different every time. Get the Hong Kong investors who are willing to sink some bucks into American ingenuity."

He gave me his adoring smile, the one that said, "I love it when you're so naive." And I adored his looking at me like that.

So I stammered out my love. "You . . . you . . . could do new theme eating places . . . a . . . a . . . Home on the Range! All the home-cooked mom stuff, mom at the kitchen range with a gingham apron and mom waitresses leaning over telling you to finish your soup.

"And maybe . . . maybe you could do a novel-menu restaurant . . . foods from fiction . . . sandwiches from Lawrence Sanders murder mysteries, just desserts from Nora Ephron's *Heartburn*. And something else with a magic theme, or jokes and gags, or . . ."

Harold actually listened to me. He took those ideas and he applied them in an educated, methodical way. He made it happen. But still, I remember, it was my idea.

And today Livotny & Associates is a growing firm of twelve

full-time people, which specializes in thematic restaurant design, what I still like to call "theme eating." Harold is the concept man, the chief architect, the designer, the person who makes the final sales presentation to a new client. I work under the interior designer, because, as Harold explains, it would not seem fair to the other employees if he promoted me just because we are now married—that was five years ago, two years after he started Livotny & Associates. And even though I am very good at what I do, I have never been formally trained in this area. When I was majoring in Asian-American studies, I took only one relevant course, in theater set design, for a college production of *Madama Butterfly*.

At Livotny & Associates, I procure the theme elements. For one restaurant called The Fisherman's Tale, one of my prized findings was a yellow varnished wood boat stenciled with the name "Overbored," and I was the one who thought the menus should dangle from miniature fishing poles, and the napkins be printed with rulers that have inches translating into feet. For a Lawrence of Arabia deli called Tray Sheik, I was the one who thought the place should have a bazaar effect, and I found the replicas of cobras lying on fake Hollywood boulders.

I love my work when I don't think about it too much. And when I do think about it, how much I get paid, how hard I work, how fair Harold is to everybody except me, I get upset.

So really, we're equals, except that Harold makes about seven times more than what I make. He knows this, too, because he signs my monthly check, and then I deposit it into my separate checking account.

Lately, however, this business about being equals started to bother me. It's been on my mind, only I didn't really know it. I just felt a little uneasy about *something*. And then about a week ago, it all became clear. I was putting the breakfast dishes away and Harold was warming up the car so we could go to work. And I saw the newspaper spread open on the kitchen counter, Harold's glasses on top, his favorite coffee mug with the chipped handle off to the side. And for some reason, seeing all these little domestic signs of familiarity, our daily ritual, made me swoon inside. But it was as if I were seeing Harold the first time we made love, this feeling of surrendering everything to him, with abandon, without caring what I got in return.

And when I got into the car, I still had the glow of that feeling and I touched his hand and said, "Harold, I love you." And he looked in the rearview mirror, backing up the car, and said, "I love you, too. Did you lock the door?" And just like that, I started to think, It's just not enough.

Harold jingles the car keys and says, "I'm going down the hill to buy stuff for dinner. Steaks okay? Want anything special?"

"We're out of rice," I say, discreetly nodding toward my mother, whose back is turned to me. She's looking out the kitchen window, at the trellis of bougainvillea. And then Harold is out the door and I hear the deep rumble of the car and then the sound of crunching gravel as he drives away.

My mother and I are alone in the house. I start to water the plants. She is standing on her tiptoes, peering at a list stuck on our refrigerator door.

The list says "Lena" and "Harold" and under each of our names are things we've bought and how much they cost:

Lena	*HAROLD*
chicken, veg., bread, broccoli, shampoo, beer $19.63	Garage stuff $25.35
	Bathroom stuff $5.41
Maria (clean + tip) $65 groceries	Car stuff $6.57
	Light Fixtures $87.26
(see shop list) $55.15	Road gravel $19.99
petunias, potting soil $14.11	Gas $22.00
	Car Smog Check $35
Photo developing $13.83	Movies & Dinner $65
	Ice Cream $4.50

The way things are going this week, Harold's already spent over a hundred dollars more, so I'll owe him around fifty from my checking account.

"What is this writing?" asks my mother in Chinese.

"Oh, nothing really. Just things we share," I say as casually as I can.

And she looks at me and frowns but doesn't say anything. She goes back to reading the list, this time more carefully, moving her finger down each item.

And I feel embarrassed, knowing what she's seeing. I'm relieved that she doesn't see the other half of it, the discussions. Through countless talks, Harold and I reached an understanding about not including personal things like "mascara," and "shaving lotion," "hair spray" or "Bic shavers," "tampons," or "athlete's foot powder."

When we got married at city hall, he insisted on paying the fee. I got my friend Robert to take photos. We held a party at our apartment and everybody brought champagne. And when we bought the house, we agreed that I should pay only a percentage of the mortgage based on what I earn and what he earns, and that I should own an equivalent percentage of community property; this is written in our prenuptial agreement. Since Harold pays more, he had the deciding vote on how the house should look. It is sleek, spare, and what he calls "fluid," nothing to disrupt the line, meaning none of my cluttered look. As for vacations, the one we choose together is fifty-fifty. The others Harold pays for, with the understanding that it's a birthday or Christmas present, or an anniversary gift.

And we've had philosophical arguments over things that have gray borders, like my birth control pills, or dinners at home when we entertain people who are really his clients or my old friends from college, or food magazines that I subscribe to but he also reads only because he's bored, not because he would have chosen them for himself.

And we still argue about Mirugai, *the* cat—not our cat, or my cat, but *the* cat that was his gift to me for my birthday last year.

"This, you do not share!" exclaims my mother in an astonished voice. And I am startled, thinking she had read my thoughts about Mirugai. But then I see she is pointing to "ice cream" on Harold's list. My mother must remember the incident on the fire escape landing, where she found me, shivering and exhausted, sitting next to that container of regurgitated ice cream. I could never stand the stuff after that. And then I am startled once again to realize that Harold has never noticed that I don't eat any of the ice cream he brings home every Friday evening.

"Why you do this?"

My mother has a wounded sound in her voice, as if I had put the list up to hurt her. I think how to explain this, recalling the words Harold and I have used with each other in the past: "So we can eliminate false dependencies . . . be equals . . . love without obligation . . ." But these are words she could never understand.

So instead I tell my mother this: "I don't really know. It's something we started before we got married. And for some reason we never stopped."

When Harold returns from the store, he starts the charcoal. I unload the groceries, marinate the steaks, cook the rice, and set the table. My mother sits on a stool at the granite counter, drinking from a mug of coffee I've poured for her. Every few minutes she wipes the bottom of the mug with a tissue she keeps stuffed in her sweater sleeve.

During dinner, Harold keeps the conversation going. He talks about the plans for the house: the skylights, expanding the deck, planting flower beds of tulips and crocuses, clearing the poison oak, adding another wing, building a Japanese-style tile bathroom. And then he clears the table and starts stacking the plates in the dishwasher.

"Who's ready for dessert?" he asks, reaching into the freezer.

"I'm full," I say.

"Lena cannot eat ice cream," says my mother.

"So it seems. She's always on a diet."

"No, she never eat it. She doesn't like."

And now Harold smiles and looks at me puzzled, expecting me to translate what my mother has said.

"It's true," I say evenly. "I've hated ice cream almost all my life."

Harold looks at me, as if I, too, were speaking Chinese and he could not understand.

"I guess I assumed you were just trying to lose weight. . . . Oh well."

"She become so thin now you cannot see her," says my mother. "She like a ghost, disappear."

"That's right! Christ, that's great," exclaims Harold, laughing, relieved in thinking my mother is graciously trying to rescue him.

After dinner, I put clean towels on the bed in the guest room. My mother is sitting on the bed. The room has Harold's minimalist look to it: the twin bed with plain white sheets and white blanket, polished wood floors, a bleached oakwood chair, and nothing on the slanted gray walls.

The only decoration is an odd-looking piece right next to the bed: an end table made out of a slab of unevenly cut marble and thin crisscrosses of black lacquer wood for the legs. My mother puts her handbag on the table and the cylindrical black vase on top starts to wobble. The freesias in the vase quiver.

"Careful, it's not too sturdy," I say. The table is a poorly designed piece that Harold made in his student days. I've always wondered why he's so proud of it. The lines are clumsy. It doesn't bear any of the traits of "fluidity" that are so important to Harold these days.

"What use for?" asks my mother, jiggling the table with her hand. "You put something else on top, everything fall down. *Chunwang chihan.*"

I leave my mother in her room and go back downstairs. Harold is opening the windows to let the night air in. He does this every evening.

"I'm cold," I say.

"What's that?"

"Could you close the windows, please."

He looks at me, sighs and smiles, pulls the windows shut, and then sits down cross-legged on the floor and flips open a magazine. I'm sitting on the sofa, seething, and I don't know why. It's not that Harold has done anything wrong. Harold is just Harold.

And before I even do it, I know I'm starting a fight that is bigger than I know how to handle. But I do it anyway. I go to the refrigerator and I cross out "ice cream" on Harold's side of the list.

"What's going on here?"

"I just don't think you should get credit for *your* ice cream anymore."

He shrugs his shoulders, amused. "Suits me."

"Why do you have to be so goddamn fair!" I shout.

Harold puts his magazine down, now wearing his open-mouthed exasperated look. "What is this? Why don't you say what's really the matter?"

"I don't know. . . . I don't know. Everything . . . the way we account for everything. What we share. What we don't share. I'm so tired of it, adding things up, subtracting, making it come out even. I'm sick of it."

"You were the one who wanted the cat."

"What are you talking about?"

"All right. If you think I'm being unfair about the exterminators, we'll both pay for it."

"That's not the point!"

"Then tell me, *please*, what is the point?"

I start to cry, which I know Harold hates. It always makes him uncomfortable, angry. He thinks it's manipulative. But I can't help it, because I realize now that I don't know what the point of this argument is. Am I asking Harold to support me? Am I asking to pay less than half? Do I really think we should stop accounting for everything? Wouldn't we continue to tally things up in our head? Wouldn't Harold wind up paying more? And then wouldn't I feel worse, less than equal? Or maybe we shouldn't have gotten married in the first place. Maybe Harold is a bad man. Maybe I've made him this way.

None of it seems right. Nothing makes sense. I can admit to nothing and I am in complete despair.

"I just think we have to change things," I say when I think

I can control my voice. Only the rest comes out like whining. "We need to think about what our marriage is really based on . . . not this balance sheet, who owes who what."

"Shit," Harold says. And then he sighs and leans back, as if he were thinking about this. Finally he says in what sounds like a hurt voice, "Well, I know our marriage is based on a lot more than a balance sheet. A lot more. And if you don't then I think you should think about what else you want, before you change things."

And now I don't know what to think. What am I saying? What's he saying? We sit in the room, not saying anything. The air feels muggy. I look out the window, and out in the distance is the valley beneath us, a sprinkling of thousands of lights shimmering in the summer fog. And then I hear the sound of glass shattering, upstairs, and a chair scrapes across a wood floor.

Harold starts to get up, but I say, "No, I'll go see."

The door is open, but the room is dark, so I call out, "Ma?"

I see it right away: the marble end table collapsed on top of its spindly black legs. Off to the side is the black vase, the smooth cylinder broken in half, the freesias strewn in a puddle of water.

And then I see my mother sitting by the open window, her dark silhouette against the night sky. She turns around in her chair, but I can't see her face.

"Fallen down," she says simply. She doesn't apologize.

"It doesn't matter," I say, and I start to pick up the broken glass shards. "I knew it would happen."

"Then why you don't stop it?" asks my mother.

And it's such a simple question.

WAVERLY JONG

Four Directions

I had taken my mother out to lunch at my favorite Chinese restaurant in hopes of putting her in a good mood, but it was a disaster.

When we met at the Four Directions Restaurant, she eyed me with immediate disapproval. "*Ai-ya!* What's the matter with your hair?" she said in Chinese.

"What do you mean, 'What's the matter,' " I said. "I had it cut." Mr. Rory had styled my hair differently this time, an asymmetrical blunt-line fringe that was shorter on the left side. It was fashionable, yet not radically so.

"Looks chopped off," she said. "You must ask for your money back."

I sighed. "Let's just have a nice lunch together, okay?"

She wore her tight-lipped, pinched-nose look as she scanned the menu, muttering, "Not too many good things, this menu." Then she tapped the waiter's arm, wiped the length of her chopsticks with her finger, and sniffed: "This greasy thing, do you expect me to eat with it?" She made a show of washing out her rice bowl with hot tea, and then warned other restaurant patrons seated near us to do the same. She told the waiter to make sure the soup was very hot, and of course, it was by her tongue's expert estimate "not even *lukewarm*."

"You shouldn't get so upset," I said to my mother after she disputed a charge of two extra dollars because she had specified chrysanthemum tea, instead of the regular green tea. "Besides, unnecessary stress isn't good for your heart."

"Nothing is wrong with my heart," she huffed as she kept a disparaging eye on the waiter.

And she was right. Despite all the tension she places on herself—and others—the doctors have proclaimed that my mother, at age sixty-nine, has the blood pressure of a sixteen-year-old and the strength of a horse. And that's what she is. A Horse, born in 1918, destined to be obstinate and frank to the point of tactlessness. She and I make a bad combination, because I'm a Rabbit, born in 1951, supposedly sensitive, with tendencies toward being thin-skinned and skittery at the first sign of criticism.

After our miserable lunch, I gave up the idea that there would ever be a good time to tell her the news: that Rich Schields and I were getting married.

"Why are you so nervous?" my friend Marlene Ferber had asked over the phone the other night. "It's not as if Rich is the scum of the earth. He's a tax attorney like you, for Chrissake. How can she criticize that?"

"You don't know my mother," I said. "She never thinks anybody is good enough for anything."

"So elope with the guy," said Marlene.

"That's what I did with Marvin." Marvin was my first husband, my high school sweetheart.

"So there you go," said Marlene.

"So when my mother found out, she threw her shoe at us," I said. "And that was just for openers."

My mother had never met Rich. In fact, every time I brought up his name—when I said, for instance, that Rich and I had gone to the symphony, that Rich had taken my four-year-old daughter, Shoshana, to the zoo—my mother found a way to change the subject.

"Did I tell you," I said as we waited for the lunch bill at Four

Directions, "what a great time Shoshana had with Rich at the Exploratorium? He—"

"Oh," interrupted my mother, "I didn't tell you. Your father, doctors say maybe need exploratory surgery. But no, now they say everything normal, just too much constipated." I gave up. And then we did the usual routine.

I paid for the bill, with a ten and three ones. My mother pulled back the dollar bills and counted out exact change, thirteen cents, and put that on the tray instead, explaining firmly: "No tip!" She tossed her head back with a triumphant smile. And while my mother used the restroom, I slipped the waiter a five-dollar bill. He nodded to me with deep understanding. While she was gone, I devised another plan.

"*Choszle!*"—Stinks to death in there!—muttered my mother when she returned. She nudged me with a little travel package of Kleenex. She did not trust other people's toilet paper. "Do you need to use?"

I shook my head. "But before I drop you off, let's stop at my place real quick. There's something I want to show you."

My mother had not been to my apartment in months. When I was first married, she used to drop by unannounced, until one day I suggested she should call ahead of time. Ever since then, she has refused to come unless I issue an official invitation.

And so I watched her, seeing her reaction to the changes in my apartment—from the pristine habitat I maintained after the divorce, when all of a sudden I had too much time to keep my life in order—to this present chaos, a home full of life and love. The hallway floor was littered with Shoshana's toys, all bright plastic things with scattered parts. There was a set of Rich's barbells in the living room, two dirty snifters on the coffee table, the disemboweled remains of a phone that Shoshana and Rich took apart the other day to see where the voices came from.

"It's back here," I said. We kept walking, all the way to the back bedroom. The bed was unmade, dresser drawers were hanging out with socks and ties spilling over. My mother stepped over running shoes, more of Shoshana's toys, Rich's black loafers, my scarves, a stack of white shirts just back from the cleaner's.

Her look was one of painful denial, reminding me of a time long ago when she took my brothers and me down to a clinic to get our polio booster shots. As the needle went into my brother's arm and he screamed, my mother looked at me with agony written all over her face and assured me, "Next one doesn't hurt."

But now, how could my mother *not* notice that we were living together, that this was serious and would not go away even if she didn't talk about it? She had to say something.

I went to the closet and then came back with a mink jacket that Rich had given me for Christmas. It was the most extravagant gift I had ever received.

I put the jacket on. "It's sort of a silly present," I said nervously. "It's hardly ever cold enough in San Francisco to wear mink. But it seems to be a fad, what people are buying their wives and girlfriends these days."

My mother was quiet. She was looking toward my open closet, bulging with racks of shoes, ties, my dresses, and Rich's suits. She ran her fingers over the mink.

"This is not so good," she said at last. "It is just leftover strips. And the fur is too short, no long hairs."

"How can you criticize a gift!" I protested. I was deeply wounded. "He gave me this from his heart."

"That is why I worry," she said.

And looking at the coat in the mirror, I couldn't fend off the strength of her will anymore, her ability to make me see black where there was once white, white where there was once black. The coat looked shabby, an imitation of romance.

"Aren't you going to say anything else?" I asked softly.

"What I should say?"

"About the apartment? About *this*?" I gestured to all the signs of Rich lying about.

She looked around the room, toward the hall, and finally she said, "You have career. You are busy. You want to live like mess. what I can say?"

•

My mother knows how to hit a nerve. And the pain I feel is worse than any other kind of misery. Because what she does always comes as a shock, exactly like an electric jolt, that grounds itself permanently in my memory. I still remember the first time I felt it.

I was ten years old. Even though I was young, I knew my ability to play chess was a gift. It was effortless, so easy. I could see things on the chessboard that other people could not. I could create barriers to protect myself that were invisible to my opponents. And this gift gave me supreme confidence. I knew what my opponents would do, move for move. I knew at exactly what point their faces would fall when my seemingly simple and childlike strategy would reveal itself as a devastating and irrevocable course. I loved to win.

And my mother loved to show me off, like one of my many trophies she polished. She used to discuss my games as if she had devised the strategies.

"I told my daughter, Use your horses to run over the enemy," she informed one shopkeeper. "She won very quickly this way." And of course, she had said this before the game—that and a hundred other useless things that had nothing to do with my winning.

To our family friends who visited she would confide, "You don't have to be so smart to win chess. It is just tricks. You blow from the North, South, East, and West. The other person becomes confused. They don't know which way to run."

I hated the way she tried to take all the credit. And one day I told her so, shouting at her on Stockton Street, in the middle of a crowd of people. I told her she didn't know anything, so she shouldn't show off. She should shut up. Words to that effect.

That evening and the next day she wouldn't speak to me. She would say stiff words to my father and brothers, as if I had become invisible and she was talking about a rotten fish she had thrown away but which had left behind its bad smell.

I knew this strategy, the sneaky way to get someone to pounce back in anger and fall into a trap. So I ignored her. I refused to speak and waited for her to come to me.

After many days had gone by in silence, I sat in my room, staring at the sixty-four squares of my chessboard, trying to think of another way. And that's when I decided to quit playing chess.

Of course I didn't mean to quit forever. At most, just for a few days. And I made a show of it. Instead of practicing in my room every night, as I always did, I marched into the living room and sat down in front of the television set with my brothers, who stared at me, an unwelcome intruder. I used my brothers to further my plan; I cracked my knuckles to annoy them.

"Ma!" they shouted. "Make her stop. Make her go away."

But my mother did not say anything.

Still I was not worried. But I could see I would have to make a stronger move. I decided to sacrifice a tournament that was coming up in one week. I would refuse to play in it. And my mother would certainly have to speak to me about this. Because the sponsors and the benevolent associations would start calling her, asking, shouting, pleading to make me play again.

And then the tournament came and went. And she did not come to me, crying, "Why are you not playing chess?" But I was crying inside, because I learned that a boy whom I had easily defeated on two other occasions had won.

I realized my mother knew more tricks than I had thought. But now I was tired of her game. I wanted to start practicing for the next tournament. So I decided to pretend to let her win. I would be the one to speak first.

"I am ready to play chess again," I announced to her. I had imagined she would smile and then ask me what special thing I wanted to eat.

But instead, she gathered her face into a frown and stared into my eyes, as if she could force some kind of truth out of me.

"Why do you tell me this?" she finally said in sharp tones. "You think it is so easy. One day quit, next day play. Everything for you is this way. So smart, so easy, so fast."

"I said I'll play," I whined.

"No!" she shouted, and I almost jumped out of my scalp. "It is not so easy anymore."

I was quivering, stunned by what she said, in not knowing what she meant. And then I went back to my room. I stared at my chessboard, its sixty-four squares, to figure out how to undo this terrible mess. And after staring like this for many hours, I actually believed that I had made the white squares black and the black squares white, and everything would be all right.

And sure enough, I won her back. That night I developed a high fever, and she sat next to my bed, scolding me for going to school without my sweater. In the morning she was there as well, feeding me rice porridge flavored with chicken broth she had strained herself. She said she was feeding me this because I had the chicken pox and one chicken knew how to fight another. And in the afternoon, she sat in a chair in my room, knitting me a pink sweater while telling me about a sweater that Auntie Suyuan had knit for her daughter June, and how it was most unattractive and of the worst yarn. I was so happy that she had become her usual self.

But after I got well, I discovered that, really, my mother had changed. She no longer hovered over me as I practiced different chess games. She did not polish my trophies every day. She did not cut out the small newspaper item that mentioned my name. It was as if she had erected an invisible wall and I was secretly groping each day to see how high and how wide it was.

At my next tournament, while I had done well overall, in the end the points were not enough. I lost. And what was worse, my mother said nothing. She seemed to walk around with this satisfied look, as if it had happened because she had devised this strategy.

I was horrified. I spent many hours every day going over in my mind what I had lost. I knew it was not just the last tournament. I examined every move, every piece, every square. And I could no longer see the secret weapons of each piece, the magic within the intersection of each square. I could see only my mistakes, my weaknesses. It was as though I had lost my magic armor. And everybody could see this, where it was easy to attack me.

Over the next few weeks and later months and years, I continued to play, but never with that same feeling of supreme confidence. I fought hard, with fear and desperation. When I won, I was grateful, relieved. And when I lost, I was filled with growing dread, and then terror that I was no longer a prodigy, that I had lost the gift and had turned into someone quite ordinary.

When I lost twice to the boy whom I had defeated so easily a few years before, I stopped playing chess altogether. And nobody protested. I was fourteen.

"You know, I really don't understand you," said Marlene when I called her the night after I had shown my mother the mink jacket. "You can tell the IRS to piss up a rope, but you can't stand up to your own mother."

"I always intend to and then she says these little sneaky things, smoke bombs and little barbs, and . . ."

"Why don't you tell her to stop torturing you," said Marlene. "Tell her to stop ruining your life. Tell her to shut up."

"That's hilarious," I said with a half-laugh. "You want me to tell my mother to shut up?"

"Sure, why not?"

"Well, I don't know if it's explicitly stated in the law, but you can't *ever* tell a Chinese mother to shut up. You could be charged as an accessory to your own murder."

I wasn't so much afraid of my mother as I was afraid for Rich. I already knew what she would do, how she would attack him, how she would criticize him. She would be quiet at first. Then she would say a word about something small, something she had noticed, and then another word, and another, each one flung out like a little piece of sand, one from this direction, another from behind, more and more, until his looks, his character, his soul would have eroded away. And even if I recognized her strategy, her sneak attack, I was afraid that some unseen speck of truth would fly into my eye, blur what I was seeing and transform him from the divine man I thought he was into someone quite mundane, mortally wounded with tiresome habits and irritating imperfections.

This happened to my first marriage, to Marvin Chen, with whom I had eloped when I was eighteen and he was nineteen. When I was in love with Marvin, he was nearly perfect. He graduated third in his class at Lowell and got a full scholarship to Stanford. He played tennis. He had bulging calf muscles and one hundred forty-six straight black hairs on his chest. He made everyone laugh and his own laugh was deep, sonorous, masculinely sexy. He prided himself on having favorite love positions for different days and hours of the week; all he had to whisper was "Wednesday afternoon" and I'd shiver.

But by the time my mother had had her say about him, I saw his brain had shrunk from laziness, so that now it was good only for thinking up excuses. He chased golf and tennis balls to run away from family responsibilities. His eye wandered up and down other girls' legs, so he didn't know how to drive straight home anymore. He liked to tell big jokes to make other people feel little. He made a loud show of leaving ten-dollar tips to strangers but was stingy with presents to family. He thought waxing his red sports car all afternoon was more important than taking his wife somewhere in it.

My feelings for Marvin never reached the level of hate. No, it was worse in a way. It went from disappointment to contempt to apathetic boredom. It wasn't until after we separated, on nights when Shoshana was asleep and I was lonely, that I wondered if perhaps my mother had poisoned my marriage.

Thank God, her poison didn't affect my daughter, Shoshana. I almost aborted her, though. When I found out I was pregnant, I was furious. I secretly referred to my pregnancy as my "growing resentment," and I dragged Marvin down to the clinic so he would have to suffer through this too. It turned out we went to the wrong kind of clinic. They made us watch a film, a terrible bit of puritanical brainwash. I saw those little things, babies they called them even at seven weeks, and they had tiny, tiny fingers. And the film said that the baby's translucent fingers could *move*, that we should imagine them clinging for life, grasping for a chance, this miracle of life. If they had shown *anything else* except tiny fingers—so thank God they did. Because Shoshana really was a miracle. She was perfect. I found every detail about her to be remarkable, especially the way she flexed and curled her fingers. From the very moment she flung her fist away from her mouth to cry, I knew my feelings for her were inviolable.

But I worried for Rich. Because I knew my feelings for him were vulnerable to being felled by my mother's suspicions, passing remarks, and innuendos. And I was afraid of what I would then lose, because Rich Schields adored me in the same way I adored Shoshana. His love was unequivocal. Nothing could change it. He expected nothing from me; my mere existence was enough. And at the same time, he said that he had changed—for the *better*—because of me. He was embarrassingly romantic; he insisted he never was until he met me. And this confession made his romantic gestures all the more ennobling. At work, for example, when he would staple "FYI—For Your Information" notes to legal briefs and corporate returns that I had to review, he signed them at the bottom: "FYI—Forever You & I." The firm didn't know about our relationship, and so that kind of reckless behavior on his part thrilled me.

The sexual chemistry was what really surprised me, though. I thought he'd be one of those quiet types who was awkwardly gentle and clumsy, the kind of mild-mannered guy who says, "Am I hurting you?" when I can't feel a thing. But he was so attuned to my every movement I was sure he was reading my mind. He had no inhibitions, and whatever ones he discovered I had he'd pry away from me like little treasures. He saw all those private aspects of me—and I mean not just sexual private parts, but my darker side, my meanness, my pettiness, my self-loathing—all the things I kept hidden. So that with him I was completely naked, and when I was, when I was feeling the most vulnerable—when the wrong word would have sent me flying out the door forever—he always said exactly the right thing at the right moment. He didn't allow me to cover myself up. He would grab my hands, look me straight in the eye and tell me something new about why he loved me.

I'd never known love so pure, and I was afraid that it would become sullied by my mother. So I tried to store every one of these endearments about Rich in my memory, and I planned to call upon them again when the time was necessary.

After much thought, I came up with a brilliant plan. I concocted a way for Rich to meet my mother and win her over. In fact, I arranged it so my mother would want to cook a meal especially for him. I had some help from Auntie Suyuan. Auntie Su was my mother's friend from way back. They were very close, which meant they were ceaselessly tormenting each other with boasts and secrets. And I gave Auntie Su a secret to boast about.

After walking through North Beach one Sunday, I suggested to Rich that we stop by for a surprise visit to my Auntie Su and Uncle Canning. They lived on Leavenworth, just a few blocks west of my mother's apartment. It was late afternoon, just in time to catch Auntie Su preparing Sunday dinner.

"Stay! Stay!" she had insisted.

"No, no. It's just that we were walking by," I said.

"Already cooked enough for you. See? One soup, four dishes. You don't eat it, only have to throw it away. Wasted!"

How could we refuse? Three days later, Auntie Suyuan had a thank-you letter from Rich and me. "Rich said it was the best Chinese food he has ever tasted," I wrote.

And the next day, my mother called me, to invite me to a belated birthday dinner for my father. My brother Vincent was bringing his girlfriend, Lisa Lum. I could bring a friend, too.

I knew she would do this, because cooking was how my mother expressed her love, her pride, her power, her proof that she knew more than Auntie Su. "Just be sure to tell her later that her cooking was the best you ever tasted, that it was far better than Auntie Su's," I told Rich. "Believe me."

The night of the dinner, I sat in the kitchen watching her cook, waiting for the right moment to tell her about our marriage plans, that we had decided to get married next July, about seven months away. She was chopping eggplant into wedges, chattering at the same time about Auntie Suyuan: "She can only cook looking at a recipe. My instructions are in my fingers. I know what secret ingredients to put in just by using my nose!" And she was slicing with such a ferocity, seemingly inattentive to her sharp cleaver, that I was afraid her fingertips would become one of the ingredients of the red-cooked eggplant and shredded pork dish.

I was hoping she would say something first about Rich. I had seen her expression when she opened the door, her forced smile as she scrutinized him from head to toe, checking her appraisal of him against that already given to her by Auntie Suyuan. I tried to anticipate what criticisms she would have.

Rich was not only *not* Chinese, he was a few years younger than I was. And unfortunately, he looked much younger with his curly red hair, smooth pale skin, and the splash of orange freckles across his nose. He was a bit on the short side, compactly built. In his dark business suits, he looked nice but easily forgettable, like somebody's nephew at a funeral. Which was why I didn't notice him the first year we worked together at the firm. But my mother noticed everything.

"So what do you think of Rich?" I finally asked, holding my breath.

She tossed the eggplant in the hot oil and it made a loud, angry hissing sound. "So many spots on his face," she said.

I could feel the pinpricks on my back. "They're freckles. Freckles are good luck, you know," I said a bit too heatedly in trying to raise my voice above the din of the kitchen.

"Oh?" she said innocently.

"Yes, the more spots the better. Everybody knows that."

She considered this a moment and then smiled and spoke in Chinese: "Maybe this is true. When you were young, you got the chicken pox. So many spots, you had to stay home for ten days. So lucky, you thought."

I couldn't save Rich in the kitchen. And I couldn't save him later at the dinner table.

He had brought a bottle of French wine, something he did not know my parents could not appreciate. My parents did not even own wineglasses. And then he also made the mistake of drinking not one but two frosted glasses full, while everybody else had a half-inch "just for taste."

When I offered Rich a fork, he insisted on using the slippery ivory chopsticks. He held them splayed like the knock-kneed legs of an ostrich while picking up a large chunk of sauce-coated eggplant. Halfway between his plate and his open mouth, the chunk fell on his crisp white shirt and then slid into his crotch. It took several minutes to get Shoshana to stop shrieking with laughter.

And then he had helped himself to big portions of the shrimp and snow peas, not realizing he should have taken only a polite spoonful, until everybody had had a morsel.

He had declined the sautéed new greens, the tender and expensive leaves of bean plants plucked before the sprouts turn into beans. And Shoshana refused to eat them also, pointing to Rich: "He didn't eat them! He didn't eat them!"

He thought he was being polite by refusing seconds, when he should have followed my father's example, who made a big show of taking small portions of seconds, thirds, and even fourths, always saying he could not resist another bite of something or other, and then groaning that he was so full he thought he would burst.

But the worst was when Rich criticized my mother's cooking, and he didn't even know what he had done. As is the Chinese cook's custom, my mother always made disparaging remarks about her own cooking. That night she chose to direct it toward her famous steamed pork and preserved vegetable dish, which she always served with special pride.

"Ai! This dish not salty enough, no flavor," she complained, after tasting a small bite. "It is too bad to eat."

This was our family's cue to eat some and proclaim it the best she had ever made. But before we could do so, Rich said, "You know, all it needs is a little soy sauce." And he proceeded to pour a riverful of the salty black stuff on the platter, right before my mother's horrified eyes.

And even though I was hoping throughout the dinner that my

mother would somehow see Rich's kindness, his sense of humor and boyish charm, I knew he had failed miserably in her eyes.

Rich obviously had had a different opinion on how the evening had gone. When we got home that night, after we put Shoshana to bed, he said modestly, "Well. I think we hit it off *A-o-kay*." He had the look of a dalmatian, panting, loyal, waiting to be petted.

"Uh-hmm," I said. I was putting on an old nightgown, a hint that I was not feeling amorous. I was still shuddering, remembering how Rich had firmly shaken both my parents' hands with that same easy familiarity he used with nervous new clients. "Linda, Tim," he said, "we'll see you again soon, I'm sure." My parents' names are Lindo and Tin Jong, and nobody, except a few older family friends, ever calls them by their first names.

"So what did she say when you told her?" And I knew he was referring to our getting married. I had told Rich earlier that I would tell my mother first and let her break the news to my father.

"I never had a chance," I said, which was true. How could I have told my mother I was getting married, when at every possible moment we were alone, she seemed to remark on how much expensive wine Rich liked to drink, or how pale and ill he looked, or how sad Shoshana seemed to be.

Rich was smiling. "How long does it take to say, Mom, Dad, I'm getting married?"

"You don't understand. You don't understand my mother."

Rich shook his head. "Whew! You can say that again. Her English was *so* bad. You know, when she was talking about that dead guy showing up on *Dynasty*, I thought she was talking about something that happened in China a long time ago."

That night, after the dinner, I lay in bed, tense. I was despairing over this latest failure, made worse by the fact that Rich seemed blind to it all. He looked so pathetic. *So pathetic*, those words! My mother was doing it again, making me see black where I once saw white. In her hands, I always became the pawn. I could only run away. And she was the queen, able to move in all directions, relentless in her pursuit, always able to find my weakest spots.

I woke up late, with teeth clenched and every nerve on edge. Rich was already up, showered, and reading the Sunday paper. "Morning, doll," he said between noisy munches of cornflakes. I put on my jogging clothes and headed out the door, got into the car, and drove to my parents' apartment.

Marlene was right. I had to tell my mother—that I knew what she was doing, her scheming ways of making me miserable. By the time I arrived, I had enough anger to fend off a thousand flying cleavers.

My father opened the door and looked surprised to see me. "Where's Ma?" I asked, trying to keep my breath even. He gestured to the living room in back.

I found her sleeping soundly on the sofa. The back of her head was resting on a white embroidered doily. Her mouth was slack and all the lines in her face were gone. With her smooth face, she looked like a young girl, frail, guileless, and innocent. One arm hung limply down the side of the sofa. Her chest was still. All her strength was gone. She had no weapons, no demons surrounding her. She looked powerless. Defeated.

And then I was seized with a fear that she looked like this because she was dead. She had died when I was having terrible thoughts about her. I had wished her out of my life, and she had acquiesced, floating out of her body to escape my terrible hatred.

"Ma!" I said sharply. "Ma!" I whined, starting to cry.

And her eyes slowly opened. She blinked. Her hands moved with life. "*Shemma?* Meimei-ah? Is that you?"

I was speechless. She had not called me Meimei, my childhood name, in many years. She sat up and the lines in her face returned, only now they seemed less harsh, soft creases of worry. "Why are you here? Why are you crying? Something has happened!"

I didn't know what to do or say. In a matter of seconds, it

seemed, I had gone from being angered by her strength, to being amazed by her innocence, and then frightened by her vulnerability. And now I felt numb, strangely weak, as if someone had unplugged me and the current running through me had stopped.

"Nothing's happened. Nothing's the matter. I don't know why I'm here," I said in a hoarse voice. "I wanted to talk to you. . . . I wanted to tell you . . . Rich and I are getting married."

I squeezed my eyes shut, waiting to hear her protests, her laments, the dry voice delivering some sort of painful verdict.

"*Irdaule*"—I already know this—she said, as if to ask why I was telling her this again.

"You know?"

"Of course. Even if you didn't tell me," she said simply.

This was worse than I had imagined. She had known all along, when she criticized the mink jacket, when she belittled his freckles and complained about his drinking habits. She disapproved of him. "I know you hate him," I said in a quavering voice. "I know you think he's not good enough, but I . . ."

"Hate? Why do you think I hate your future husband?"

"You never want to talk about him. The other day, when I started to tell you about him and Shoshana at the Exploratorium, you . . . you changed the subject . . . you started talking about Dad's exploratory surgery and then . . ."

"What is more important, explore fun or explore sickness?"

I wasn't going to let her escape this time. "And then when you met him, you said he had spots on his face."

She looked at me, puzzled. "Is this not true?"

"Yes, but, you said it just to be mean, to hurt me, to . . ."

"Ai-ya, why do you think these bad things about me?" Her face looked old and full of sorrow. "So you think your mother is this bad. You think I have a secret meaning. But it is you who has this meaning. Ai-ya! She thinks I am this bad!" She sat straight and proud on the sofa, her mouth clamped tight, her hands clasped together, her eyes sparkling with angry tears.

Oh, her strength! her weakness!—both pulling me apart. My mind was flying one way, my heart another. I sat down on the sofa next to her, the two of us stricken by the other.

I felt as if I had lost a battle, but one that I didn't know I had been fighting. I was weary. "I'm going home," I finally said. "I'm not feeling too good right now."

"You have become ill?" she murmured, putting her hand on my forehead.

"No," I said. I wanted to leave. "I . . . I just don't know what's inside me right now."

"Then I will tell you," she said simply. And I stared at her. "Half of everything inside you," she explained in Chinese, "is from your father's side. This is natural. They are the Jong clan, Cantonese people. Good, honest people. Although sometimes they are bad-tempered and stingy. You know this from your father, how he can be unless I remind him."

And I was thinking to myself, Why is she telling me this? What does this have to do with anything? But my mother continued to speak, smiling broadly, sweeping her hand. "And half of everything inside you is from me, your mother's side, from the Sun clan in Taiyuan." She wrote the characters out on the back of an envelope, forgetting that I cannot read Chinese.

"We are a smart people, very strong, tricky, and famous for winning wars. You know Sun Yat-sen, hah?"

I nodded.

"He is from the Sun clan. But his family moved to the south many centuries ago, so he is not exactly the same clan. My family has always live in Taiyuan, from before the days of even Sun Wei. Do you know Sun Wei?"

I shook my head. And although I still didn't know where this conversation was going, I felt soothed. It seemed like the first time we had had an almost normal conversation.

"He went to battle with Genghis Khan. And when the Mongol soldiers shot at Sun Wei's warriors—heh!—their arrows bounced off the shields like rain on stone. Sun Wei had made a kind of armor so strong Genghis Khan believed it was magic!"

"Genghis Khan must have invented some magic arrows, then," I said. "After all, he conquered China."

My mother acted as if she hadn't heard me right. "This is true, we always know how to win. So now you know what is inside you, almost all good stuff from Taiyuan."

"I guess we've evolved to just winning in the toy and electronics market," I said.

"How do you know this?" she asked eagerly.

"You see it on everything. Made in Taiwan."

"Ai!" she cried loudly. "I'm not from Taiwan!"

And just like that, the fragile connection we were starting to build snapped.

"I was born in China, in *Taiyuan*," she said. "Taiwan is not China."

"Well, I only thought you said 'Taiwan' because it sounds the same," I argued, irritated that she was upset by such an unintentional mistake.

"Sound is completely different! Country is completely different!" she said in a huff. "People there only dream that it is China, because if you are Chinese you can never let go of China in your mind."

We sank into silence, a stalemate. And then her eyes lighted up. "Now listen. You can also say the name of Taiyuan is Bing. Everyone from that city calls it that. Easier for you to say. Bing, it is a nickname."

She wrote down the character, and I nodded as if this made everything perfectly clear. "The same as here," she added in English. "You call Apple for New York. Frisco for San Francisco."

"Nobody calls San Francisco that!" I said, laughing. "People who call it that don't know any better."

"Now you understand my meaning," said my mother triumphantly.

I smiled.

And really, I did understand finally. Not what she had just said. But what had been true all along.

I saw what I had been fighting for: It was for me, a scared child, who had run away a long time ago to what I had imagined was a safer place. And hiding in this place, behind my invisible barriers, I knew what lay on the other side: Her side attacks. Her secret weapons. Her uncanny ability to find my weakest spots. But in the brief instant that I had peered over the barriers I could finally see what was really there: an old woman, a wok for her armor, a knitting needle for her sword, getting a little crabby as she waited patiently for her daughter to invite her in.

Rich and I have decided to postpone our wedding. My mother says July is not a good time to go to China on our honeymoon. She knows this because she and my father have just returned from a trip to Beijing and Taiyuan.

"It is too hot in the summer. You will only grow more spots and then your whole face will become red!" she tells Rich. And Rich grins, gestures his thumb toward my mother, and says to me, "Can you believe what comes out of her mouth? Now I know where you get your sweet, tactful nature."

"You must go in October. That is the best time. Not too hot, not too cold. I am thinking of going back then too," she says authoritatively. And then she hastily adds: "Of course not with you!"

I laugh nervously, and Rich jokes: "That'd be great, Lindo. You could translate all the menus for us, make sure we're not eating snakes or dogs by mistake." I almost kick him.

"No, this is not my meaning," insists my mother. "Really, I am not asking."

And I know what she really means. She would love to go to China with us. And I would hate it. Three weeks' worth of her complaining about dirty chopsticks and cold soup, three meals a day—well, it would be a disaster.

Yet part of me also thinks the whole idea makes perfect sense. The three of us, leaving our differences behind, stepping on the plane together, sitting side by side, lifting off, moving West to reach the East.

ROSE HSU JORDAN

Without Wood

I used to believe everything my mother said, even when I didn't know what she meant. Once when I was little, she told me she knew it would rain because lost ghosts were circling near our windows, calling "Woo-woo" to be let in. She said doors would unlock themselves in the middle of the night unless we checked twice. She said a mirror could see only my face, but she could see me inside out even when I was not in the room.

And all these things seemed true to me. The power of her words was that strong.

She said that if I listened to her, later I would know what she knew: where true words came from, always from up high, above everything else. And if I didn't listen to her, she said my ear would bend too easily to other people, all saying words that had no lasting meaning, because they came from the bottom of their hearts, where their own desires lived, a place where I could not belong.

The words my mother spoke did come from up high. As I recall, I was always looking up at her face as I lay on my pillow. In those days my sisters and I all slept in the same double bed. Janice, my oldest sister, had an allergy that made one nostril sing like a bird at night, so we called her Whistling Nose. Ruth was Ugly Foot because she could spread her toes out in the shape of a witch's claw. I was Scaredy Eyes because I would squeeze shut my eyes so I wouldn't have to see the dark, which Janice and Ruth said was a dumb thing to do. During those early years, I was the last to fall asleep. I clung to the bed, refusing to leave this world for dreams.

"Your sisters have already gone to see Old Mr. Chou," my mother would whisper in Chinese. According to my mother, Old Mr. Chou was the guardian of a door that opened into dreams. "Are you ready to go see Old Mr. Chou, too?" And every night I would shake my head.

"Old Mr. Chou takes me to bad places," I cried.

Old Mr. Chou took my sisters to sleep. They never remembered anything from the night before. But Old Mr. Chou would swing the door wide open for me, and as I tried to walk in, he would slam it fast, hoping to squash me like a fly. That's why I would always dart back into wakefulness.

But eventually Old Mr. Chou would get tired and leave the door unwatched. The bed would grow heavy at the top and slowly tilt. And I would slide headfirst, in through Old Mr. Chou's door, and land in a house without doors or windows.

I remember one time I dreamt of falling through a hole in Old Mr. Chou's floor. I found myself in a nighttime garden and Old Mr. Chou was shouting, "Who's in my backyard?" I ran away. Soon I found myself stomping on plants with veins of blood, running through fields of snapdragons that changed colors like stoplights, until I came to a giant playground filled with row after row of square sandboxes. In each sandbox was a new doll. And my mother, who was not there but could see me inside out, told Old Mr. Chou she knew which doll I would pick. So I decided to pick one that was entirely different.

"Stop her! Stop her!" cried my mother. As I tried to run away, Old Mr. Chou chased me, shouting, "See what happens when you don't listen to your mother!" And I became paralyzed, too scared to move in any direction.

The next morning, I told my mother what happened, and she laughed and said, "Don't pay attention to Old Mr. Chou. He is only a dream. You only have to listen to me."

And I cried, "But Old Mr. Chou listens to you too."

＊

More than thirty years later, my mother was still trying to make me listen. A month after I told her that Ted and I were getting a divorce, I met her at church, at the funeral of China Mary, a wonderful ninety-two-year-old woman who had played godmother to every child who passed through the doors of the First Chinese Baptist Church.

"You are getting too thin," my mother said in her pained voice when I sat down next to her. "You must eat more."

"I'm fine," I said, and I smiled for proof. "And besides, wasn't it you who said my clothes were always too tight?"

"Eat more," she insisted, and then she nudged me with a little spiral-bound book hand-titled "Cooking the Chinese Way by China Mary Chan." They were selling them at the door, only five dollars each, to raise money for the Refugee Scholarship Fund.

The organ music stopped and the minister cleared his throat. He was not the regular pastor; I recognized him as Wing, a boy who used to steal baseball cards with my brother Luke. Only later Wing went to divinity school, thanks to China Mary, and Luke went to the county jail for selling stolen car stereos.

"I can still hear her voice," Wing said to the mourners. "She said God made me with all the right ingredients, so it'd be a shame if I burned in hell."

"Already cre-*mated*," my mother whispered matter-of-factly, nodding toward the altar, where a framed color photo of China Mary stood. I held my finger to my lips the way librarians do, but she didn't get it.

"That one, we bought it." She was pointing to a large spray of yellow chrysanthemums and red roses. "Thirty-four dollars. All artificial, so it will last forever. You can pay me later. Janice and Matthew also chip in some. You have money?"

"Yes, Ted sent me a check."

Then the minister asked everyone to bow in prayer. My mother was quiet at last, dabbing her nose with Kleenex while the minister talked: "I can just see her now, wowing the angels with her Chinese cooking and gung-ho attitude."

And when heads lifted, everyone rose to sing hymn number

335, China Mary's favorite: "You can be an an-gel, ev-ery day on earth . . ."

But my mother was not singing. She was staring at me. "Why does he send you a check?" I kept looking at the hymnal, singing: "Send-ing rays of sun-shine, full of joy from birth."

And so she grimly answered her own question: "He is doing monkey business with someone else."

Monkey business? Ted? I wanted to laugh—her choice of words, but also the idea! Cool, silent, hairless Ted, whose breathing pattern didn't alter one bit in the height of passion? I could just see him, grunting "Ooh-ooh-ooh" while scratching his armpits, then bouncing and shrieking across the mattress trying to grab a breast.

"No, I don't think so," I said.

"Why not?"

"I don't think we should talk about Ted now, not here."

"Why can you talk about this with a psyche-atric and not with mother?"

"Psychiatrist."

"Psyche-atricks," she corrected herself.

"A mother is best. A mother knows what is inside you," she said above the singing voices. "A psyche-atricks will only make you *hulihudu*, make you see *heimongmong*."

Back home, I thought about what she said. And it was true. Lately I had been feeling *hulihudu*. And everything around me seemed to be *heimongmong*. These were words I had never thought about in English terms. I suppose the closest in meaning would be "confused" and "dark fog."

But really, the words mean much more than that. Maybe they can't be easily translated because they refer to a sensation that only Chinese people have, as if you were falling headfirst through Old Mr. Chou's door, then trying to find your way back. But you're so scared you can't open your eyes, so you get on your hands and knees and grope in the dark, listening for voices to tell you which way to go.

I had been talking to too many people, my friends, everybody it seems, except Ted. To each person I told a different story.

Yet each version was true, I was certain of it, at least at the moment that I told it.

To my friend Waverly, I said I never knew how much I loved Ted until I saw how much he could hurt me. I felt such pain, literally a *physical* pain, as if someone had torn off both my arms without anesthesia, without sewing me back up.

"Have you ever had them torn off *with* anesthesia? God! I've never seen you so hysterical," said Waverly. "You want my opinion, you're better off without him. It hurts only because it's taken you fifteen years to see what an emotional wimp he is. Listen, I know what it feels like."

To my friend Lena, I said I was better off without Ted. After the initial shock, I realized I didn't miss him at all. I just missed the way I felt when I was with him.

"Which was what?" Lena gasped. "You were depressed. You were manipulated into thinking you were nothing next to him. And now you think you're nothing without him. If I were you, I'd get the name of a good lawyer and go for everything you can. Get even."

I told my psychiatrist I was obsessed with revenge. I dreamt of calling Ted up and inviting him to dinner, to one of those trendy who's-who places, like Café Majestic or Rosalie's. And after he started the first course and was nice and relaxed, I would say, "It's not that easy, Ted." From my purse I would take out a voodoo doll which Lena had already lent me from her props department. I would aim my escargot fork at a strategic spot on the voodoo doll and I would say, out loud, in front of all the fashionable restaurant patrons, "Ted, you're just such an impotent bastard and I'm going to make sure you stay that way." *Wham!*

Saying this, I felt I had raced to the top of a big turning point in my life, a new me after just two weeks of psychotherapy. But my psychiatrist just looked bored, his hand still propped under his chin. "It seems you've been experiencing some very powerful feelings," he said, sleepy-eyed. "I think we should think about them more next week."

And so I didn't know what to think anymore. For the next

few weeks, I inventoried my life, going from room to room trying to remember the history of everything in the house: things I had collected before I met Ted (the hand-blown glasses, the macrame wall hangings, and the rocker I had recaned); things we bought together right after we were married (most of the big furniture); things people gave us (the glass-domed clock that no longer worked, three sake sets, four teapots); things he picked out (the signed lithographs, none of them beyond number twenty-five in a series of two hundred fifty, the Steuben crystal strawberries); and things I picked out because I couldn't bear to see them left behind (the mismatched candlestick holders from garage sales, an antique quilt with a hole in it, odd-shaped vials that once contained ointments, spices, and perfumes).

I had started to inventory the bookshelves when I got a letter from Ted, a note actually, written hurriedly in ballpoint on his prescription notepad. "Sign 4x where indicated," it read. And then in fountain-pen blue ink, "enc: check, to tide you over until settlement."

The note was clipped to our divorce papers, along with a check for ten thousand dollars, signed in the same fountain-pen blue ink on the note. And instead of being grateful, I was hurt.

Why had he sent the check with the papers? Why the two different pens? Was the check an afterthought? How long had he sat in his office determining how much money was enough? And why had he chosen to sign it with *that* pen?

I still remember the look on his face last year when he carefully undid the gold foil wrap, the surprise in his eyes as he slowly examined every angle of the pen by the light of the Christmas tree. He kissed my forehead. "I'll use it only to sign important things," he had promised me.

Remembering that, holding the check, all I could do was sit on the edge of the couch feeling my head getting heavy at the top. I stared at the x's on the divorce papers, the wording on the prescription notepad, the two colors of ink, the date of the check, the careful way in which he wrote, "Ten thousand only and no cents."

I sat there quietly, trying to listen to my heart, to make the right decision. But then I realized I didn't know what the choices were. And so I put the papers and the check away, in a drawer where I kept store coupons which I never threw away and which I never used either.

My mother once told me why I was so confused all the time. She said I was without wood. Born without wood so that I listened to too many people. She knew this, because once she had almost become this way.

"A girl is like a young tree," she said. "You must stand tall and listen to your mother standing next to you. That is the only way to grow strong and straight. But if you bend to listen to other people, you will grow crooked and weak. You will fall to the ground with the first strong wind. And then you will be like a weed, growing wild in any direction, running along the ground until someone pulls you out and throws you away."

But by the time she told me this, it was too late. I had already begun to bend. I had started going to school, where a teacher named Mrs. Berry lined us up and marched us in and out of rooms, up and down hallways while she called out, "Boys and girls, follow me." And if you didn't listen to her, she would make you bend over and whack you with a yardstick ten times.

I still listened to my mother, but I also learned how to let her words blow through me. And sometimes I filled my mind with other people's thoughts—all in English—so that when she looked at me inside out, she would be confused by what she saw.

Over the years, I learned to choose from the best opinions. Chinese people had Chinese opinions. American people had American opinions. And in almost every case, the American version was much better.

It was only later that I discovered there was a serious flaw with the American version. There were too many choices, so it was easy to get confused and pick the wrong thing. That's how I felt about my situation with Ted. There was so much to think about, so much to decide. Each decision meant a turn in another direction.

The check, for example. I wondered if Ted was really trying to trick me, to get me to admit that I was giving up, that I wouldn't fight the divorce. And if I cashed it, he might later say the amount was the whole settlement. Then I got a little sentimental and imagined, only for a moment, that he had sent me ten thousand dollars because he truly loved me; he was telling me in his own way how much I meant to him. Until I realized that ten thousand dollars was nothing to him, that I was nothing to him.

I thought about putting an end to this torture and signing the divorce papers. And I was just about to take the papers out of the coupon drawer when I remembered the house.

I thought to myself, I love this house. The big oak door that opens into a foyer filled with stained-glass windows. The sunlight in the breakfast room, the south view of the city from the front parlor. The herb and flower garden Ted had planted. He used to work in the garden every weekend, kneeling on a green rubber pad, obsessively inspecting every leaf as if he were manicuring fingernails. He assigned plants to certain planter boxes. Tulips could not be mixed with perennials. A cutting of aloe vera that Lena gave me did not belong anywhere because we had no other succulents.

I looked out the window and saw the calla lilies had fallen and turned brown, the daisies had been crushed down by their own weight, the lettuce gone to seed. Runner weeds were growing between the flagstone walkways that wound between the planter boxes. The whole thing had grown wild from months of neglect.

And seeing the garden in this forgotten condition reminded me of something I once read in a fortune cookie: When a husband stops paying attention to the garden, he's thinking of pulling up roots. When was the last time Ted pruned the rosemary back? When was the last time he squirted Snail B-Gone around the flower beds?

I quickly walked down to the garden shed, looking for pesticides and weed killer, as if the amount left in the bottle, the expiration date, anything would give me some idea of what was happening in my life. And then I put the bottle down. I had the sense someone was watching me and laughing.

I went back in the house, this time to call a lawyer. But as I started to dial, I became confused. I put the receiver down. What could I say? What did I want from divorce—when I never knew what I had wanted from marriage?

The next morning, I was still thinking about my marriage: fifteen years of living in Ted's shadow. I lay in bed, my eyes squeezed shut, unable to make the simplest decisions.

I stayed in bed for three days, getting up only to go to the bathroom or to heat up another can of chicken noodle soup. But mostly I slept. I took the sleeping pills Ted had left behind in the medicine cabinet. And for the first time I can recall, I had no dreams. All I could remember was falling smoothly into a dark space with no feeling of dimension or direction. I was the only person in this blackness. And every time I woke up, I took another pill and went back to this place.

But on the fourth day, I had a nightmare. In the dark, I couldn't see Old Mr. Chou, but he said he would find me, and when he did, he would squish me into the ground. He was sounding a bell, and the louder the bell rang the closer he was to finding me. I held my breath to keep from screaming, but the bell got louder and louder until I burst awake.

It was the phone. It must have rung for an hour nonstop. I picked it up.

"Now that you are up, I am bringing you leftover dishes," said my mother. She sounded as if she could see me now. But the room was dark, the curtains closed tight.

"Ma, I can't . . . " I said. "I can't see you now. I'm busy."

"Too busy for mother?"

"I have an appointment . . . with my psychiatrist."

She was quiet for a while. "Why do you not speak up for yourself?" she finally said in her pained voice. "Why can you not talk to your husband?"

"Ma," I said, feeling drained. "Please. Don't tell me to save my marriage anymore. It's hard enough as it is."

"I am not telling you to save your marriage," she protested. "I only say you should speak up."

When I hung up, the phone rang again. It was my psychiatrist's receptionist. I had missed my appointment that morning, as well as two days ago. Did I want to reschedule? I said I would look at my schedule and call back.

And five minutes later the phone rang again.

"Where've you been?" It was Ted.

I began to shake. "Out," I said.

"I've been trying to reach you for the last three days. I even called the phone company to check the line."

And I knew he had done that, not out of any concern for me, but because when he wants something, he gets impatient and irrational about people who make him wait.

"You know it's been two weeks," he said with obvious irritation.

"Two weeks?"

"You haven't cashed the check or returned the papers. I wanted to be nice about this, Rose. I can get someone to officially serve the papers, you know."

"You can?"

And then without missing a beat, he proceeded to say what he really wanted, which was more despicable than all the terrible things I had imagined.

He wanted the papers returned, signed. He wanted the house. He wanted the whole thing to be over as soon as possible. Because he wanted to get married again, to someone else.

Before I could stop myself, I gasped. "You mean you *were* doing monkey business with someone else?" I was so humiliated I almost started to cry.

And then for the first time in months, after being in limbo all that time, everything stopped. All the questions: gone. There were no choices. I had an empty feeling—and I felt free, wild. From high inside my head I could hear someone laughing.

"What's so funny?" said Ted angrily.

"Sorry," I said. "It's just that . . ." and I was trying hard to stifle my giggles, but one of them escaped through my nose with a snort, which made me laugh more. And then Ted's silence made me laugh even harder.

I was still gasping when I tried to begin again in a more even voice: "Listen, Ted, sorry . . . I think the best thing is for you to come over after work." I didn't know why I said that, but I felt right saying it.

"There's nothing to talk about, Rose."

"I know," I said in a voice so calm it surprised even me. "I just want to show you something. And don't worry, you'll get your papers. Believe me."

I had no plan. I didn't know what I would say to him later. I knew only that I wanted Ted to see me one more time before the divorce.

What I ended up showing him was the garden. By the time he arrived, the late-afternoon summer fog had already blown in. I had the divorce papers in the pocket of my windbreaker. Ted was shivering in his sports jacket as he surveyed the damage to the garden.

"What a mess," I heard him mutter to himself, trying to shake his pant leg loose of a blackberry vine that had meandered onto the walkway. And I knew he was calculating how long it would take to get the place back into order.

"I like it this way," I said, patting the tops of overgrown carrots, their orange heads pushing through the earth as if about to be born. And then I saw the weeds: Some had sprouted in and out of the cracks in the patio. Others had anchored on the side of the house. And even more had found refuge under loose shingles and were on their way to climbing up to the roof. No way to pull them out once they've buried themselves in the masonry; you'd end up pulling the whole building down.

Ted was picking up plums from the ground and tossing them over the fence into the neighbor's yard. "Where are the papers?" he finally said.

I handed them to him and he stuffed them in the inside pocket of his jacket. He faced me and I saw his eyes, the look I had once mistaken for kindness and protection. "You don't have to move out right away," he said. "I know you'll want at least a month to find a place."

"I've already found a place," I said quickly, because right

then I knew where I was going to live. His eyebrows raised in surprise and he smiled—for the briefest moment—until I said, "Here."

"What's that?" he said sharply. His eyebrows were still up, but now there was no smile.

"I said I'm staying here," I announced again.

"Who says?" He folded his arms across his chest, squinted his eyes, examining my face as if he knew it would crack at any moment. That expression of his used to terrify me into stammers.

Now I felt nothing, no fear, no anger. "I say I'm staying, and my lawyer will too, once we serve you the papers," I said.

Ted pulled out the divorce papers and stared at them. His x's were still there, the blanks were still blank. "What do you think you're doing? Exactly what?" he said.

And the answer, the one that was important above everything else, ran through my body and fell from my lips: "You can't just pull me out of your life and throw me away."

I saw what I wanted: his eyes, confused, then scared. He was *hulihudu*. The power of my words was that strong.

That night I dreamt I was wandering through the garden. The trees and bushes were covered with mist. And then I spotted Old Mr. Chou and my mother off in the distance, their busy movements swirling the fog around them. They were bending over one of the planter boxes.

"There she is!" cried my mother. Old Mr. Chou smiled at me and waved. I walked up to my mother and saw that she was hovering over something, as if she were tending a baby.

"See," she said, beaming. "I have just planted them this morning, some for you, some for me."

And below the *heimongmong*, all along the ground, were weeds already spilling out over the edges, running wild in every direction.

JING-MEI WOO

Best Quality

Five months ago, after a crab dinner celebrating Chinese New Year, my mother gave me my "life's importance," a jade pendant on a gold chain. The pendant was not a piece of jewelry I would have chosen for myself. It was almost the size of my little finger, a mottled green and white color, intricately carved. To me, the whole effect looked wrong: too large, too green, too garishly ornate. I stuffed the necklace in my lacquer box and forgot about it.

But these days, I think about my life's importance. I wonder what it means, because my mother died three months ago, six days before my thirty-sixth birthday. And she's the only person I could have asked, to tell me about life's importance, to help me understand my grief.

I now wear that pendant every day. I think the carvings mean something, because shapes and details, which I never seem to notice until after they're pointed out to me, always mean something to Chinese people. I know I could ask Auntie Lindo, Auntie An-mei, or other Chinese friends, but I also know they would tell me a meaning that is different from what my mother intended. What if they tell me this curving line branching into three oval shapes is a pomegranate and that my mother was wishing me fertility and posterity? What if my mother really meant the carvings were a branch of pears to give me purity and

197

honesty? Or ten-thousand-year droplets from the magic mountain, giving me my life's direction and a thousand years of fame and immortality?

And because I think about this all the time, I always notice other people wearing these same jade pendants—not the flat rectangular medallions or the round white ones with holes in the middle but ones like mine, a two-inch oblong of bright apple green. It's as though we were all sworn to the same secret covenant, so secret we don't even know what we belong to. Last weekend, for example, I saw a bartender wearing one. As I fingered mine, I asked him, "Where'd you get yours?"

"My mother gave it to me," he said.

I asked him why, which is a nosy question that only one Chinese person can ask another; in a crowd of Caucasians, two Chinese people are already like family.

"She gave it to me after I got divorced. I guess my mother's telling me I'm still worth something."

And I knew by the wonder in his voice that he had no idea what the pendant really meant.

At last year's Chinese New Year dinner, my mother had cooked eleven crabs, one crab for each person, plus an extra. She and I had bought them on Stockton Street in Chinatown. We had walked down the steep hill from my parents' flat, which was actually the first floor of a six-unit building they owned on Leavenworth near California. Their place was only six blocks from where I worked as a copywriter for a small ad agency, so two or three times a week I would drop by after work. My mother always had enough food to insist that I stay for dinner.

That year, Chinese New Year fell on a Thursday, so I got off work early to help my mother shop. My mother was seventy-one, but she still walked briskly along, her small body straight and purposeful, carrying a colorful flowery plastic bag. I dragged the metal shopping cart behind.

Every time I went with her to Chinatown, she pointed out other Chinese women her age. "Hong Kong ladies," she said, eyeing two finely dressed women in long, dark mink coats and perfect black hairdos. "Cantonese, village people," she whispered as we passed women in knitted caps, bent over in layers of padded tops and men's vests. And my mother—wearing light-blue polyester pants, a red sweater, and a child's green down jacket—she didn't look like anybody else. She had come here in 1949, at the end of a long journey that started in Kweilin in 1944; she had gone north to Chungking, where she met my father, and then they went southeast to Shanghai and fled farther south to Hong Kong, where the boat departed for San Francisco. My mother came from many different directions.

And now she was huffing complaints in rhythm to her walk downhill. "Even you don't want them, you stuck," she said. She was fuming again about the tenants who lived on the second floor. Two years ago, she had tried to evict them on the pretext that relatives from China were coming to live there. But the couple saw through her ruse to get around rent control. They said they wouldn't budge until she produced the relatives. And after that I had to listen to her recount every new injustice this couple inflicted on her.

My mother said the gray-haired man put too many bags in the garbage cans: "Cost me extra."

And the woman, a very elegant artist type with blond hair, had supposedly painted the apartment in terrible red and green colors. "Awful," moaned my mother. "And they take bath, two three times every day. Running the water, running, running, running, never stop!"

"Last week," she said, growing angrier at each step, "the *waigoren* accuse me." She referred to all Caucasians as *waigoren*, foreigners. "They say I put poison in a fish, kill that cat."

"What cat?" I asked, even though I knew exactly which one she was talking about. I had seen that cat many times. It was a big one-eared tom with gray stripes who had learned to jump on the outside sill of my mother's kitchen window. My mother would stand on her tiptoes and bang the kitchen window to scare the cat away. And the cat would stand his ground, hissing back in response to her shouts.

"That cat always raising his tail to put a stink on my door," complained my mother.

I once saw her chase him from her stairwell with a pot of

boiling water. I was tempted to ask if she really had put poison in a fish, but I had learned never to take sides against my mother.

"So what happened to that cat?" I asked.

"That cat gone! Disappear!" She threw her hands in the air and smiled, looking pleased for a moment before the scowl came back. "And that man, he raise his hand like this, show me his ugly fist and call me worst Fukien landlady. I not from Fukien. Hunh! He know nothing!" she said, satisfied she had put him in his place.

On Stockton Street, we wandered from one fish store to another, looking for the liveliest crabs.

"Don't get a dead one," warned my mother in Chinese. "Even a beggar won't eat a dead one."

I poked the crabs with a pencil to see how feisty they were. If a crab grabbed on, I lifted it out and into a plastic sack. I lifted one crab this way, only to find one of its legs had been clamped onto by another crab. In the brief tug-of-war, my crab lost a limb.

"Put it back," whispered my mother. "A missing leg is a bad sign on Chinese New Year."

But a man in a white smock came up to us. He started talking loudly to my mother in Cantonese, and my mother, who spoke Cantonese so poorly it sounded just like her Mandarin, was talking loudly back, pointing to the crab and its missing leg. And after more sharp words, that crab and its leg were put into our sack.

"Doesn't matter," said my mother. "This number eleven, extra one."

Back home, my mother unwrapped the crabs from their newspaper liners and then dumped them into a sinkful of cold water. She brought out her old wooden board and cleaver, then chopped the ginger and scallions, and poured soy sauce and sesame oil into a shallow dish. The kitchen smelled of wet newspapers and Chinese fragrances.

Then, one by one, she grabbed the crabs by their back, hoisted them out of the sink and shook them dry and awake. The crabs flexed their legs in midair between sink and stove. She stacked the crabs in a multileveled steamer that sat over two burners on the stove, put a lid on top, and lit the burners. I couldn't bear to watch so I went into the dining room.

When I was eight, I had played with a crab my mother had brought home for my birthday dinner. I had poked it, and jumped back every time its claws reached out. And I determined that the crab and I had come to a great understanding when it finally heaved itself up and walked clear across the counter. But before I could even decide what to name my new pet, my mother had dropped it into a pot of cold water and placed it on the tall stove. I had watched with growing dread, as the water heated up and the pot began to clatter with this crab trying to tap his way out of his own hot soup. To this day, I remember that crab screaming as he thrust one bright red claw out over the side of the bubbling pot. It must have been my own voice, because now I know, of course, that crabs have no vocal cords. And I also try to convince myself that they don't have enough brains to know the difference between a hot bath and a slow death.

For our New Year celebration, my mother had invited her longtime friends Lindo and Tin Jong. Without even asking, my mother knew that meant including the Jongs' children: their son Vincent, who was thirty-eight years old and still living at home, and their daughter, Waverly, who was around my age. Vincent called to see if he could also bring his girlfriend, Lisa Lum. Waverly said she would bring her new fiancé, Rich Shields, who, like Waverly, was a tax attorney at Price Waterhouse. And she added that Shoshana, her four-year-old daughter from a previous marriage, wanted to know if my parents had a VCR so she could watch *Pinocchio*, just in case she got bored. My mother also reminded me to invite Mr. Chong, my old piano teacher, who still lived three blocks away at our old apartment.

Including my mother, father, and me, that made eleven people. But my mother had counted only ten, because to her way of thinking Shoshana was just a child and didn't count, at least not as far as crabs were concerned. She hadn't considered that Waverly might not think the same way.

When the platter of steaming crabs was passed around, Waverly was first and she picked the best crab, the brightest, the plumpest, and put it on her daughter's plate. And then she picked the next best for Rich and another good one for herself. And because she had learned this skill, of choosing the best, from her mother, it was only natural that her mother knew how to pick the next-best ones for her husband, her son, his girlfriend, and herself. And my mother, of course, considered the four remaining crabs and gave the one that looked the best to Old Chong, because he was nearly ninety and deserved that kind of respect, and then she picked another good one for my father. That left two on the platter: a large crab with a faded orange color, and number eleven, which had the torn-off leg.

My mother shook the platter in front of me. "Take it, already cold," said my mother.

I was not too fond of crab, every since I saw my birthday crab boiled alive, but I knew I could not refuse. That's the way Chinese mothers show they love their children, not through hugs and kisses but with stern offerings of steamed dumplings, duck's gizzards, and crab.

I thought I was doing the right thing, taking the crab with the missing leg. But my mother cried, "No! No! Big one, you eat it. I cannot finish."

I remember the hungry sounds everybody else was making—cracking the shells, sucking the crab meat out, scraping out tidbits with the ends of chopsticks—and my mother's quiet plate. I was the only one who noticed her prying open the shell, sniffing the crab's body and then getting up to go to the kitchen, plate in hand. She returned, without the crab, but with more bowls of soy sauce, ginger, and scallions.

And then as stomachs filled, everybody started talking at once.

"Suyuan!" called Auntie Lindo to my mother. "Why you wear that color?" Auntie Lindo gestured with a crab leg to my mother's red sweater.

"How can you wear this color anymore? Too young!" she scolded.

My mother acted as though this were a compliment. "Emporium Capwell," she said. "Nineteen dollar. Cheaper than knit it myself."

Auntie Lindo nodded her head, as if the color were worth this price. And then she pointed her crab leg toward her future son-in-law, Rich, and said, "See how this one doesn't know how to eat Chinese food."

"Crab isn't Chinese," said Waverly in her complaining voice. It was amazing how Waverly still sounded the way she did twenty-five years ago, when we were ten and she had announced to me in that same voice, "You aren't a genius like me."

Auntie Lindo looked at her daughter with exasperation. "How do you know what is Chinese, what is not Chinese?" And then she turned to Rich and said with much authority, "Why you are not eating the best part?"

And I saw Rich smiling back, with amusement, and not humility, showing in his face. He had the same coloring as the crab on his plate: reddish hair, pale cream skin, and large dots of orange freckles. While he smirked, Auntie Lindo demonstrated the proper technique, poking her chopstick into the orange spongy part: "You have to dig in here, get this out. The brain is most tastiest, you try."

Waverly and Rich grimaced at each other, united in disgust. I heard Vincent and Lisa whisper to each other, "Gross," and then they snickered too.

Uncle Tin started laughing to himself, to let us know he also had a private joke. Judging by his preamble of snorts and leg slaps, I figured he must have practiced this joke many times: "I tell my daughter, Hey, why be poor? Marry rich!" He laughed loudly and then nudged Lisa, who was sitting next to him, "Hey, don't you get it? Look what happen. She gonna marry this guy here. Rich. 'Cause I tell her to, *marry Rich*."

"When *are* you guys getting married?" asked Vincent.

"I should ask you the same thing," said Waverly. Lisa looked embarrassed when Vincent ignored the question.

"Mom, I don't *like* crab!" whined Shoshana.

"Nice haircut," Waverly said to me from across the table.

"Thanks, David always does a great job."

"You mean you still go to that guy on Howard Street?" Waverly asked, arching one eyebrow. "Aren't you afraid?"

I could sense the danger, but I said it anyway: "What do you mean, afraid? He's always very good."

"I mean, he *is* gay," Waverly said. "He could have AIDS. And he is cutting your hair, which is like cutting a living tissue. Maybe I'm being paranoid, being a mother, but you just can't be too safe these days. . . . "

And I sat there feeling as if my hair were coated with disease.

"You should go see my guy," said Waverly. "Mr. Rory. He does fabulous work, although he probably charges more than you're used to."

I felt like screaming. She could be so sneaky with her insults. Every time I asked her the simplest of tax questions, for example, she could turn the conversation around and make it seem as if I were too cheap to pay for her legal advice.

She'd say things like, "I really don't like to talk about important tax matters except in my office. I mean, what if you say something casual over lunch and I give you some casual advice. And then you follow it, and it's wrong because you didn't give me the full information. I'd feel terrible. And you would too, wouldn't you?"

At that crab dinner, I was so mad about what she said about my hair that I wanted to embarrass her, to reveal in front of everybody how petty she was. So I decided to confront her about the free-lance work I'd done for her firm, eight pages of brochure copy on its tax services. The firm was now more than thirty days late in paying my invoice.

"Maybe I could afford Mr. Rory's prices if someone's firm paid me on time," I said with a teasing grin. And I was pleased to see Waverly's reaction. She was genuinely flustered, speechless.

I couldn't resist rubbing it in: "I think it's pretty ironic that a big accounting firm can't even pay its own bills on time. I mean, really, Waverly, what kind of place are you working for?"

Her face was dark and quiet.

"Hey, hey, you girls, no more fighting!" said my father, as if

Waverly and I were still children arguing over tricycles and crayon colors.

"That's right, we don't want to talk about this now," said Waverly quietly.

"So how do you think the Giants are going to do?" said Vincent, trying to be funny. Nobody laughed.

I wasn't about to let her slip away this time. "Well, every time I call you on the phone, you can't talk about it then either," I said.

Waverly looked at Rich, who shrugged his shoulders. She turned back to me and sighed.

"Listen, June, I don't know how to tell you this. That stuff you wrote, well, the firm decided it was unacceptable."

"You're lying. You said it was great."

Waverly sighed again. "I know I did. I didn't want to hurt your feelings. I was trying to see if we could fix it somehow. But it won't work."

And just like that, I was starting to flail, tossed without warning into deep water, drowning and desperate. "Most copy needs fine-tuning," I said. "It's . . . normal not to be perfect the first time. I should have explained the process better."

"June, I really don't think . . ."

"Rewrites are free. I'm just as concerned about making it perfect as you are."

Waverly acted as if she didn't even hear me. "I'm trying to convince them to at least pay you for some of your time. I know you put a lot of work into it. . . . I owe you at least that for even suggesting you do it."

"Just tell me what they want changed. I'll call you next week so we can go over it, line by line."

"June—I can't," Waverly said with cool finality. "It's just not . . . sophisticated. I'm sure what you write for your other clients is *wonderful*. But we're a big firm. We need somebody who understands that . . . our style." She said this touching her hand to her chest, as if she were referring to *her* style.

Then she laughed in a lighthearted way. "I mean, really, June." And then she started speaking in a deep television-announcer

voice: "*Three* benefits, *three* needs, *three* reasons to buy . . .
Satisfaction *guaranteed* . . . for today's and tomorrow's tax
needs . . ."

She said this in such a funny way that everybody thought it
was a good joke and laughed. And then, to make matters worse,
I heard my mother saying to Waverly: "True, cannot teach style.
June not sophisticate like you. Must be born this way."

I was surprised at myself, how humiliated I felt. I had been
outsmarted by Waverly once again, and now betrayed by my
own mother. I was smiling so hard my lower lip was twitching
from the strain. I tried to find something else to concentrate on,
and I remember picking up my plate, and then Mr. Chong's, as
if I were clearing the table, and seeing so sharply through my
tears the chips on the edges of these old plates, wondering why
my mother didn't use the new set I had bought her five years
ago.

The table was littered with crab carcasses. Waverly and Rich
lit cigarettes and put a crab shell between them for an ashtray.
Shoshana had wandered over to the piano and was banging notes
out with a crab claw in each hand. Mr. Chong, who had grown
totally deaf over the years, watched Shoshana and applauded:
"Bravo! Bravo!" And except for his strange shouts, nobody said
a word. My mother went to the kitchen and returned with a
plate of oranges sliced into wedges. My father poked at the
remnants of his crab. Vincent cleared his throat, twice, and then
patted Lisa's hand.

It was Auntie Lindo who finally spoke: "Waverly, you let her
try again. You make her do too fast first time. Of course she
cannot get it right."

I could hear my mother eating an orange slice. She was the
only person I knew who crunched oranges, making it sound as
if she were eating crisp apples instead. The sound of it was worse
than gnashing teeth.

"Good one take time," continued Auntie Lindo, nodding her
head in agreement with herself.

"Put in lotta action," advised Uncle Tin. "Lotta action, boy,
that's what I like. Hey, that's all you need, make it right."

"Probably not," I said, and smiled before carrying the plates to the sink.

That was the night, in the kitchen, that I realized I was no better than who I was. I was a copywriter. I worked for a small ad agency. I promised every new client, "We can provide the sizzle for the meat." The sizzle always boiled down to "Three Benefits, Three Needs, Three Reasons to Buy." The meat was always coaxial cable, T-1 multiplexers, protocol converters, and the like. I was very good at what I did, succeeding at something small like that.

I turned on the water to wash the dishes. And I no longer felt angry at Waverly. I felt tired and foolish, as if I had been running to escape someone chasing me, only to look behind and discover there was no one there.

I picked up my mother's plate, the one she had carried into the kitchen at the start of the dinner. The crab was untouched. I lifted the shell and smelled the crab. Maybe it was because I didn't like crab in the first place. I couldn't tell what was wrong with it.

After everybody left, my mother joined me in the kitchen. I was putting dishes away. She put water on for more tea and sat down at the small kitchen table. I waited for her to chastise me.

"Good dinner, Ma," I said politely.

"Not so good," she said, jabbing at her mouth with a toothpick.

"What happened to your crab? Why'd you throw it away?"

"Not so good," she said again. "That crab die. Even a beggar don't want it."

"How could you tell? I didn't smell anything wrong."

"Can tell even before cook!" She was standing now, looking out the kitchen window into the night. "I shake that crab before cook. His legs—droopy. His mouth—wide open, already like a dead person."

"Why'd you cook it if you knew it was already dead?"

"I thought . . . maybe only just die. Maybe taste not too bad. But I can smell, dead taste, not firm."

"What if someone else had picked that crab?"

My mother looked at me and smiled. "Only *you* pick that crab. Nobody else take it. I already know this. Everybody else want best quality. You thinking different."

She said it in a way as if this were proof—proof of something good. She always said things that didn't make any sense, that sounded both good and bad at the same time.

I was putting away the last of the chipped plates and then I remembered something else. "Ma, why don't you ever use those new dishes I bought you? If you didn't like them, you should have told me. I could have changed the pattern."

"Of course, I like," she said, irritated. "Sometime I think something is so good, I want to save it. Then I forget I save it."

And then, as if she had just now remembered, she unhooked the clasp of her gold necklace and took it off, wadding the chain and the jade pendant in her palm. She grabbed my hand and put the necklace in my palm, then shut my fingers around it.

"No, Ma," I protested. "I can't take this."

"*Nala, nala*"—Take it, take it—she said, as if she were scolding me. And then she continued in Chinese. "For a long time, I wanted to give you this necklace. See, I wore this on my skin, so when you put it on your skin, then you know my meaning. This is your life's importance."

I looked at the necklace, the pendant with the light green jade. I wanted to give it back. I didn't want to accept it. And yet I also felt as if I had already swallowed it.

"You're giving this to me only because of what happened tonight," I finally said.

"What happen?"

"What Waverly said. What everybody said."

"Tss! Why you listen to her? Why you want to follow behind her, chasing her words? She is like this crab." My mother poked a shell in the garbage can. "Always walking sideways, moving crooked. You can make your legs go the other way."

I put the necklace on. It felt cool.

"Not so good, this jade," she said matter-of-factly, touching the pendant, and then she added in Chinese: "This is young jade. It is a very light color now, but if you wear it every day it will become more green."

My father hasn't eaten well since my mother died. So I am here, in the kitchen, to cook him dinner. I'm slicing tofu. I've decided to make him a spicy bean-curd dish. My mother used to tell me how hot things restore the spirit and health. But I'm making this mostly because I know my father loves this dish and I know how to cook it. I like the smell of it: ginger, scallions, and a red chili sauce that tickles my nose the minute I open the jar.

Above me, I hear the old pipes shake into action with a *thunk!* and then the water running in my sink dwindles to a trickle. One of the tenants upstairs must be taking a shower. I remember my mother complaining: "Even you don't want them, you stuck." And now I know what she meant.

As I rinse the tofu in the sink, I am startled by a dark mass that appears suddenly at the window. It's the one-eared tomcat from upstairs. He's balancing on the sill, rubbing his flank against the window.

My mother didn't kill that damn cat after all, and I'm relieved. And then I see this cat rubbing more vigorously on the window and he starts to raise his tail.

"Get away from there!" I shout, and slap my hand on the window three times. But the cat just narrows his eyes, flattens his one ear, and hisses back at me.

QUEEN MOTHER OF THE WESTERN SKIES

"O! Hwai dungsyi"—*You bad little thing*—said the woman, teasing her baby granddaughter. *"Is Buddha teaching you to laugh for no reason?"* As the baby continued to gurgle, the woman felt a deep wish stirring in her heart.

"Even if I could live forever," she said to the baby, *"I still don't know which way I would teach you. I was once so free and innocent. I too laughed for no reason.*

"But later I threw away my foolish innocence to protect myself. And then I taught my daughter, your mother, to shed her innocence so she would not be hurt as well.

"Hwai dungsyi, was this kind of thinking wrong? If I now recognize evil in other people, is it not because I have become evil too? If I see someone has a suspicious nose, have I not smelled the same bad things?"

The baby laughed, listening to her grandmother's laments.

"O! O! You say you are laughing because you have already lived forever, over and over again? You say you are Syi Wang Mu, Queen Mother of the Western Skies, now come back to give me the answer! Good, good, I am listening. . . .

"Thank you, Little Queen. Then you must teach my daughter this same lesson. How to lose your innocence but not your hope. How to laugh forever."

AN-MEI HSU

Magpies

Yesterday my daughter said to me, "My marriage is falling apart."

And now all she can do is watch it falling. She lies down on a psychiatrist couch, squeezing tears out about this shame. And, I think, she will lie there until there is nothing more to fall, nothing left to cry about, everything dry.

She cried, "No choice! No choice!" She doesn't know. If she doesn't speak, she is making a choice. If she doesn't try, she can lose her chance forever.

I know this, because I was raised the Chinese way: I was taught to desire nothing, to swallow other people's misery, to eat my own bitterness.

And even though I taught my daughter the opposite, still she came out the same way! Maybe it is because she was born to me and she was born a girl. And I was born to my mother and I was born a girl. All of us are like stairs, one step after another, going up and down, but all going the same way.

I know how it is to be quiet, to listen and watch, as if your life were a dream. You can close your eyes when you no longer want to watch. But when you no longer want to listen, what can you do? I can still hear what happened more than sixty years ago.

My mother was a stranger to me when she first arrived at my uncle's house in Ningpo. I was nine years old and had not seen her for many years. But I knew she was my mother, because I could feel her pain.

"Do not look at that woman," warned my aunt. "She has thrown her face into the eastward-flowing stream. Her ancestral spirit is lost forever. The person you see is just decayed flesh, evil, rotted to the bone."

And I would stare at my mother. She did not look evil. I wanted to touch her face, the one that looked like mine.

It is true, she wore strange foreign clothes. But she did not speak back when my aunt cursed her. Her head bowed even lower when my uncle slapped her for calling him Brother. She cried from her heart when Popo died, even though Popo, her mother, had sent her away so many years before. And after Popo's funeral, she obeyed my uncle. She prepared herself to return to Tientsin, where she had dishonored her widowhood by becoming the third concubine to a rich man.

How could she leave without me? This was a question I could not ask. I was a child. I could only watch and listen.

The night before she was to leave, she held my head against her body, as if to protect me from a danger I could not see. I was crying to bring her back before she was even gone. And as I lay in her lap, she told me a story.

"An-mei," she whispered, "have you seen the little turtle that lives in the pond?" I nodded. This was a pond in our courtyard and I often poked a stick in the still water to make the turtle swim out from underneath the rocks.

"I also knew that turtle when I was a small child," said my mother. "I used to sit by the pond and watch him swimming to the surface, biting the air with his little beak. He is a very old turtle."

I could see that turtle in my mind and I knew my mother was seeing the same one.

"This turtle feeds on our thoughts," said my mother. "I learned this one day, when I was your age, and Popo said I could no longer be a child. She said I could not shout, or run, or sit on the ground to catch crickets. I could not cry if I was disappointed. I had to be silent and listen to my elders. And if I did not do this, Popo said she would cut off my hair and send me to a place where Buddhist nuns lived.

"That night, after Popo told me this, I sat by the pond, looking into the water. And because I was weak, I began to cry. Then I saw this turtle swimming to the top and his beak was eating my tears as soon as they touched the water. He ate them quickly, five, six, seven tears, then climbed out of the pond, crawled onto a smooth rock and began to speak.

"The turtle said, 'I have eaten your tears, and this is why I know your misery. But I must warn you. If you cry, your life will always be sad.'

"Then the turtle opened his beak and out poured five, six, seven pearly eggs. The eggs broke open and from them emerged seven birds, who immediately began to chatter and sing. I knew from their snow-white bellies and pretty voices that they were magpies, birds of joy. These birds bent their beaks to the pond and began to drink greedily. And when I reached out my hand to capture one, they all rose up, beat their black wings in my face, and flew up into the air, laughing.

" 'Now you see,' said the turtle, drifting back into the pond, 'why it is useless to cry. Your tears do not wash away your sorrows. They feed someone else's joy. And that is why you must learn to swallow your own tears.' "

But after my mother finished her story, I looked at her and saw she was crying. And I also began to cry again, that this was our fate, to live like two turtles seeing the watery world together from the bottom of the little pond.

In the morning, I awoke to hear—not the bird of joy—but angry sounds in the distance. I jumped out of my bed and ran quietly to my window.

Out in the front courtyard, I saw my mother kneeling, scratching the stone pathway with her fingers, as if she had lost something and knew she could not find it again. In front of her stood Uncle, my mother's brother, and he was shouting.

"You want to take your daughter and ruin her life as well!" Uncle stamped his foot at this impertinent thought. "You should already be gone."

My mother did not say anything. She remained bent on the ground, her back as rounded as the turtle in the pond. She was crying with her mouth closed. And I began to cry in the same way, swallowing those bitter tears.

I hurried to get dressed. And by the time I ran down the stairs and into the front room, my mother was about to leave. A servant was taking her trunk outside. My auntie was holding onto my little brother's hand. Before I could remember to close my mouth, I shouted, "Ma!"

"See how your evil influence has already spread to your daughter!" exclaimed my uncle.

And my mother, her head still bowed, looked up at me and saw my face. I could not stop my tears from running down. And I think, seeing my face like this, my mother changed. She stood up tall, with her back straight, so that now she was almost taller than my uncle. She held her hand out to me and I ran to her. She said in a quiet, calm voice: "An-mei, I am not asking you. But I am going back to Tientsin now and you can follow me."

My auntie heard this and immediately hissed. "A girl is no better than what she follows! An-mei, you think you can see something new, riding on top of a new cart. But in front of you, it is just the ass of the same old mule. Your life is what you see in front of you."

And hearing this made me more determined to leave. Because the life in front of me was my uncle's house. And it was full of dark riddles and suffering that I could not understand. So I turned my head away from my auntie's strange words and looked at my mother.

Now my uncle picked up a porcelain vase. "Is this what you want to do?" said my uncle. "Throw your life away? If you follow this woman, you can never lift your head again." He threw that vase on the ground, where it smashed into many pieces. I jumped, and my mother took my hand.

Her hand was warm. "Come, An-mei. We must hurry," she said, as if observing a rainy sky.

"An-mei!" I heard my aunt call piteously from behind, but then my uncle said, *"Swanle!"*—Finished!—"She is already changed."

As I walked away from my old life, I wondered if it were true, what my uncle had said, that I was changed and could never lift my head again. So I tried. I lifted it.

And I saw my little brother, crying so hard as my auntie held onto his hand. My mother did not dare take my brother. A son can never go to somebody else's house to live. If he went, he would lose any hope for a future. But I knew he was not thinking this. He was crying, angry and scared, because my mother had not asked him to follow.

What my uncle had said was true. After I saw my brother this way, I could not keep my head lifted.

In the rickshaw on our way to the railway station, my mother murmured, "Poor An-mei, only you know. Only you know what I have suffered." When she said this, I felt proud, that only I could see these delicate and rare thoughts.

But on the train, I realized how far behind I was leaving my life. And I became scared. We traveled for seven days, one day by rail, six days by steamer boat. At first, my mother was very lively. She told me stories of Tientsin whenever my face looked back at where we had just been.

She talked of clever peddlers who served every kind of simple food: steamed dumplings, boiled peanuts, and my mother's favorite, a thin pancake with an egg dropped in the middle, brushed with black bean paste, then rolled up—still finger-hot off the griddle!—and handed to the hungry buyer.

She described the port and its seafood and claimed it was even better than what we ate in Ningpo. Big clams, prawns, crab, all kinds of fish, salty and freshwater, the best—otherwise why would so many foreigners come to this port?

She told me about narrow streets with crowded bazaars. In the early morning peasants sold vegetables I had never seen or eaten before in my life—and my mother assured me I would find them so sweet, so tender, so fresh. And there were sections of the city where different foreigners lived—Japanese, White Russians, Americans, and Germans—but never together, all with their own separate habits, some dirty, some clean. And they had houses of all shapes and colors, one painted in pink, another with rooms that jutted out at every angle like the backs and fronts of Victorian dresses, others with roofs like pointed hats and wood carvings painted white to look like ivory.

And in the wintertime I would see snow, she said. My mother said, In just a few months, the period of the Cold Dew would come, then it would start to rain, and then the rain would fall more softly, more slowly until it became white and dry as the petals of quince blossoms in the spring. She would wrap me up in fur-lined coats and pants, so if it was bitter cold, no matter!

She told me many stories until my face was turned forward, looking toward my new home in Tientsin. But when the fifth day came, as we sailed closer toward the Tientsin gulf, the waters changed from muddy yellow to black and the boat began to rock and groan. I became fearful and sick. And at night I dreamed of the eastward-flowing stream my aunt had warned me about, the dark waters that changed a person forever. And watching those dark waters from my sickbed on the boat, I was scared that my aunt's words had come true. I saw how my mother was already beginning to change, how dark and angry her face had become, looking out over the sea, thinking her own thoughts. And my thoughts, too, became cloudy and confused.

On the morning of the day we were supposed to arrive in Tientsin, she went into our sleeping cabin wearing her white Chinese mourning dress. And when she returned to the sitting room on the top deck, she looked like a stranger. Her eyebrows were painted thick at the center, then long and sharp at the corners. Her eyes had dark smudges around them and her face was pale white, her lips dark red. On top of her head, she wore a small brown felt hat with one large brown-speckled feather swept across the front. Her short hair was tucked into this hat, except for two perfect curls on her forehead that faced each other like black lacquer carvings. She had on a long brown dress with a white lace collar that fell all the way to her waist and was fastened down with a silk rose.

This was a shocking sight. We were in mourning. But I could not say anything. I was a child. How could I scold my own mother? I could only feel shame seeing my mother wear her shame so boldly.

In her gloved hands she held a large cream-colored box with foreign words written on top: "Fine English-Tailored Apparel, Tientsin." I remember she had put the box down between us and told me: "Open it! Quickly!" She was breathless and smiling. I was so surprised by my mother's new strange manner, it was not until many years later, when I was using this box to store letters and photographs, that I wondered how my mother had known. Even though she had not seen me for many years, she had known that I would someday follow her and that I should wear a new dress when I did.

And when I opened that box, all my shame, my fears, they fell away. Inside was a new starch-white dress. It had ruffles at the collar and along the sleeves and six tiers of ruffles for a skirt. The box also contained white stockings, white leather shoes, and an enormous white hair bow, already shaped and ready to be fastened on with two loose ties.

Everything was too big. My shoulders kept slipping out of the large neck hole. The waist was big enough to fit two of me. But I did not mind. She did not mind. I raised my arms and stood perfectly still. She drew out pins and thread and with little tucks here and there stuffed in the loose materials, then filled the toes of the shoes with tissue paper, until everything fit. Wearing those clothes, I felt as if I had grown new hands and feet and I would now have to learn to walk in a new way.

And then my mother became somber again. She sat with her hands folded in her lap, watching as our boat drew closer and closer to the dock.

"An-mei, now you are ready to start your new life. You will

live in a new house. You will have a new father. Many sisters. Another little brother. Dresses and good things to eat. Do you think all this will be enough to be happy?"

I nodded quietly, thinking about the unhappiness of my brother in Ningpo. My mother did not say anything more about the house, or my new family, or my happiness. And I did not ask any questions, because now a bell was sounding and a ship's steward was calling our arrival in Tientsin. My mother gave quick instructions to our porter, pointed to our two small trunks and handed him money, as if she had done this every day of her life. And then she carefully opened another box and pulled out what looked to be five or six dead foxes with open beady eyes, limp paws, and fluffy tails. She put this scary sight around her neck and shoulders, then grabbed my hand tight as we moved down the aisle with the crowd of people.

There was no one at the harbor to meet us. My mother walked slowly down the rampway, through the baggage platform, looking nervously from side to side.

"An-mei, come! Why are you so slow!" she said, her voice filled with fear. I was dragging my feet, trying to stay in those too-large shoes as the ground beneath me swayed. And when I was not watching which way my feet were moving, I looked up and saw everybody was in a hurry, everybody seemed unhappy: families with old mothers and fathers, all wearing dark, somber colors, pushing and pulling bags and crates of their life's possessions; pale foreign ladies dressed like my mother, walking with foreign men in hats; rich wives scolding maids and servants following behind carrying trunks and babies and baskets of food.

We stood near the street, where rickshaws and trucks came and went. We held hands, thinking our own thoughts, watching people arriving at the station, watching others hurrying away. It was late morning, and although it seemed warm outside, the sky was gray and clouding over.

After a long time of standing and seeing no one, my mother sighed and finally shouted for a rickshaw.

During this ride, my mother argued with the rickshaw puller, who wanted extra cash to carry the two of us and our luggage.

Then she complained about the dust from the ride, the smell of the street, the bumpiness of the road, the lateness of the day, the ache in her stomach. And when she had finished with these laments, she turned her complaints to me: a spot on my new dress, a tangle in my hair, my twisted stockings. I tried to win back my mother, pointing to ask her about a small park, a bird flying above us, a long electric streetcar that passed us sounding its horn.

But she became only more cross and said: "An-mei, sit still. Do not look so eager. We are only going home."

And when we finally arrived home, we were both exhausted.

I knew from the beginning our new home would not be an ordinary house. My mother had told me we would live in the household of Wu Tsing, who was a very rich merchant. She said this man owned many carpet factories and lived in a mansion located in the British Concession of Tientsin, the best section of the city where Chinese people could live. We lived not too far from Paima Di, Racehorse Street, where only Westerners could live. And we were also close to little shops that sold only one kind of thing: only tea, or only fabric, or only soap.

The house, she said, was foreign-built; Wu Tsing liked foreign things because foreigners had made him rich. And I concluded that was why my mother had to wear foreign-style clothes, in the manner of newly rich Chinese people who liked to display their wealth on the outside.

And even though I knew all this before I arrived, I was still amazed at what I saw.

The front of the house had a Chinese stone gate, rounded at the top, with big black lacquer doors and a threshold you had to step over. Within the gates I saw the courtyard and I was surprised. There were no willows or sweet-smelling cassia trees, no garden pavilions, no benches sitting by a pond, no tubs of fish. Instead, there were long rows of bushes on both sides of a wide brick walkway and to each side of those bushes was a big lawn area with fountains. And as we walked down the walkway and got closer to the house, I saw this house had been built in the Western style. It was three stories high, of mortar and stone, with long metal balconies on each floor and chimneys at every corner.

When we arrived, a young servant woman ran out and greeted my mother with cries of joy. She had a high scratchy voice: "Oh Taitai, you've already arrived! How can this be?" This was Yan Chang, my mother's personal maid, and she knew how to fuss over my mother just the right amount. She had called my mother Taitai, the simple honorable title of Wife, as if my mother were the first wife, the only wife.

Yan Chang called loudly to other servants to take our luggage, called another servant to bring tea and draw a hot bath. And then she hastily explained that Second Wife had told everyone not to expect us for another week at least. "What a shame! No one to greet you! Second Wife, the others, gone to Peking to visit her relatives. Your daughter, so pretty, your same look. She's so shy, eh? First Wife, her daughters . . . gone on a pilgrimage to another Buddhist temple . . . Last week, a cousin's uncle, just a little crazy, came to visit, turned out not to be a cousin, not an uncle, who knows who he was. . . ."

As soon as we walked into that big house, I became lost with too many things to see: a curved staircase that wound up and up, a ceiling with faces in every corner, then hallways twisting and turning into one room then another. To my right was a large room, larger than I had ever seen, and it was filled with stiff teakwood furniture: sofas and tables and chairs. And at the other end of this long, long room, I could see doors leading into more rooms, more furniture, then more doors. To my left was a darker room, another sitting room, this one filled with foreign furniture: dark green leather sofas, paintings with hunting dogs, armchairs, and mahogany desks. And as I glanced in these rooms I would see different people, and Yan Chang would explain: "This young lady, she is Second Wife's servant. That one, she is nobody, just the daughter of cook's helper. This man takes care of the garden."

And then we were walking up the staircase. We came to the top of the stairs and I found myself in another large sitting room.

We walked to the left, down a hall, past one room, and then stepped into another. "This is your mother's room," Yan Chang told me proudly. "This is where you will sleep."

And the first thing I saw, the only thing I could see at first, was a magnificent bed. It was heavy and light at the same time: soft rose silk and heavy, dark shiny wood carved all around with dragons. Four posts held up a silk canopy and at each post dangled large silk ties holding back curtains. The bed sat on four squat lion's paws, as if the weight of it had crushed the lion underneath. Yan Chang showed me how to use a small step stool to climb onto the bed. And when I tumbled onto the silk coverings, I laughed to discover a soft mattress that was ten times the thickness of my bed in Ningpo.

Sitting in this bed, I admired everything as if I were a princess. This room had a glass door that led to a balcony. In front of the window door was a round table of the same wood as the bed. It too sat on carved lion's legs and was surrounded by four chairs. A servant had already put tea and sweet cakes on the table and was now lighting the *houlu*, a small stove for burning coal.

It was not that my uncle's house in Ningpo had been poor. He was actually quite well-to-do. But this house in Tientsin was amazing. And I thought to myself, My uncle was wrong. There was no shame in my mother's marrying Wu Tsing.

While thinking this, I was startled by a sudden clang! clang! clang! followed by music. On the wall opposite the bed was a big wooden clock with a forest and bears carved into it. The door on the clock had burst open and a tiny room full of people was coming out. There was a bearded man in a pointed cap seated at a table. He was bending his head over and over again to drink soup, but his beard would dip in the bowl first and stop him. A girl in a white scarf and blue dress was standing next to the table and she was bending over and over again to give the man more of this soup. And next to the man and girl was another girl with a skirt and short jacket. She was swinging her arm back and forth, playing violin music. She always played the same dark song. I can still hear it in my head after these many years— ni-ah! nah! nah! nah! nah-ni-nah!

225

This was a wonderful clock to see, but after I heard it that first hour, then the next, and then always, this clock became an extravagant nuisance. I could not sleep for many nights. And later, I found I had an ability: to not listen to something meaningless calling to me.

I was so happy those first few nights, in this amusing house, sleeping in the big soft bed with my mother. I would lie in this comfortable bed, thinking about my uncle's house in Ningpo, realizing how unhappy I had been, feeling sorry for my little brother. But most of my thoughts flew to all the new things to see and do in this house.

I watched hot water pouring out of pipes not just in the kitchen but also into washbasins and bathtubs on all three floors of the house. I saw chamber pots that flushed clean without servants having to empty them. I saw rooms as fancy as my mother's. Yan Chang explained which ones belonged to First Wife and the other concubines, who were called Second Wife and Third Wife. And some rooms belonged to no one. "They are for guests," said Yan Chang.

On the third floor were rooms for only the men servants, said Yan Chang, and one of the rooms even had a door to a cabinet that was really a secret hiding place from sea pirates.

Thinking back, I find it hard to remember everything that was in that house; too many good things all seem the same after a while. I tired of anything that was not a novelty. "Oh, this," I said when Yan Chang brought me the same sweet meats as the day before. "I've tasted this already."

My mother seemed to regain her pleasant nature. She put her old clothes back on, long Chinese gowns and skirts now with white mourning bands sewn at the bottoms. During the day, she pointed to strange and funny things, naming them for me: bidet, Brownie camera, salad fork, napkin. In the evening, when there was nothing to do, we talked about the servants: who was clever, who was diligent, who was loyal. We gossiped as we cooked small eggs and sweet potatoes on top of the *houlu* just to enjoy their smell. And at night, my mother would again tell me stories as I lay in her arms falling asleep.

If I look upon my whole life, I cannot think of another time when I felt more comfortable: when I had no worries, fears, or desires, when my life seemed as soft and lovely as lying inside a cocoon of rose silk. But I remember clearly when all that comfort became no longer comfortable.

It was perhaps two weeks after we had arrived. I was in the large garden in back, kicking a ball and watching two dogs chase it. My mother sat at a table watching me play. And then I heard a horn off in the distance, shouts, and those two dogs forgot the ball and ran off barking in high happy voices.

My mother had the same fearful look she wore in the harbor station. She walked quickly into the house. I walked around the side of the house toward the front. Two shiny black rickshaws had arrived and behind them a large black motorcar. A manservant was taking luggage out of one rickshaw. From another rickshaw, a young maid jumped out.

All the servants crowded around the motorcar, looking at their faces in the polished metal, admiring the curtained windows, the velvet seats. Then the driver opened the back door and out stepped a young girl. She had short hair with rows of waves. She looked to be only a few years older than I, but she had on a woman's dress, stockings, and high heels. I looked down at my own white dress covered with grass stains and I felt ashamed.

And then I saw the servants reaching into the backseat of the motorcar and a man was slowly being lifted by both arms. This was Wu Tsing. He was a big man, not tall, but puffed out like a bird. He was much older than my mother, with a high shiny forehead and a large black mole on one nostril. He wore a Western suit jacket with a vest that closed too tightly around his stomach, but his pants were very loose. He groaned and grunted as he heaved himself out and into view. And as soon as his shoes touched the ground, he began to walk toward the house, acting as though he saw no one, even though people greeted him and were busy opening doors, carrying his bags, taking his long coat. He walked into the house like that, with this young girl following him. She was looking behind at everyone with a simpering smile, as if they were there to honor her. And when she was hardly in the door, I heard one servant remark to another, "Fifth Wife is so young she did not bring any of her own servants, only a wet nurse."

I looked up at the house and saw my mother looking down from her window, watching everything. So in this clumsy way, my mother found out that Wu Tsing had taken his fourth concubine, who was actually just an afterthought, a foolish bit of decoration for his new motorcar.

My mother was not jealous of this young girl who would now be called Fifth Wife. Why should she be? My mother did not love Wu Tsing. A girl in China did not marry for love. She married for position, and my mother's position, I later learned, was the worst.

After Wu Tsing and Fifth Wife arrived home, my mother often stayed in her room working on her embroidery. In the afternoon, she and I would go on long silent rides in the city, searching for a bolt of silk in a color she could not seem to name. Her unhappiness was this same way. She could not name it.

And so, while everything seemed peaceful, I knew it was not. You may wonder how a small child, only nine years old, can know these things. Now I wonder about it myself. I can remember only how uncomfortable I felt, how I could feel the truth with my stomach, knowing something terrible was going to happen. And I can tell you, it was almost as bad as how I felt some fifteen years later when the Japanese bombs started to fall and, listening in the distance, I could hear soft rumbles and knew that what was coming was unstoppable.

A few days after Wu Tsing had arrived home, I awoke in the middle of the night. My mother was rocking my shoulder gently.

"An-mei, be a good girl," she said in a tired voice. "Go to Yan Chang's room now."

I rubbed my eyes and as I awoke I saw a dark shadow and began to cry. It was Wu Tsing.

"Be quiet. Nothing is the matter. Go to Yan Chang," my mother whispered.

And then she lifted me down slowly to the cold floor. I heard the wooden clock begin to sing and Wu Tsing's deep voice complaining of the chill. And when I went to Yan Chang, it was as though she had expected me and knew I would be crying.

The next morning I could not look at my mother. But I saw that Fifth Wife had a swollen face like mine. And at breakfast that morning, in front of everybody, her anger finally erupted when she shouted rudely to a servant for serving her so slowly. Everyone, even my mother, stared at her for her bad manners, criticizing a servant that way. I saw Wu Tsing throw her a sharp look, like a father, and she began to cry. But later that morning, Fifth Wife was smiling again, prancing around in a new dress and new shoes.

In the afternoon, my mother spoke of her unhappiness for the first time. We were in a rickshaw going to a store to find embroidery thread. "Do you see how shameful my life is?" she cried. "Do you see how I have no position? He brought home a new wife, a low-class girl, dark-skinned, no manners! Bought her for a few dollars from a poor village family that makes mud-brick tiles. And at night when he can no longer use her, he comes to me, smelling of her mud."

She was crying now, rambling like a crazy woman: "You can see now, a fourth wife is less than a fifth wife. An-mei, you must not forget. I was a first wife, *yi tai*, the wife of a scholar. Your mother was not always Fourth Wife, *Sz Tai!*"

She said this word, *sz*, so hatefully I shuddered. It sounded like the *sz* that means "die." And I remembered Popo once telling me four is a very unlucky number because if you say it in an angry way, it always comes out wrong.

The Cold Dew came. It became chilly, and Second Wife and Third Wife, their children and servants returned home to Tientsin. There was a big commotion when they arrived. Wu Tsing had allowed the new motorcar to be sent to the railway station, but of course that was not enough to carry them all back. So behind the motorcar came a dozen or so rickshaws, bouncing up and down like crickets following a large shiny beetle. Women began to pour out of the motorcar.

My mother was standing behind me, ready to greet everybody. A woman wearing a plain foreign dress and large, ugly shoes walked toward us. Three girls, one of whom was my age, followed behind.

"This is Third Wife and her three daughters," said my mother.

Those three girls were even more shy than I. They crowded around their mother with bowed heads and did not speak. But I continued to stare. They were as plain as their mother, with big teeth, thick lips, and eyebrows as bushy as a caterpillar. Third Wife welcomed me warmly and allowed me to carry one of her packages.

I felt my mother's hand stiffen on my shoulder. "And there is Second Wife. She will want you to call her Big Mother," she whispered.

I saw a woman wearing a long black fur coat and dark Western clothes, very fancy. And in her arms she held a little boy with fat rosy cheeks who looked to be two years old.

"He is Syaudi, your littlest brother," my mother whispered. He wore a cap made out of the same dark fur and was winding his little finger around Second Wife's long pearl necklace. I wondered how she could have a baby this young. Second Wife was handsome enough and seemed healthy, but she was quite old, perhaps forty-five. She handed the baby to a servant and then began to give instructions to the many people who still crowded around her.

And then Second Wife walked toward me, smiling, her fur coat gleaming with every step. She stared, as if she were examining me, as if she recognized me. Finally she smiled and patted my head. And then with a swift, graceful movement of her small hands, she removed her long pearly strand and put it around my neck.

This was the most beautiful piece of jewelry I had ever touched. It was designed in the Western style, a long strand, each bead the same size and of an identical pinkish tone, with a heavy brooch of ornate silver to clasp the ends together.

My mother immediately protested: "This is too much for a small child. She will break it. She will lose it."

But Second Wife simply said to me: "Such a pretty girl needs something to put the light on her face."

I could see by the way my mother shrank back and became quiet that she was angry. She did not like Second Wife. I had to be careful how I showed my feelings: not to let my mother think Second Wife had won me over. Yet I had this reckless feeling. I was overjoyed that Second Wife had shown me this special favor.

"Thank you, Big Mother," I said to Second Wife. And I was looking down to avoid showing her my face, but still I could not help smiling.

When my mother and I had tea in her room later that afternoon, I knew she was angry.

"Be careful, An-mei," she said. "What you hear is not genuine. She makes clouds with one hand, rain with the other. She is trying to trick you, so you will do anything for her."

I sat quietly, trying not to listen to my mother. I was thinking how much my mother complained, that perhaps all of her unhappiness sprang from her complaints. I was thinking how I should not listen to her.

"Give the necklace to me," she said suddenly.

I looked at her without moving.

"You do not believe me, so you must give me the necklace. I will not let her buy you for such a cheap price."

And when I still did not move, she stood up and walked over, and lifted that necklace off. And before I could cry to stop her, she put the necklace under her shoe and stepped on it. When she put it on the table, I saw what she had done. This necklace that had almost bought my heart and mind now had one bead of crushed glass.

Later she removed that broken bead and knotted the space together so the necklace looked whole again. She told me to wear the necklace every day for one week so I would remember how easy it is to lose myself to something false. And after I wore those fake pearls long enough to learn this lesson, she let me take them off. Then she opened a box, and turned to me: "Now can you recognize what is true?" And I nodded.

She put something in my hand. It was a heavy ring of watery

blue sapphire, with a star in its center so pure that I never ceased to look at that ring with wonder.

Before the second cold month began, First Wife returned from Peking, where she kept a house and lived with her two unmarried daughters. I remember thinking that First Wife would make Second Wife bow to her ways. First Wife was the head wife, by law and by custom.

But First Wife turned out to be a living ghost, no threat to Second Wife, who had her strong spirit intact. First Wife looked quite ancient and frail with her rounded body, bound feet, her old-style padded jacket and pants, and plain, lined face. But now that I remember her, she must not have been too old, maybe Wu Tsing's age, so she was perhaps fifty.

When I met First Wife, I thought she was blind. She acted as if she did not see me. She did not see Wu Tsing. She did not see my mother. And yet she could see her two daughters, two spinsters beyond the marriageable age; they were at least twenty-five. And she always regained her sight in time to scold the two dogs for sniffing in her room, digging in the garden outside her window, or wetting on a table leg.

"Why does First Wife sometimes see and sometimes not see?" I asked Yan Chang one night as she helped me bathe.

"First Wife says she sees only what is Buddha perfection," said Yan Chang. "She says she is blind to most faults."

Yan Chang said that First Wife chose to be blind to the unhappiness of her marriage. She and Wu Tsing had been joined in *tyandi*, heaven and earth, so theirs was a spiritual marriage arranged by a matchmaker, ordered by his parents, and protected by the spirits of their ancestors. But after the first year of marriage, First Wife had given birth to a girl with one leg too short. And this misfortune led First Wife to begin a trek to Buddhist temples, to offer alms and tailored silk gowns in honor of Buddha's image, to burn incense and pray to Buddha to lengthen her daughter's leg. As it happened, Buddha chose instead to bless First Wife with another daughter, this one with two perfect legs, but—alas!—with a brown tea stain splashed over half her face. With this second misfortune, First Wife began to go on so many pilgrimages to Tsinan, just a half-day's train ride to the south, that Wu Tsing bought her a house near the Thousand Buddha Cliff and Bubbling Springs Bamboo Grove. And every year he increased the allowance she needed to manage her own household there. So twice a year, during the coldest and hottest months of the year, she returned to Tientsin to pay her respects and suffer sight unseen in her husband's household. And each time she returned, she remained in her bedroom, sitting all day like a Buddha, smoking her opium, talking softly to herself. She did not come downstairs for meals. Instead she fasted or ate vegetarian meals in her room. And Wu Tsing would make a mid-morning visit in her bedroom once a week, drinking tea for half an hour, inquiring about her health. He did not bother her at night.

This ghost of a woman should have caused no suffering to my mother, but in fact she put ideas into her head. My mother believed she too had suffered enough to deserve her own house-hold, perhaps not in Tsinan, but one to the east, in little Petaiho, which was a beautiful seaside resort filled with terraces and gardens and wealthy widows.

"We are going to live in a house of our own," she told me happily the day snow fell on the ground all around our house. She was wearing a new silk fur-lined gown the bright turquoise color of kingfisher feathers. "The house will not be as big as this one. It will be very small. But we can live by ourselves, with Yan Chang and a few other servants. Wu Tsing has promised this already."

During the coldest winter month, we were all bored, adults and children alike. We did not dare go outside. Yan Chang warned me that my skin would freeze and crack into a thousand pieces. And the other servants always gossiped about everyday sights they had seen in town: the back stoops of stores always blocked with the frozen bodies of beggars. Man or woman, you couldn't tell, they were so dusty with a thick cover of snow.

So every day we stayed in the house, thinking of ways to amuse ourselves. My mother looked at foreign magazines and clipped out pictures of dresses she liked, and then she went downstairs to discuss with the tailor how such a dress could be made using the materials available.

I did not like to play with Third Wife's daughters, who were as docile and dull as their mother. Those girls were content looking out the window all day, watching the sun come up and go down. So instead, Yan Chang and I roasted chestnuts on top of the little coal stove. And burning our fingers while eating these sweet nuggets, we naturally started to giggle and gossip. Then I heard the clock clang and the same song began to play. Yan Chang pretended to sing badly in the classic opera style and we both laughed out loud, remembering how Second Wife had sung yesterday evening, accompanying her quavering voice on a three-stringed lute and making many mistakes. She had caused everyone to suffer through this evening's entertainment, until Wu Tsing declared it was enough suffering by falling asleep in his chair. And laughing about this, Yan Chang told me a story about Second Wife.

"Twenty years ago, she had been a famous Shantung sing-song girl, a woman of some respect, especially among married men who frequented teahouses. While she had never been pretty, she was clever, an enchantress. She could play several musical instruments, sing ancient tales with heartbreaking clarity, and touch her finger to her cheek and cross her tiny feet in just the right manner.

"Wu Tsing had asked her to be his concubine, not for love, but because of the prestige of owning what so many other men wanted. And this sing-song girl, after she had seen his enormous wealth and his feebleminded first wife, consented to become his concubine.

"From the start, Second Wife knew how to control Wu Tsing's money. She knew by the way his face paled at the sound of the wind that he was fearful of ghosts. And everybody knows that suicide is the only way a woman can escape a marriage and gain revenge, to come back as a ghost and scatter tea leaves and good fortune. So when he refused her a bigger allowance, she did pretend-suicide. She ate a piece of raw opium, enough to make her sick, and then sent her maid to tell Wu Tsing she was dying. Three days later, Second Wife had an allowance even bigger than what she had asked.

"She did so many pretend-suicides, we servants began to suspect she no longer bothered to eat the opium. Her acting was potent enough. Soon she had a better room in the house, her own private rickshaw, a house for her elderly parents, a sum for buying blessings at temples.

"But one thing she could not have: children. And she knew Wu Tsing would soon become anxious to have a son who could perform the ancestral rites and therefore guarantee his own spiritual eternity. So before Wu Tsing could complain about Second Wife's lack of sons, she said: 'I have already found her, a concubine suitable to bear your sons. By her very nature, you can see she is a virgin.' And this was quite true. As you can see, Third Wife is quite ugly. She does not even have small feet.

"Third Wife was of course indebted to Second Wife for arranging this, so there was no argument over management of the household. And even though Second Wife did not need to lift a finger, she oversaw the purchase of food and supplies, she approved the hiring of servants, she invited relatives on festival days. She found wet nurses for each of the three daughters Third Wife bore for Wu Tsing. And later, when Wu Tsing was again impatient for a son and began to spend too much money in teahouses in other cities, Second Wife arranged it so that your mother became Wu Tsing's third concubine and fourth wife!"

Yan Chang revealed this story in such a natural and lively way that I applauded her clever ending. We continued to crack chestnuts open, until I could no longer remain quiet.

"What did Second Wife do so my mother would marry Wu Tsing?" I asked timidly.

"A little child cannot understand such things!" she scolded.

I immediately looked down and remained silent, until Yan Chang became restless again to hear her own voice speak on this quiet afternoon.

"Your mother," said Yan Chang, as if talking to herself, "is too good for this family."

"Five years ago—your father had died only one year before—she and I went to Hangchow to visit the Six Harmonies Pagoda on the far side of West Lake. Your father had been a respected scholar and also devoted to the six virtues of Buddhism enshrined in this pagoda. So your mother kowtowed in the pagoda, pledging to observe the right harmony of body, thoughts, and speech, to refrain from giving opinions, and to shun wealth. And when we boarded the boat to cross the lake again, we sat opposite a man and a woman. This was Wu Tsing and Second Wife.

"Wu Tsing must have seen her beauty immediately. Back then your mother had hair down to her waist, which she tied high up on her head. And she had unusual skin, a lustrous pink color. Even in her white widow's clothes she was beautiful! But because she was a widow, she was worthless in many respects. She could not remarry.

"But this did not stop Second Wife from thinking of a way. She was tired of watching her household's money being washed away in so many different teahouses. The money he spent was enough to support five more wives! She was anxious to quiet Wu Tsing's outside appetite. So she conspired with Wu Tsing to lure your mother to his bed.

"She chatted with your mother, discovered that she planned to go to the Monastery of the Spirits' Retreat the next day. And Second Wife showed up at that place as well. And after more friendly talk, she invited your mother to dinner. Your mother was so lonely for good conversation she gladly accepted. And after the dinner, Second Wife said to your mother, 'Do you play mah jong? Oh, it doesn't matter if you play badly. We are only three people now and cannot play at all unless you would be kind enough to join us tomorrow night.'

"The next night, after a long evening of mah jong, Second Wife yawned and insisted my mother spend the night. 'Stay! Stay! Don't be so polite. No, your politeness is really more inconvenient. Why wake the rickshaw boy?' said Second Wife. 'Look here, my bed is certainly big enough for two.'

"As your mother slept soundly in Second Wife's bed, Second Wife got up in the middle of the night and left the dark room, and Wu Tsing took her place. When your mother awoke to find him touching her beneath her undergarments, she jumped out of bed. He grabbed her by her hair and threw her on the floor, then put his foot on her throat and told her to undress. Your mother did not scream or cry when he fell on her.

"In the early morning, she left in a rickshaw, her hair undone and with tears streaming down her face. She told no one but me what had happened. But Second Wife complained to many people about the shameless widow who had enchanted Wu Tsing into bed. How could a worthless widow accuse a rich woman of lying?

"So when Wu Tsing asked your mother to be his third concubine, to bear him a son, what choice did she have? She was already as low as a prostitute. And when she returned to her brother's house and kowtowed three times to say good-bye, her brother kicked her, and her own mother banned her from the family house forever. That is why you did not see your mother again until your grandmother died. Your mother went to live in Tientsin, to hide her shame with Wu Tsing's wealth. And three years later, she gave birth to a son, which Second Wife claimed as her own.

"And that is how I came to live in Wu Tsing's house," concluded Yan Chang proudly.

And that was how I learned that the baby Syaudi was really my mother's son, my littlest brother.

In truth, this was a bad thing that Yan Chang had done, telling me my mother's story. Secrets are kept from children, a lid on top of the soup kettle, so they do not boil over with too much truth.

After Yan Chang told me this story, I saw everything. I heard things I had never understood before.

I saw Second Wife's true nature.

I saw how she often gave Fifth Wife money to go visit her poor village, encouraging this silly girl to "show your friends and family how rich you've become!" And of course, her visits always reminded Wu Tsing of Fifth Wife's low-class background and how foolish he had been to be lured by her earthy flesh.

I saw Second Wife *koutou* to First Wife, bowing with deep

respect while offering her more opium. And I knew why First Wife's power had been drained away.

I saw how fearful Third Wife became when Second Wife told her stories of old concubines who were kicked out into the streets. And I knew why Third Wife watched over Second Wife's health and happiness.

And I saw my mother's terrible pain as Second Wife bounced Syaudi on her lap, kissing my mother's son and telling this baby, "As long as I am your mother, you will never be poor. You will never be unhappy. You will grow up to own this household and care for me in my old age."

And I knew why my mother cried in her room so often. Wu Tsing's promise of a house—for becoming the mother of his only son—had disappeared the day Second Wife collapsed from another bout of pretend-suicide. And my mother knew she could do nothing to bring the promise back.

I suffered so much after Yan Chang told me my mother's story. I wanted my mother to shout at Wu Tsing, to shout at Second Wife, to shout at Yan Chang and say she was wrong to tell me these stories. But my mother did not even have the right to do this. She had no choice.

Two days before the lunar new year, Yan Chang woke me when it was still black outside.

"Quickly!" she cried, pulling me along before my mind and eyes could work together.

My mother's room was brightly lit. As soon as I walked in I could see her. I ran to her bed and stood on the footstool. Her arms and legs were moving back and forth as she lay on her back. She was like a soldier, marching to nowhere, her head looking right then left. And now her whole body became straight and stiff as if to stretch herself out of her body. Her jaw was pulled down and I saw her tongue was swollen and she was coughing to try to make it fall out.

"Wake up!" I whispered, and then I turned and saw everybody standing there: Wu Tsing, Yan Chang, Second Wife, Third Wife, Fifth Wife, the doctor.

"She has taken too much opium," cried Yan Chang. "The doctor says he can do nothing. She has poisoned herself."

So they were doing nothing, only waiting. I also waited those many hours.

The only sounds were that of the girl in the clock playing the violin. And I wanted to shout to the clock and make its meaningless noise be silent, but I did not.

I watched my mother march in her bed. I wanted to say the words that would quiet her body and spirit. But I stood there like the others, waiting and saying nothing.

And then I recalled her story about the little turtle, his warning not to cry. And I wanted to shout to her that it was no use. There were already too many tears. And I tried to swallow them one by one, but they came too fast, until finally my closed lips burst open and I cried and cried, then cried all over again, letting everybody in the room feed on my tears.

I fainted with all this grief and they carried me back to Yan Chang's bed. So that morning, while my mother was dying, I was dreaming.

I was falling from the sky down to the ground, into a pond. And I became a little turtle lying at the bottom of this watery place. Above me I could see the beaks of a thousand magpies drinking from the pond, drinking and singing happily and filling their snow-white bellies. I was crying hard, so many tears, but they drank and drank, so many of them, until I had no more tears left and the pond was empty, everything as dry as sand.

Yan Chang later told me my mother had listened to Second Wife and tried to do pretend-suicide. False words! Lies! She would never listen to this woman who caused her so much suffering.

I know my mother listened to her own heart, to no longer pretend. I know this because why else did she die two days before the lunar new year? Why else did she plan her death so carefully that it became a weapon?

Three days before the lunar new year, she had eaten *ywansyau*, the sticky sweet dumpling that everybody eats to celebrate. She ate one after the other. And I remember her strange remark.

239

"You see how this life is. You cannot eat enough of this bitterness." And what she had done was eat *ywansyau* filled with a kind of bitter poison, not candied seeds or the dull happiness of opium as Yan Chang and the others had thought. When the poison broke into her body, she whispered to me that she would rather kill her own weak spirit so she could give me a stronger one.

The stickiness clung to her body. They could not remove the poison and so she died, two days before the new year. They laid her on a wooden board in the hallway. She wore funeral clothes far richer than those she had worn in life. Silk undergarments to keep her warm without the heavy burden of a fur coat. A silk gown, sewn with gold thread. A headdress of gold and lapis and jade. And two delicate slippers with the softest leather soles and two giant pearls on each toe, to light her way to nirvana.

Seeing her this last time, I threw myself on her body. And she opened her eyes slowly. I was not scared. I knew she could see me and what she had finally done. So I shut her eyes with my fingers and told her with my heart: I can see the truth, too. I am strong, too.

Because we both knew this: that on the third day after someone dies, the soul comes back to settle scores. In my mother's case, this would be the first day of the lunar new year. And because it is the new year, all debts must be paid, or disaster and misfortune will follow.

So on that day, Wu Tsing, fearful of my mother's vengeful spirit, wore the coarsest of white cotton mourning clothes. He promised her visiting ghost that he would raise Syaudi and me as his honored children. He promised to revere her as if she had been First Wife, his only wife.

And on that day, I showed Second Wife the fake pearl necklace she had given me and crushed it under my foot.

And on that day, Second Wife's hair began to turn white.

And on that day, I learned to shout.

I know how it is to live your life like a dream. To listen and watch, to wake up and try to understand what has already happened.

You do not need a psychiatrist to do this. A psychiatrist does not want you to wake up. He tells you to dream some more, to find the pond and pour more tears into it. And really, he is just another bird drinking from your misery.

My mother, she suffered. She lost her face and tried to hide it. She found only greater misery and finally could not hide that. There is nothing more to understand. That was China. That was what people did back then. They had no choice. They could not speak up. They could not run away. That was their fate.

But now they can do something else. Now they no longer have to swallow their own tears or suffer the taunts of magpies. I know this because I read this news in a magazine from China.

It said that for thousands of years birds had been tormenting the peasants. They flocked to watch peasants bent over in the fields, digging the hard dirt, crying into the furrows to water the seeds. And when the people stood up, the birds would fly down and drink the tears and eat the seeds. So children starved.

But one day, all these tired peasants—from all over China— they gathered in fields everywhere. They watched the birds eating and drinking. And they said, "Enough of this suffering and silence!" They began to clap their hands, and bang sticks on pots and pans and shout, *"Sz! Sz! Sz!"*—Die! Die! Die!

And all these birds rose in the air, alarmed and confused by this new anger, beating their black wings, flying just above, waiting for the noise to stop. But the people's shouts only grew stronger, angrier. The birds became more exhausted, unable to land, unable to eat. And this continued for many hours, for many days, until all those birds—hundreds, thousands, and then millions!—fluttered to the ground, dead and still, until not one bird remained in the sky.

What would your psychiatrist say if I told him that I shouted for joy when I read that this had happened?

YING-YING ST. CLAIR

Waiting Between the Trees

My daughter has put me in the tiniest of rooms in her new house.

"This is the guest bedroom," Lena said in her proud American way.

I smiled. But to Chinese ways of thinking, the guest bedroom is the best bedroom, where she and her husband sleep. I do not tell her this. Her wisdom is like a bottomless pond. You throw stones in and they sink into the darkness and dissolve. Her eyes looking back do not reflect anything.

I think this to myself even though I love my daughter. She and I have shared the same body. There is a part of her mind that is part of mine. But when she was born, she sprang from me like a slippery fish, and has been swimming away ever since. All her life, I have watched her as though from another shore. And now I must tell her everything about my past. It is the only way to penetrate her skin and pull her to where she can be saved.

This room has ceilings that slope downward toward the pillow of my bed. Its walls close in like a coffin. I should remind my daughter not to put any babies in this room. But I know she will not listen. She has already said she does not want any babies. She and her husband are too busy drawing places that someone else will build and someone else will live in. I cannot say the American word that she and her husband are. It is an ugly word.

"Arty-tecky," I once pronounced it to my sister-in-law.

My daughter had laughed when she heard this. When she was a child, I should have slapped her more often for disrespect. But now it is too late. Now she and her husband give me money to add to my so-so security. So the burning feeling I have in my hand sometimes, I must pull it back into my heart and keep it inside.

What good does it do to draw fancy buildings and then live in one that is useless? My daughter has money, but everything in her house is for looking, not even for good-looking. Look at this end table. It is heavy white marble on skinny black legs. A person must always think not to put a heavy bag on this table or it will break. The only thing that can sit on the table is a tall black vase. The vase is like a spider leg, so thin only one flower can be put in. If you shake the table, the vase and flower will fall down.

All around this house I see the signs. My daughter looks but does not see. This is a house that will break into pieces. How do I know? I have always known a thing before it happens.

When I was a young girl in Wushi, I was *lihai*. Wild and stubborn. I wore a smirk on my face. Too good to listen. I was small and pretty. I had tiny feet which made me very vain. If a pair of silk slippers became dusty, I threw them away. I wore costly imported calfskin shoes with little heels. I broke many pairs and ruined many stockings running across the cobblestone courtyard.

I often unraveled my hair and wore it loose. My mother would look at my wild tangles and scold me: "Aii-ya, Ying-ying, you are like the lady ghosts at the bottom of the lake."

These were the ladies who drowned their shame and floated in living people's houses with their hair undone to show their everlasting despair. My mother said I would bring shame into the house, but I only giggled as she tried to tuck my hair up with long pins. She loved me too much to get angry. I was like her. That was why she named me Ying-ying, Clear Reflection.

We were one of the richest families in Wushi. We had many rooms, each filled with big, heavy tables. On each table was a jade jar sealed airtight with a jade lid. Each jar held unfiltered British cigarettes, always the right amount. Not too much, not too little. The jars were made just for these cigarettes. I thought nothing of these jars. They were junk in my mind. Once my brothers and I stole a jar and poured the cigarettes out onto the streets. We ran down to a large hole that had opened up in the street, where underneath water flowed. There we squatted along with the children who lived by the gutter. We scooped up cups of dirty water, hoping to find a fish or unknown treasure. We found nothing, and soon our clothes were washed over with mud and we were unrecognizable from the children who lived on the streets.

We had many riches in that house. Silk rugs and jewels. Rare bowls and carved ivory. But when I think back on that house, and it is not often, I think of that jade jar, the muddied treasure I did not know I was holding in my hand.

There is another thing I remember clearly about that house. I was sixteen. It was the night my youngest aunt got married. She and her new husband had already retired to the room they would share in the big house with her new mother-in-law and the rest of her new family.

Many of the visiting family members lingered at our house, sitting around the big table in the main room, everybody laughing and eating peanuts, peeling oranges, and laughing more. A man from another town was seated with us, a friend of my aunt's new husband. He was older than my oldest brother, so I called him Uncle. His face was reddened from drinking whiskey.

"Ying-ying," he called hoarsely to me as he rose from his chair. "Maybe you are still hungry, isn't it so?"

I looked around the table, smiling at everyone because of this special attention given to me. I thought he would pull a special treat from a large sack he was reaching into. I hoped for some sweetened cookies. But he pulled out a watermelon and put it on the table with a loud *pung*.

"*Kai gwa?*"—Open the watermelon—he said, poising a large knife over the perfect fruit.

Then he sank the knife in with a mighty push and his huge mouth roared a laugh so big I could see all the way back to his gold teeth. Everyone at the table laughed loudly. My face burned from embarrassment, because at that time I did not understand.

Yes, it is true I was a wild girl, but I was innocent. I did not know what an evil thing he did when he cut open that watermelon. I did not understand until six months later when I was married to this man and he hissed drunkenly to me that he was ready to *kai gwa*.

This was a man so bad that even today I cannot speak his name. Why did I marry this man? It was because the night after my youngest aunt's wedding, I began to know a thing before it happened.

Most of the relatives had left the next morning. And by the evening, my half-sisters and I were bored. We were sitting at the same large table, drinking tea and eating roasted watermelon seeds. My half-sisters gossiped loudly, while I sat cracking seeds and laying their flesh in a pile.

My half-sisters were all dreaming of being married to worthless young boys from families not as good as ours. My half-sisters did not know how to reach very high for a good thing. They were the daughters of my father's concubines. I was the daughter of my father's wife.

"His mother will treat you like a servant . . ." chided one half-sister upon hearing the other's choice.

"A madness on his uncle's side . . ." retorted the other half-sister.

When they tired of teasing one another, they asked me whom I wanted to marry.

"I know of no one," I told them haughtily.

It was not that boys did not interest me. I knew how to attract attention and be admired. But I was too vain to think any one boy was good enough for me.

Those were the thoughts in my head. But thoughts are of two kinds. Some are seeds that are planted when you are born, placed there by your father and mother and their ancestors before them. And some thoughts are planted by others. Maybe it was the watermelon seeds I was eating: I thought of that laughing man from the night before. And just then, a large wind blew in from the north and the flower on the table split from its stem and fell at my feet.

This is the truth. It was as if a knife had cut the flower's head off as a sign. Right then, I knew I would marry this man. It was not with joy that I thought this, but wonderment that I could know it.

And soon I began to hear this man mentioned by my father and uncle and aunt's new husband. At dinner his name was spooned into my bowl along with my soup. I found him staring at me across from my uncle's courtyard, hu-huing, "See, she cannot turn away. She is already mine."

True enough, I did not turn away. I fought his eyes with mine. I listened to him with my nose held high, sniffing the stink of his words when he told me my father would not likely give the dowry he required. I pushed so hard to keep him from my thoughts that I fell into a marriage bed with him.

My daughter does not know that I was married to this man so long ago, twenty years before she was even born.

She does not know how beautiful I was when I married this man. I was far more pretty than my daughter, who has country feet and a large nose like her father's.

Even today, my skin is still smooth, my figure like a girl's. But there are deep lines in my mouth where I used to wear smiles. And my poor feet, once so small and pretty! Now they are swollen, callused, and cracked at the heels. My eyes, so bright and flashy at sixteen, are now yellow-stained, clouded.

But I still see almost everything clearly. When I want to remember, it is like looking into a bowl and finding the last grains of rice you did not finish.

There was an afternoon on Tai Lake soon after this man and I married. I remember this is when I came to love him. This man had turned my face toward the late-afternoon sun. He held my chin and stroked my cheek and said, "Ying-ying, you have tiger eyes. They gather fire in the day. At night they shine golden."

I did not laugh, even though this was a poem he said very badly. I cried with honest joy. I had a swimming feeling in my heart like a creature thrashing to get out and wanting to stay in at the same time. That is how much I came to love this man. This is how it is when a person joins your body and there is a part of your mind that swims to join that person against your will.

I became a stranger to myself. I was pretty for him. If I put slippers on my feet, it was to choose a pair that I knew would please him. I brushed my hair ninety-nine times a night to bring luck to our marital bed, in hopes of conceiving a son.

The night he planted the baby, I again knew a thing before it happened. I knew it was a boy. I could see this little boy in my womb. He had my husband's eyes, large and wide apart. He had long tapered fingers, fat earlobes, and slick hair that rose high to reveal a large forehead.

It is because I had so much joy then that I came to have so much hate. But even when I was my happiest, I had a worry that started right above my brow, where you know a thing. This worry later trickled down to my heart, where you feel a thing and it becomes true.

My husband started to take many business trips to the north. These trips began soon after we married, but they became longer after the baby was put in my womb. I remembered that the north wind had blown luck and my husband my way, so at night when he was away, I opened wide my bedroom windows, even on cold nights, to blow his spirit and heart back my way.

What I did not know is that the north wind is the coldest. It penetrates the heart and takes the warmth away. The wind gathered such a force that it blew my husband past my bedroom and out the back door. I found out from my youngest aunt that he had left me to live with an opera singer.

Later still, when I overcame my grief and came to have nothing in my heart but loathing despair, my youngest aunt told me of others. Dancers and American ladies. Prostitutes. A girl cousin younger even than I was. She left mysteriously for Hong Kong soon after my husband disappeared.

247

So I will tell Lena of my shame. That I was rich and pretty. I was too good for any one man. That I became abandoned goods. I will tell her that at eighteen the prettiness drained from my cheeks. That I thought of throwing myself in the lake like the other ladies of shame. And I will tell her of the baby I killed because I came to hate this man so much.

I took this baby from my womb before it could be born. This was not a bad thing to do in China back then, to kill a baby before it is born. But even then, I thought it was bad, because my body flowed with terrible revenge as the juices of this man's firstborn son poured from me.

When the nurses asked what they should do with the lifeless baby, I hurled a newspaper at them and said to wrap it like a fish and throw it in the lake. My daughter thinks I do not know what it means to not want a baby.

When my daughter looks at me, she sees a small old lady. That is because she sees only with her outside eyes. She has no *chuming*, no inside knowing of things. If she had *chuming*, she would see a tiger lady. And she would have careful fear.

I was born in the year of the Tiger. It was a very bad year to be born, a very good year to be a Tiger. That was the year a very bad spirit entered the world. People in the countryside died like chickens on a hot summer day. People in the city became shadows, went into their homes and disappeared. Babies were born and did not get fatter. The flesh fell off their bones in days and they died.

The bad spirit stayed in the world for four years. But I came from a spirit even stronger, and I lived. This is what my mother told me when I was old enough to know why I was so heartstrong in my ways.

Then she told me why a tiger is gold and black. It has two ways. The gold side leaps with its fierce heart. The black side stands still with cunning, hiding its gold between trees, seeing and not being seen, waiting patiently for things to come. I did not learn to use my black side until after the bad man left me.

I became like the ladies of the lake. I threw white clothes

over the mirrors in my bedroom so I did not have to see my grief. I lost my strength, so I could not even lift my hands to place pins in my hair. And then I floated like a dead leaf on the water until I drifted out of my mother-in-law's house and back to my family home.

I went to the country outside of Shanghai to live with a second cousin's family. I stayed in this country home for ten years. If you ask me what I did during these long years, I can only say I waited between the trees. I had one eye asleep, the other open and watching.

I did not work. My cousin's family treated me well because I was the daughter of the family who supported them. The house was shabby, crowded with three families. It was not a comfort to be there, and that is what I wanted. Babies crawled on the floor with the mice. Chickens came in and out like my relatives' graceless peasant guests. We all ate in the kitchen amidst the hot frying grease. And the flies! If you left a bowl with even a few grains of rice, you would find it covered with hungry flies so thick it looked like a living bowl of black bean soup. This is how poor the country was.

After ten years, I was ready. I was no longer a girl but a strange woman. A still-married woman with no husband. I went to the city with both eyes open. It was as if the bowl of black flies had been poured out onto the streets. Everywhere there were people moving, unknown men pushing against unknown women and no one caring.

With the money from my family, I bought fresh clothes, modern straight suits. I cut off my long hair in the manner that was stylish, like a young boy. I was so tired of doing nothing for so many years I decided to work. I became a shopgirl.

I did not need to learn to flatter women. I knew the words they wanted to hear. A tiger can make a soft prrrn-prrn noise deep within its chest and make even rabbits feel safe and content.

Even though I was a grown woman, I became pretty again. This was a gift. I wore clothes far better and more expensive than what was sold in the store. And this made women buy the cheap clothes, because they thought they could look as pretty as I.

It was at this shop, working like a peasant, that I met Clifford St. Clair. He was a large, pale American man who bought the store's cheap-style clothes and sent them overseas. It was his name that made me know I would marry him.

"Mistah Saint Clair," he said in English when he introduced himself to me.

And then he added in his thick, flat Chinese, "Like the angel of light."

I neither liked him nor disliked him. I thought him neither attractive nor unattractive. But this I knew. I knew he was the sign that the black side of me would soon go away.

Saint courted me for four years in his strange way. Even though I was not the owner of the shop, he always greeted me, shaking hands, holding them too long. From his palms water always poured, even after we married. He was clean and pleasant. But he smelled like a foreigner, a lamb-smell stink that can never be washed away.

I was not unkind. But he was *kechi*, too polite. He bought me cheap gifts: a glass figurine, a prickly brooch of cut glass, a silver-colored cigarette lighter. Saint acted as if these gifts were nothing, as if he were a rich man treating a poor country girl to things we had never seen in China.

But I saw his look as he watched me open the boxes. Anxious and eager to please. He did not know that such things were nothing to me, that I was raised with riches he could not even imagine.

I always accepted these gifts graciously, always protesting just enough, not too little, not too much. I did not encourage him. But because I knew this man would someday be my husband, I put these worthless trinkets carefully into a box, wrapping each with tissue. I knew that someday he would ask to see them again.

Lena thinks Saint saved me from the poor country village that I said I was from. She is right. She is wrong. My daughter does not know that Saint had to wait patiently for four years like a dog in front of a butcher shop.

How is it that I finally came out and let him marry me? I was waiting for the sign I knew would come. I had to wait until 1946.

A letter came from Tientsin, not from my family, who thought I was dead. It was from my youngest aunt. Even before I opened the letter I knew. My husband was dead. He had long since left his opera singer. He was with some worthless girl, a young servant. But she had a strong spirit and was reckless, more so than even he. When he tried to leave her, she had already sharpened her longest kitchen knife.

I thought this man had long ago drained everything from my heart. But now something strong and bitter flowed and made me feel another emptiness in a place I didn't know was there. I cursed this man aloud so he could hear. You had dog eyes. You jumped and followed whoever called you. Now you chase your own tail.

So I decided. I decided to let Saint marry me. So easy for me. I was the daughter of my father's wife. I spoke in a trembly voice. I became pale, ill, and more thin. I let myself become a wounded animal. I let the hunter come to me and turn me into a tiger ghost. I willingly gave up my *chi*, the spirit that caused me so much pain.

Now I was a tiger that neither pounced nor lay waiting between the trees. I became an unseen spirit.

Saint took me to America, where I lived in houses smaller than the one in the country. I wore large American clothes. I did servant's tasks. I learned the Western ways. I tried to speak with a thick tongue. I raised a daughter, watching her from another shore. I accepted her American ways.

With all these things, I did not care. I had no spirit.

Can I tell my daughter that I loved her father? This was a man who rubbed my feet at night. He praised the food that I cooked. He cried honestly when I brought out the trinkets I had saved for the right day, the day he gave me my daughter, a tiger girl.

How could I not love this man? But it was the love of a ghost. Arms that encircled but did not touch. A bowl full of rice but without my appetite to eat it. No hunger. No fullness.

Now Saint is a ghost. He and I can now love equally. He knows the things I have been hiding all these years. Now I must tell my daughter everything. That she is the daughter of a ghost. She has no *chi*. This is my greatest shame. How can I leave this world without leaving her my spirit?

So this is what I will do. I will gather together my past and look. I will see a thing that has already happened. The pain that cut my spirit loose. I will hold that pain in my hand until it becomes hard and shiny, more clear. And then my fierceness can come back, my golden side, my black side. I will use this sharp pain to penetrate my daughter's tough skin and cut her tiger spirit loose. She will fight me, because this is the nature of two tigers. But I will win and give her my spirit, because this is the way a mother loves her daughter.

I hear my daughter speaking to her husband downstairs. They say words that mean nothing. They sit in a room with no life in it.

I know a thing before it happens. She will hear the vase and table crashing to the floor. She will come up the stairs and into my room. Her eyes will see nothing in the darkness, where I am waiting between the trees.

LINDO JONG

Double Face

My daughter wanted to go to China for her second honeymoon, but now she is afraid.

"What if I blend in so well they think I'm one of them?" Waverly asked me. "What if they don't let me come back to the United States?"

"When you go to China," I told her, "you don't even need to open your mouth. They already know you are an outsider."

"What are you talking about?" she asked. My daughter likes to speak back. She likes to question what I say.

"Aii-ya," I said. "Even if you put on their clothes, even if you take off your makeup and hide your fancy jewelry, they know. They know just watching the way you walk, the way you carry your face. They know you do not belong."

My daughter did not look pleased when I told her this, that she didn't look Chinese. She had a sour American look on her face. Oh, maybe ten years ago, she would have clapped her hands—hurray!—as if this were good news. But now she wants to be Chinese, it is so fashionable. And I know it is too late. All those years I tried to teach her! She followed my Chinese ways only until she learned how to walk out the door by herself and go to school. So now the only Chinese words she can say are *sh-sh, houche, chr fan,* and *gwan deng shweijyau.* How can she talk to people in China with these words? Pee-pee, choo-choo train, eat, close light sleep. How can she think she can blend in? Only her skin and her hair are Chinese. Inside—she is all American-made.

It's my fault she is this way. I wanted my children to have the best combination: American circumstances and Chinese character. How could I know these two things do not mix?

I taught her how American circumstances work. If you are born poor here, it's no lasting shame. You are first in line for a scholarship. If the roof crashes on your head, no need to cry over this bad luck. You can sue anybody, make the landlord fix it. You do not have to sit like a Buddha under a tree letting pigeons drop their dirty business on your head. You can buy an umbrella. Or go inside a Catholic church. In America, nobody says you have to keep the circumstances somebody else gives you.

She learned these things, but I couldn't teach her about Chinese character. How to obey parents and listen to your mother's mind. How not to show your own thoughts, to put your feelings behind your face so you can take advantage of hidden opportunities. Why easy things are not worth pursuing. How to know your own worth and polish it, never flashing it around like a cheap ring. Why Chinese thinking is best.

No, this kind of thinking didn't stick to her. She was too busy chewing gum, blowing bubbles bigger than her cheeks. Only that kind of thinking stuck.

"Finish your coffee," I told her yesterday. "Don't throw your blessings away."

"Don't be so old-fashioned, Ma," she told me, finishing her coffee down the sink. "I'm my own person."

And I think, How can she be her own person? When did I give her up?

My daughter is getting married a second time. So she asked me to go to her beauty parlor, her famous Mr. Rory. I know her meaning. She is ashamed of my looks. What will her husband's parents and his important lawyer friends think of this backward old Chinese woman?

"Auntie An-mei can cut me," I say.

"Rory is famous," says my daughter, as if she had no ears. "He does fabulous work."

So I sit in Mr. Rory's chair. He pumps me up and down until I am the right height. Then my daughter criticizes me as if I were not there. "See how it's flat on one side," she accuses my head. "She needs a cut and a perm. And this purple tint in her hair, she's been doing it at home. She's never had anything professionally done."

She is looking at Mr. Rory in the mirror. He is looking at me in the mirror. I have seen this professional look before. Americans don't really look at one another when talking. They talk to their reflections. They look at others or themselves only when they think nobody is watching. So they never see how they really look. They see themselves smiling without their mouth open, or turned to the side where they cannot see their faults.

"How does she want it?" asked Mr. Rory. He thinks I do not understand English. He is floating his fingers through my hair. He is showing how his magic can make my hair thicker and longer.

"Ma, how do you want it?" Why does my daughter think she is translating English for me? Before I can even speak, she explains my thoughts: "She wants a soft wave. We probably shouldn't cut it too short. Otherwise it'll be too tight for the wedding. She doesn't want it to look kinky or weird."

And now she says to me in a loud voice, as if I had lost my hearing, "Isn't that right, Ma? Not too tight?"

I smile. I use my American face. That's the face Americans think is Chinese, the one they cannot understand. But inside I am becoming ashamed. I am ashamed she is ashamed. Because she is my daughter and I am proud of her, and I am her mother but she is not proud of me.

Mr. Rory pats my hair more. He looks at me. He looks at my daughter. Then he says something to my daughter that really displeases her: "It's uncanny how much you two look alike!"

I smile, this time with my Chinese face. But my daughter's eyes and her smile become very narrow, the way a cat pulls itself small just before it bites. Now Mr. Rory goes away so we can think about this. I hear him snap his fingers, "Wash! Mrs. Jong is next!"

So my daughter and I are alone in this crowded beauty parlor. She is frowning at herself in the mirror. She sees me looking at her.

"The same cheeks," she says. She points to mine and then pokes her cheeks. She sucks them outside in to look like a starved person. She puts her face next to mine, side by side, and we look at each other in the mirror.

"You can see your character in your face," I say to my daughter without thinking. "You can see your future."

"What do you mean?" she says.

And now I have to fight back my feelings. These two faces, I think, so much the same! The same happiness, the same sadness, the same good fortune, the same faults.

I am seeing myself and my mother, back in China, when I was a young girl.

My mother—your grandmother—once told me my fortune, how my character could lead to good and bad circumstances. She was sitting at her table with the big mirror. I was standing behind her, my chin resting on her shoulder. The next day was the start of the new year. I would be ten years by my Chinese age, so it was an important birthday for me. For this reason maybe she did not criticize me too much. She was looking at my face.

She touched my ear. "You are lucky," she said. "You have my ears, a big thick lobe, lots of meat at the bottom, full of blessings. Some people are born so poor. Their ears are so thin, so close to their head, they can never hear luck calling to them. You have the right ears, but you must listen to your opportunities."

She ran her thin finger down my nose. "You have my nose.

The hole is not too big, so your money will not be running out. The nose is straight and smooth, a good sign. A girl with a crooked nose is bound for misfortune. She is always following the wrong things, the wrong people, the worst luck."

She tapped my chin and then hers. "Not too short, not too long. Our longevity will be adequate, not cut off too soon, not so long we become a burden."

She pushed my hair away from my forehead. "We are the same," concluded my mother. "Perhaps your forehead is wider, so you will be even more clever. And your hair is thick, the hairline is low on your forehead. This means you will have some hardships in your early life. This happened to me. But look at my hairline now. High! Such a blessing for my old age. Later you will learn to worry and lose your hair, too."

She took my chin in her hand. She turned my face toward her, eyes facing eyes. She moved my face to one side, then the other. "The eyes are honest, eager," she said. "They follow me and show respect. They do not look down in shame. They do not resist and turn the opposite way. You will be a good wife, mother, and daughter-in-law."

When my mother told me these things, I was still so young. And even though she said we looked the same, I wanted to look more the same. If her eye went up and looked surprised, I wanted my eye to do the same. If her mouth fell down and was unhappy, I too wanted to feel unhappy.

I was so much like my mother. This was before our circumstances separated us: a flood that caused my family to leave me behind, my first marriage to a family that did not want me, a war from all sides, and later, an ocean that took me to a new country. She did not see how my face changed over the years. How my mouth began to droop. How I began to worry but still did not lose my hair. How my eyes began to follow the American way. She did not see that I twisted my nose bouncing forward on a crowded bus in San Francisco. Your father and I, we were on our way to church to give many thanks to God for all our blessings, but I had to subtract some for my nose.

*

It's hard to keep your Chinese face in America. At the beginning, before I even arrived, I had to hide my true self. I paid an American-raised Chinese girl in Peking to show me how.

"In America," she said, "you cannot say you want to live there forever. If you are Chinese, you must say you admire their schools, their ways of thinking. You must say you want to be a scholar and come back to teach Chinese people what you have learned."

"What should I say I want to learn?" I asked. "If they ask me questions, if I cannot answer . . ."

"Religion, you must say you want to study religion," said this smart girl. "Americans all have different ideas about religion, so there are no right and wrong answers. Say to them, I'm going for God's sake, and they will respect you."

For another sum of money, this girl gave me a form filled out with English words. I had to copy these words over and over again as if they were English words formed from my own head. Next to the word NAME, I wrote *Lindo Sun*. Next to the word BIRTHDATE, I wrote *May 11, 1918,* which this girl insisted was the same as three months after the Chinese lunar new year. Next to the word BIRTHPLACE, I put down *Taiyuan, China*. And next to the word OCCUPATION, I wrote *student of theology*.

I gave the girl even more money for a list of addresses in San Francisco, people with big connections. And finally, this girl gave me, free of charge, instructions for changing my circumstances. "First," she said, "you must find a husband. An American citizen is best."

She saw my surprise and quickly added, "Chinese! Of course, he must be Chinese. 'Citizen' does not mean Caucasian. But if he is not a citizen, you should immediately do number two. See here, you should have a baby. Boy or girl, it doesn't matter in the United States. Neither will take care of you in your old age, isn't that true?" And we both laughed.

"Be careful, though," she said. "The authorities there will ask you if you have children now or if you are thinking of having some. You must say no. You should look sincere and say you are not married, you are religious, you know it is wrong to have a baby."

I must have looked puzzled, because she explained further: "Look here now, how can an unborn baby know what it is not supposed to do? And once it has arrived, it is an American citizen and can do anything it wants. It can ask its mother to stay. Isn't that true?"

But that is not the reason I was puzzled. I wondered why she said I should look sincere. How could I look any other way when telling the truth?

See how truthful my face still looks. Why didn't I give this look to you? Why do you always tell your friends that I arrived in the United States on a slow boat from China? This is not true. I was not that poor. I took a plane. I had saved the money my first husband's family gave me when they sent me away. And I had saved money from my twelve years' work as a telephone operator. But it is true I did not take the fastest plane. The plane took three weeks. It stopped everywhere: Hong Kong, Vietnam, the Philippines, Hawaii. So by the time I arrived, I did not look sincerely glad to be here.

Why do you always tell people that I met your father in the Cathay House, that I broke open a fortune cookie and it said I would marry a dark, handsome stranger, and that when I looked up, there he was, the waiter, your father. Why do you make this joke? This is not sincere. This was not true! Your father was not a waiter, I never ate in that restaurant. The Cathay House had a sign that said "Chinese Food," so only Americans went there before it was torn down. Now it is a McDonald's restaurant with a big Chinese sign that says *mai dong lou*—"wheat," "east," "building." All nonsense. Why are you attracted only to Chinese nonsense? You must understand my real circumstances, how I arrived, how I married, how I lost my Chinese face, why you are the way you are.

When I arrived, nobody asked me questions. The authorities looked at my papers and stamped me in. I decided to go first to a San Francisco address given to me by this girl in Peking. The bus put me down on a wide street with cable cars. This was California Street. I walked up this hill and then I saw a tall building. This was Old St. Mary's. Under the church sign, in handwritten Chinese characters, someone had added: "A Chinese Ceremony to Save Ghosts from Spiritual Unrest 7 A.M. and 8:30 A.M." I memorized this information in case the authorities asked me where I worshipped my religion. And then I saw another sign across the street. It was painted on the outside of a short building: "Save Today for Tomorrow, at Bank of America." And I thought to myself, This is where American people worship. See, even then I was not so dumb! Today that church is the same size, but where that short bank used to be, now there is a tall building, fifty stories high, where you and your husband-to-be work and look down on everybody.

My daughter laughed when I said this. Her mother can make a good joke.

So I kept walking up this hill. I saw two pagodas, one on each side of the street, as though they were the entrance to a great Buddha temple. But when I looked carefully, I saw the pagoda was really just a building topped with stacks of tile roofs, no walls, nothing else under its head. I was surprised how they tried to make everything look like an old imperial city or an emperor's tomb. But if you looked on either side of these pretend-pagodas, you could see the streets became narrow and crowded, dark, and dirty. I thought to myself, Why did they choose only the worst Chinese parts for the inside? Why didn't they build gardens and ponds instead? Oh, here and there was the look of a famous ancient cave or a Chinese opera. But inside it was always the same cheap stuff.

So by the time I found the address the girl in Peking gave me, I knew not to expect too much. The address was a large green building, so noisy, children running up and down the outside stairs and hallways. Inside number 402, I found an old woman who told me right away she had wasted her time waiting for me all week. She quickly wrote down some addresses and gave them to me, keeping her hand out after I took the paper. So I gave her an American dollar and she looked at it and said, *"Syaujye"*—Miss—"we are in America now. Even a beggar can starve on this dollar." So I gave her another dollar and she said, "Aii, you think it is so easy getting this information?" So I gave her another and she closed her hand and her mouth.

With the addresses this old woman gave me, I found a cheap apartment on Washington Street. It was like all the other places, sitting on top of a little store. And through this three-dollar list, I found a terrible job paying me seventy-five cents an hour. Oh, I tried to get a job as a salesgirl, but you had to know English for that. I tried for another job as a Chinese hostess, but they also wanted me to rub my hands up and down foreign men, and I knew right away this was as bad as fourth-class prostitutes in China! So I rubbed that address out with black ink. And some of the other jobs required you to have a special relationship. They were jobs held by families from Canton and Toishan and the Four Districts, southern people who had come many years ago to make their fortune and were still holding onto them with the hands of their great-grandchildren.

So my mother was right about my hardships. This job in the cookie factory was one of the worst. Big black machines worked all day and night pouring little pancakes onto moving round griddles. The other women and I sat on high stools, and as the little pancakes went by, we had to grab them off the hot griddle just as they turned golden. We would put a strip of paper in the center, then fold the cookie in half and bend its arms back just as it turned hard. If you grabbed the pancake too soon, you would burn your fingers on the hot, wet dough. But if you grabbed too late, the cookie would harden before you could even complete the first bend. And then you had to throw these mistakes in a barrel, which counted against you because the owner could sell those only as scraps.

After the first day, I suffered ten red fingers. This was not a job for a stupid person. You had to learn fast or your fingers would turn into fried sausages. So the next day only my eyes burned, from never taking them off the pancakes. And the day after that, my arms ached from holding them out ready to catch the pancakes at just the right moment. But by the end of my first week, it became mindless work and I could relax enough to notice who else was working on each side of me. One was an older woman who never smiled and spoke to herself in Cantonese when she was angry. She talked like a crazy person. On my other side was a woman around my age. Her barrel contained very few mistakes. But I suspected she ate them. She was quite plump.

"Eh, *Syaujye*," she called to me over the loud noise of the machines. I was grateful to hear her voice, to discover we both spoke Mandarin, although her dialect was coarse-sounding. "Did you ever think you would be so powerful you could determine someone else's fortune?" she asked.

I didn't understand what she meant. So she picked up one of the strips of paper and read it aloud, first in English: "Do not fight and air your dirty laundry in public. To the victor go the soils." Then she translated in Chinese: "You shouldn't fight and do your laundry at the same time. If you win, your clothes will get dirty."

I still did not know what she meant. So she picked up another one and read in English: "Money is the root of all evil. Look around you and dig deep." And then in Chinese: "Money is a bad influence. You become restless and rob graves."

"What is this nonsense?" I asked her, putting the strips of paper in my pocket, thinking I should study these classical American sayings.

"They are fortunes," she explained. "American people think Chinese people write these sayings."

"But we never say such things!" I said. "These things don't make sense. These are not fortunes, they are bad instructions."

"No, Miss," she said, laughing, "it is our bad fortune to be here making these and somebody else's bad fortune to pay to get them."

So that is how I met An-mei Hsu. Yes, yes, Auntie An-mei, now so old-fashioned. An-mei and I still laugh over those bad fortunes and how they later became quite useful in helping me catch a husband.

"Eh, Lindo," An-mei said to me one day at our workplace. "Come to my church this Sunday. My husband has a friend who is looking for a good Chinese wife. He is not a citizen, but I'm sure he knows how to make one." So that is how I first heard about Tin Jong, your father. It was not like my first marriage, where everything was arranged. I had a choice. I could choose to marry your father, or I could choose not to marry him and go back to China.

I knew something was not right when I saw him: He was Cantonese! How could An-mei think I could marry such a person? But she just said: "We are not in China anymore. You don't have to marry the village boy. Here everybody is now from the same village even if they come from different parts of China." See how changed Auntie An-mei is from those old days.

So we were shy at first, your father and I, neither of us able to speak to each other in our Chinese dialects. We went to English class together, speaking to each other in those new words and sometimes taking out a piece of paper to write a Chinese character to show what we meant. At least we had that, a piece of paper to hold us together. But it's hard to tell someone's marriage intentions when you can't say things aloud. All those little signs—the teasing, the bossy, scolding words—that's how you know if it is serious. But we could talk only in the manner of our English teacher. I see cat. I see rat. I see hat.

But I saw soon enough how much your father liked me. He would pretend he was in a Chinese play to show me what he meant. He ran back and forth, jumped up and down, pulling his fingers through his hair, so I knew—*mang jile!*—what a busy, exciting place this Pacific Telephone was, this place where he worked. You didn't know this about your father—that he could be such a good actor? You didn't know your father had so much hair?

Oh, I found out later his job was not the way he decribed it. It was not so good. Even today, now that I can speak Cantonese to your father, I always ask him why he doesn't find a better situation. But he acts as if we were in those old days, when he couldn't understand anything I said.

Sometimes I wonder why I wanted to catch a marriage with your father. I think An-mei put the thought in my mind. She said, "In the movies, boys and girls are always passing notes in class. That's how they fall into trouble. You need to start trouble to get this man to realize his intentions. Otherwise, you will be an old lady before it comes to his mind."

That evening An-mei and I went to work and searched through strips of fortune cookie papers, trying to find the right instructions to give to your father. An-mei read them aloud, putting aside ones that might work: "Diamonds are a girl's best friend. Don't ever settle for a pal." "If such thoughts are in your head, it's time to be wed." "Confucius say a woman is worth a thousand words. Tell your wife she's used up her total."

We laughed over those. But I knew the right one when I read it. It said: "A house is not home when a spouse is not at home." I did not laugh. I wrapped up this saying in a pancake, bending the cookie with all my heart.

After school the next afternoon, I put my hand in my purse and then made a look, as if a mouse had bitten my hand. "What's this?" I cried. Then I pulled out the cookie and handed it to your father. "Eh! So many cookies, just to see them makes me sick. You take this cookie."

I knew even then he had a nature that did not waste anything. He opened the cookie and he crunched it in his mouth, and then read the piece of paper.

"What does it say?" I asked. I tried to act as if it did not matter. And when he still did not speak, I said, "Translate, please."

We were walking in Portsmouth Square and already the fog had blown in and I was very cold in my thin coat. So I hoped your father would hurry and ask me to marry him. But instead, he kept his serious look and said, "I don't know this word 'spouse.' Tonight I will look in my dictionary. Then I can tell you the meaning tomorrow."

The next day he asked me in English, "Lindo, can you spouse me?" And I laughed at him and said he used that word incorrectly. So he came back and made a Confucius joke, that if the words were wrong, then his intentions must also be wrong. We scolded and joked with each other all day long like this, and that is how we decided to get married.

One month later we had a ceremony in the First Chinese Baptist Church, where we met. And nine months later your father and I had our proof of citizenship, a baby boy, your big brother Winston. I named him Winston because I liked the meaning of those two words "wins ton." I wanted to raise a son who would win many things, praise, money, a good life. Back then, I thought to myself, At last I have everything I wanted. I was so happy, I didn't see we were poor. I saw only what we had. How did I know Winston would die later in a car accident? So young! Only sixteen!

Two years after Winston was born, I had your other brother, Vincent. I named him Vincent, which sounds like "win cent," the sound of making money, because I was beginning to think we did not have enough. And then I bumped my nose riding on the bus. Soon after that you were born.

I don't know what caused me to change. Maybe it was my crooked nose that damaged my thinking. Maybe it was seeing you as a baby, how you looked so much like me, and this made me dissatisfied with my life. I wanted everything for you to be better. I wanted you to have the best circumstances, the best character. I didn't want you to regret anything. And that's why I named you Waverly. It was the name of the street we lived on. And I wanted you to think, This is where I belong. But I also knew if I named you after this street, soon you would grow up, leave this place, and take a piece of me with you.

Mr. Rory is brushing my hair. Everything is soft. Everything is black.

"You look great, Ma," says my daughter. "Everyone at the wedding will think you're my sister."

I look at my face in the beauty parlor mirror. I see my reflection. I cannot see my faults, but I know they are there. I gave my daughter these faults. The same eyes, the same cheeks, the same chin. Her character, it came from my circumstances. I look at my daughter and now it is the first time I have seen it.

"Ai-ya! What happened to your nose?"

She looks in the mirror. She sees nothing wrong. "What do you mean? Nothing happened," she says. "It's just the same nose."

"But how did you get it crooked?" I ask. One side of her nose is bending lower, dragging her cheek with it.

"What do you mean?" she asks. "It's your nose. You gave me this nose."

"How can that be? It's drooping. You must get plastic surgery and correct it."

But my daughter has no ears for my words. She puts her smiling face next to my worried one. "Don't be silly. Our nose isn't so bad," she says. "It makes us look devious." She looks pleased.

"What is this word, 'devious,' " I ask.

"It means we're looking one way, while following another. We're for one side and also the other. We mean what we say, but our intentions are different."

"People can see this in our face?"

My daughter laughs. "Well, not everything that we're thinking. They just know we're two-faced."

"This is good?"

"This is good if you get what you want."

I think about our two faces. I think about my intentions. Which one is American? Which one is Chinese? Which one is better? If you show one, you must always sacrifice the other.

It is like what happened when I went back to China last year, after I had not been there for almost forty years. I had taken off my fancy jewelry. I did not wear loud colors. I spoke their language. I used their local money. But still, they knew. They knew my face was not one hundred percent Chinese. They still charged me high foreign prices.

So now I think, What did I lose? What did I get back in return? I will ask my daughter what she thinks.

JING-MEI WOO

A Pair of Tickets

The minute our train leaves the Hong Kong border and enters Shenzhen, China, I feel different. I can feel the skin on my forehead tingling, my blood rushing through a new course, my bones aching with a familiar old pain. And I think, My mother was right. I am becoming Chinese.

"Cannot be helped," my mother said when I was fifteen and had vigorously denied that I had any Chinese whatsoever below my skin. I was a sophomore at Galileo High in San Francisco, and all my Caucasian friends agreed: I was about as Chinese as they were. But my mother had studied at a famous nursing school in Shanghai, and she said she knew all about genetics. So there was no doubt in her mind, whether I agreed or not: Once you are born Chinese, you cannot help but feel and think Chinese.

"Someday you will see," said my mother. "It is in your blood, waiting to be let go."

And when she said this, I saw myself transforming like a werewolf, a mutant tag of DNA suddenly triggered, replicating itself insidiously into a *syndrome*, a cluster of telltale Chinese behaviors, all those things my mother did to embarrass me—haggling with store owners, pecking her mouth with a toothpick in public, being color-blind to the fact that lemon yellow and pale pink are not good combinations for winter clothes.

But today I realize I've never really known what it means to be Chinese. I am thirty-six years old. My mother is dead and I am on a train, carrying with me her dreams of coming home. I am going to China.

We are first going to Guangzhou, my seventy-two-year-old father, Canning Woo, and I, where we will visit his aunt, whom he has not seen since he was ten years old. And I don't know whether it's the prospect of seeing his aunt or if it's because he's back in China, but now he looks like he's a young boy, so innocent and happy I want to button his sweater and pat his head. We are sitting across from each other, separated by a little table with two cold cups of tea. For the first time I can ever remember, my father has tears in his eyes, and all he is seeing out the train window is a sectioned field of yellow, green, and brown, a narrow canal flanking the tracks, low rising hills, and three people in blue jackets riding an ox-driven cart on this early October morning. And I can't help myself. I also have misty eyes, as if I had seen this a long, long time ago, and had almost forgotten.

In less than three hours, we will be in Guangzhou, which my guidebook tells me is how one properly refers to Canton these days. It seems all the cities I have heard of, except Shanghai, have changed their spellings. I think they are saying China has changed in other ways as well. Chungking is Chongqing. And Kweilin is Guilin. I have looked these names up, because after we see my father's aunt in Guangzhou, we will catch a plane to Shanghai, where I will meet my two half-sisters for the first time.

They are my mother's twin daughters from her first marriage, little babies she was forced to abandon on a road as she was fleeing Kweilin for Chungking in 1944. That was all my mother had told me about these daughters, so they had remained babies in my mind, all these years, sitting on the side of a road, listening to bombs whistling in the distance while sucking their patient red thumbs.

And it was only this year that someone found them and wrote with this joyful news. A letter came from Shanghai, addressed to my mother. When I first heard about this, that they were alive, I imagined my identical sisters transforming from little babies into six-year-old girls. In my mind, they were seated next to each other at a table, taking turns with the fountain pen. One would write a neat row of characters: *Dearest Mama. We are alive.* She would brush back her wispy bangs and hand the other sister the pen, and she would write: *Come get us. Please hurry.*

Of course they could not know that my mother had died three months before, suddenly, when a blood vessel in her brain burst. One minute she was talking to my father, complaining about the tenants upstairs, scheming how to evict them under the pretense that relatives from China were moving in. The next minute she was holding her head, her eyes squeezed shut, groping for the sofa, and then crumpling softly to the floor with fluttering hands.

So my father had been the first one to open the letter, a long letter it turned out. And they did call her Mama. They said they always revered her as their true mother. They kept a framed picture of her. They told her about their life, from the time my mother last saw them on the road leaving Kweilin to when they were finally found.

And the letter had broken my father's heart so much—these daughters calling my mother from another life he never knew— that he gave the letter to my mother's old friend Auntie Lindo and asked her to write back and tell my sisters, in the gentlest way possible, that my mother was dead.

But instead Auntie Lindo took the letter to the Joy Luck Club and discussed with Auntie Ying and Auntie An-mei what should be done, because they had known for many years about my mother's search for her twin daughters, her endless hope. Auntie Lindo and the others cried over this double tragedy, of losing my mother three months before, and now again. And so they couldn't help but think of some miracle, some possible way of reviving her from the dead, so my mother could fulfill her dream.

So this is what they wrote to my sisters in Shanghai: "Dearest Daughters, I too have never forgotten you in my memory or in my heart. I never gave up hope that we would see each other again in a joyous reunion. I am only sorry it has been too long.

I want to tell you everything about my life since I last saw you. I want to tell you this when our family comes to see you in China. . . ." They signed it with my mother's name.

It wasn't until all this had been done that they first told me about my sisters, the letter they received, the one they wrote back.

"They'll think she's coming, then," I murmured. And I had imagined my sisters now being ten or eleven, jumping up and down, holding hands, their pigtails bouncing, excited that their mother—*their* mother—was coming, whereas my mother was dead.

"How can you say she is not coming in a letter?" said Auntie Lindo. "She is their mother. She is your mother. You must be the one to tell them. All these years, they have been dreaming of her." And I thought she was right.

But then I started dreaming, too, of my mother and my sisters and how it would be if I arrived in Shanghai. All these years, while they waited to be found, I had lived with my mother and then had lost her. I imagined seeing my sisters at the airport. They would be standing on their tiptoes, looking anxiously, scanning from one dark head to another as we got off the plane. And I would recognize them instantly, their faces with the identical worried look.

"*Jyejye, Jyejye.* Sister, Sister. We are here," I saw myself saying in my poor version of Chinese.

"Where is Mama?" they would say, and look around, still smiling, two flushed and eager faces. "Is she hiding?" And this would have been like my mother, to stand behind just a bit, to tease a little and make people's patience pull a little on their hearts. I would shake my head and tell my sisters she was not hiding.

"Oh, that must be Mama, no?" one of my sisters would whisper excitedly, pointing to another small woman completely engulfed in a tower of presents. And that, too, would have been like my mother, to bring mountains of gifts, food, and toys for children—all bought on sale—shunning thanks, saying the gifts were nothing, and later turning the labels over to show my sisters, "Calvin Klein, 100% wool."

I imagined myself starting to say, "Sisters, I am sorry, I have come alone . . ." and before I could tell them—they could see it in my face—they were wailing, pulling their hair, their lips twisted in pain, as they ran away from me. And then I saw myself getting back on the plane and coming home.

After I had dreamed this scene many times—watching their despair turn from horror into anger—I begged Auntie Lindo to write another letter. And at first she refused.

"How can I say she is dead? I cannot write this," said Auntie Lindo with a stubborn look.

"But it's cruel to have them believe she's coming on the plane," I said. "When they see it's just me, they'll hate me."

"Hate you? Cannot be." She was scowling. "You are their own sister, their only family."

"You don't understand," I protested.

"What I don't understand?" she said.

And I whispered, "They'll think I'm responsible, that she died because I didn't appreciate her."

And Auntie Lindo looked satisfied and sad at the same time, as if this were true and I had finally realized it. She sat down for an hour, and when she stood up she handed me a two-page letter. She had tears in her eyes. I realized that the very thing I had feared, she had done. So even if she had written the news of my mother's death in English, I wouldn't have had the heart to read it.

"Thank you," I whispered.

The landscape has become gray, filled with low flat cement buildings, old factories, and then tracks and more tracks filled with trains like ours passing by in the opposite direction. I see platforms crowded with people wearing drab Western clothes, with spots of bright colors: little children wearing pink and yellow, red and peach. And there are soldiers in olive green and red, and old ladies in gray tops and pants that stop mid-calf. We are in Guangzhou.

Before the train even comes to a stop, people are bringing down their belongings from above their seats. For a moment there is a dangerous shower of heavy suitcases laden with gifts to relatives, half-broken boxes wrapped in miles of string to keep the contents from spilling out, plastic bags filled with yarn and vegetables and packages of dried mushrooms, and camera cases. And then we are caught in a stream of people rushing, shoving, pushing us along, until we find ourselves in one of a dozen lines waiting to go through customs. I feel as if I were getting on the number 30 Stockton bus in San Francisco. I am in China, I remind myself. And somehow the crowds don't bother me. It feels right. I start pushing too.

I take out the declaration forms and my passport. "Woo," it says at the top, and below that, "June May," who was born in "California, U.S.A.," in 1951. I wonder if the customs people will question whether I'm the same person as in the passport photo. In this picture, my chin-length hair is swept back and artfully styled. I am wearing false eyelashes, eye shadow, and lip liner. My cheeks are hollowed out by bronze blusher. But I had not expected the heat in October. And now my hair hangs limp with the humidity. I wear no makeup; in Hong Kong my mascara had melted into dark circles and everything else had felt like layers of grease. So today my face is plain, unadorned except for a thin mist of shiny sweat on my forehead and nose.

Even without makeup, I could never pass for true Chinese. I stand five-foot-six, and my head pokes above the crowd so that I am eye level only with other tourists. My mother once told me my height came from my grandfather, who was a northerner, and may have even had some Mongol blood. "This is what your grandmother once told me," explained my mother. "But now it is too late to ask her. They are all dead, your grandparents, your uncles, and their wives and children, all killed in the war, when a bomb fell on our house. So many generations in one instant."

She had said this so matter-of-factly that I thought she had long since gotten over any grief she had. And then I wondered how she knew they were all dead.

"Maybe they left the house before the bomb fell," I suggested.

"No," said my mother. "Our whole family is gone. It is just you and I."

"But how do you know? Some of them could have escaped."

"Cannot be," said my mother, this time almost angrily. And then her frown was washed over by a puzzled blank look, and she began to talk as if she were trying to remember where she had misplaced something. "I went back to that house. I kept looking up to where the house used to be. And it wasn't a house, just the sky. And below, underneath my feet, were four stories of burnt bricks and wood, all the life of our house. Then off to the side I saw things blown into the yard, nothing valuable. There was a bed someone used to sleep in, really just a metal frame twisted up at one corner. And a book, I don't know what kind, because every page had turned black. And I saw a teacup which was unbroken but filled with ashes. And then I found my doll, with her hands and legs broken, her hair burned off. . . . When I was a little girl, I had cried for that doll, seeing it all alone in the store window, and my mother had bought it for me. It was an American doll with yellow hair. It could turn its legs and arms. The eyes moved up and down. And when I married and left my family home, I gave the doll to my youngest niece, because she was like me. She cried if that doll was not with her always. Do you see? If she was in the house with that doll, her parents were there, and so everybody was there, waiting together, because that's how our family was."

The woman in the customs booth stares at my documents, then glances at me briefly, and with two quick movements stamps everything and sternly nods me along. And soon my father and I find ourselves in a large area filled with thousands of people and suitcases. I feel lost and my father looks helpless.

"Excuse me," I say to a man who looks like an American. "Can you tell me where I can get a taxi?" He mumbles something that sounds Swedish or Dutch.

"Syau Yen! Syau Yen!" I hear a piercing voice shout from behind me. An old woman in a yellow knit beret is holding up a pink plastic bag filled with wrapped trinkets. I guess she is trying to sell us something. But my father is staring down at this tiny sparrow of a woman, squinting into her eyes. And then his eyes widen, his face opens up and he smiles like a pleased little boy.

"*Aiyi! Aiyi!*"—Auntie Auntie!—he says softly.

"Syau Yen!" coos my great-aunt. I think it's funny she has just called my father "Little Wild Goose." It must be his baby milk name, the name used to discourage ghosts from stealing children.

They clasp each other's hands—they do not hug—and hold on like this, taking turns saying, "Look at you! You are so old. Look how old you've become!" They are both crying openly, laughing at the same time, and I bite my lip, trying not to cry. I'm afraid to feel their joy. Because I am thinking how different our arrival in Shanghai will be tomorrow, how awkward it will feel.

Now Aiyi beams and points to a Polaroid picture of my father. My father had wisely sent pictures when he wrote and said we were coming. See how smart she was, she seems to intone as she compares the picture to my father. In the letter, my father had said we would call her from the hotel once we arrived, so this is a surprise, that they've come to meet us. I wonder if my sisters will be at the airport.

It is only then that I remember the camera. I had meant to take a picture of my father and his aunt the moment they met. It's not too late.

"Here, stand together over here," I say, holding up the Polaroid. The camera flashes and I hand them the snapshot. Aiyi and my father still stand close together, each of them holding a corner of the picture, watching as their images begin to form. They are almost reverentially quiet. Aiyi is only five years older than my father, which makes her around seventy-seven. But she looks ancient, shrunken, a mummified relic. Her thin hair is pure white, her teeth are brown with decay. So much for stories of Chinese women looking young forever, I think to myself.

Now Aiyi is crooning to me: "*Jandale.*" So big already. She looks up at me, at my full height, and then peers into her pink plastic bag—her gifts to us, I have figured out—as if she is wondering what she will give to me, now that I am so old and big. And then she grabs my elbow with her sharp pincerlike grasp and turns me around. A man and woman in their fifties are shaking hands with my father, everybody smiling and saying, "Ah! Ah!" They are Aiyi's oldest son and his wife, and standing next to them are four other people, around my age, and a little girl who's around ten. The introductions go by so fast, all I know is that one of them is Aiyi's grandson, with his wife, and the other is her granddaughter, with her husband. And the little girl is Lili, Aiyi's great-granddaughter.

Aiyi and my father speak the Mandarin dialect from their childhood, but the rest of the family speaks only the Cantonese of their village. I understand only Mandarin but can't speak it that well. So Aiyi and my father gossip unrestrained in Mandarin, exchanging news about people from their old village. And they stop only occasionally to talk to the rest of us, sometimes in Cantonese, sometimes in English.

"Oh, it is as I suspected," says my father, turning to me. "He died last summer." And I already understood this. I just don't know who this person, Li Gong, is. I feel as if I were in the United Nations and the translators had run amok.

"Hello," I say to the little girl. "My name is Jing-mei." But the little girl squirms to look away, causing her parents to laugh with embarrassment. I try to think of Cantonese words I can say to her, stuff I learned from friends in Chinatown, but all I can think of are swear words, terms for bodily functions, and short phrases like "tastes good," "tastes like garbage," and "she's really ugly." And then I have another plan: I hold up the Polaroid camera, beckoning Lili with my finger. She immediately jumps forward, places one hand on her hip in the manner of a fashion model, juts out her chest, and flashes me a toothy smile. As soon as I take the picture she is standing next to me, jumping and giggling every few seconds as she watches herself appear on the greenish film.

By the time we hail taxis for the ride to the hotel, Lili is holding tight onto my hand, pulling me along.

In the taxi, Aiyi talks nonstop, so I have no chance to ask her about the different sights we are passing by.

"You wrote and said you would come only for one day," says Aiyi to my father in an agitated tone. "One day! How can you see your family in one day! Toishan is many hours' drive from Guangzhou. And this idea to call us when you arrive. This is nonsense. We have no telephone."

My heart races a little. I wonder if Auntie Lindo told my sisters we would call from the hotel in Shanghai?

Aiyi continues to scold my father. "I was so beside myself, ask my son, almost turned heaven and earth upside down trying to think of a way! So we decided the best was for us to take the bus from Toishan and come into Guangzhou—meet you right from the start."

And now I am holding my breath as the taxi driver dodges between trucks and buses, honking his horn constantly. We seem to be on some sort of long freeway overpass, like a bridge above the city. I can see row after row of apartments, each floor cluttered with laundry hanging out to dry on the balcony. We pass a public bus, with people jammed in so tight their faces are nearly wedged against the window. Then I see the skyline of what must be downtown Guangzhou. From a distance, it looks like a major American city, with highrises and construction going on everywhere. As we slow down in the more congested part of the city, I see scores of little shops, dark inside, lined with counters and shelves. And then there is a building, its front laced with scaffolding made of bamboo poles held together with plastic strips. Men and women are standing on narrow platforms, scraping the sides, working without safety straps or helmets. Oh, would OSHA have a field day here, I think.

Aiyi's shrill voice rises up again: "So it is a shame you can't see our village, our house. My sons have been quite successful, selling our vegetables in the free market. We had enough these last few years to build a big house, three stories, all of new brick, big enough for our whole family and then some. And every year, the money is even better. You Americans aren't the only ones who know how to get rich!"

The taxi stops and I assume we've arrived, but then I peer out at what looks like a grander version of the Hyatt Regency. "This is communist China?" I wonder out loud. And then I shake my head toward my father. "This must be the wrong hotel." I quickly pull out our itinerary, travel tickets, and reservations. I had explicitly instructed my travel agent to choose something inexpensive, in the thirty-to-forty-dollar range. I'm sure of this. And there it says on our itinerary: Garden Hotel, Huanshi Dong Lu. Well, our travel agent had better be prepared to eat the extra, that's all I have to say.

The hotel is magnificent. A bellboy complete with uniform and sharp-creased cap jumps forward and begins to carry our bags into the lobby. Inside, the hotel looks like an orgy of shopping arcades and restaurants all encased in granite and glass. And rather than be impressed, I am worried about the expense, as well as the appearance it must give Aiyi, that we rich Americans cannot be without our luxuries even for one night.

But when I step up to the reservation desk, ready to haggle over this booking mistake, it is confirmed. Our rooms are pre-paid, thirty-four dollars each. I feel sheepish, and Aiyi and the others seem delighted by our temporary surroundings. Lili is looking wide-eyed at an arcade filled with video games.

Our whole family crowds into one elevator, and the bellboy waves, saying he will meet us on the eighteenth floor. As soon as the elevator door shuts, everybody becomes very quiet, and when the door finally opens again, everybody talks at once in what sounds like relieved voices. I have the feeling Aiyi and the others have never been on such a long elevator ride.

Our rooms are next to each other and are identical. The rugs, drapes, bedspreads are all in shades of taupe. There's a color television with remote-control panels built into the lamp table between the two twin beds. The bathroom has marble walls and floors. I find a built-in wet bar with a small refrigerator stocked with Heineken beer, Coke Classic, and Seven-Up, mini-bottles of Johnnie Walker Red, Bacardi rum, and Smirnoff vodka, and packets of M & M's, honey-roasted cashews, and Cadbury chocolate bars. And again I say out loud, "This is communist China?"

My father comes into my room. "They decided we should just stay here and visit," he says, shrugging his shoulders. "They say, Less trouble that way. More time to talk."

"What about dinner?" I ask. I have been envisioning my first real Chinese feast for many days already, a big banquet with one of those soups steaming out of a carved winter melon, chicken wrapped in clay, Peking duck, the works.

My father walks over and picks up a room service book next to a *Travel & Leisure* magazine. He flips through the pages quickly and then points to the menu. "This is what they want," says my father.

So it's decided. We are going to dine tonight in our rooms, with our family, sharing hamburgers, french fries, and apple pie à la mode.

Aiyi and her family are browsing the shops while we clean up. After a hot ride on the train, I'm eager for a shower and cooler clothes.

The hotel has provided little packets of shampoo which, upon opening, I discover is the consistency and color of hoisin sauce. This is more like it, I think. This is China. And I rub some in my damp hair.

Standing in the shower, I realize this is the first time I've been by myself in what seems like days. But instead of feeling relieved, I feel forlorn. I think about what my mother said, about activating my genes and becoming Chinese. And I wonder what she meant.

Right after my mother died, I asked myself a lot of things, things that couldn't be answered, to force myself to grieve more. It seemed as if I wanted to sustain my grief, to assure myself that I had cared deeply enough.

But now I ask the questions mostly because I want to know the answers. What was that pork stuff she used to make that had the texture of sawdust? What were the names of the uncles who died in Shanghai? What had she dreamt all these years about her other daughters? All the times when she got mad at me, was she really thinking about them? Did she wish I were they? Did she regret that I wasn't?

At one o'clock in the morning, I awake to tapping sounds on the window. I must have dozed off and now I feel my body uncramping itself. I'm sitting on the floor, leaning against one of the twin beds. Lili is lying next to me. The others are asleep, too, sprawled out on the beds and floor. Aiyi is seated at a little table, looking very sleepy. And my father is staring out the window, tapping his fingers on the glass. The last time I listened my father was telling Aiyi about his life since he last saw her. How he had gone to Yenching University, later got a post with a newspaper in Chungking, met my mother there, a young widow. How they later fled together to Shanghai to try to find my mother's family house, but there was nothing there. And then they traveled eventually to Canton and then to Hong Kong, then Haiphong and finally to San Francisco. . . .

"Suyuan didn't tell me she was trying all these years to find her daughters," he is now saying in a quiet voice. "Naturally, I did not discuss her daughters with her. I thought she was ashamed she had left them behind."

"Where did she leave them?" asks Aiyi. "How were they found?"

I am wide awake now. Although I have heard parts of this story from my mother's friends.

"It happened when the Japanese took over Kweilin," says my father.

"Japanese in Kweilin?" says Aiyi. "That was never the case. Couldn't be. The Japanese never came to Kweilin."

"Yes, that is what the newspapers reported. I know this because I was working for the news bureau at the time. The Kuomintang often told us what we could say and could not say. But we knew the Japanese had come into Kwangsi Province. We had sources who told us how they had captured the Wuchang-Canton railway. How they were coming overland, making very fast progress, marching toward the provincial capital."

Aiyi looks astonished. "If people did not know this, how could Suyuan know the Japanese were coming?"

"An officer of the Kuomintang secretly warned her," explains my father. "Suyuan's husband also was an officer and everybody knew that officers and their families would be the first to be killed. So she gathered a few possessions and, in the middle of the night, she picked up her daughters and fled on foot. The babies were not even one year old."

"How could she give up those babies!" sighs Aiyi. "Twin girls. We have never had such luck in our family." And then she yawns again.

"What were they named?" she asks. I listen carefully. I had been planning on using just the familiar "Sister" to address them both. But now I want to know how to pronounce their names.

"They have their father's surname, Wang," says my father. "And their given names are Chwun Yu and Chwun Hwa."

"What do the names mean?" I ask.

"Ah." My father draws imaginary characters on the window. "One means 'Spring Rain,' the other 'Spring Flower,' " he explains in English, "because they born in the spring, and of course rain come before flower, same order these girls are born. Your mother like a poet, don't you think?"

I nod my head. I see Aiyi nod her head forward, too. But it falls forward and stays there. She is breathing deeply, noisily. She is asleep.

"And what does Ma's name mean?" I whisper.

" 'Suyuan,' " he says, writing more invisible characters on the glass. "The way she write it in Chinese, it mean 'Long-Cherished Wish.' Quite a fancy name, not so ordinary like flower name. See this first character, it mean something like 'Forever Never Forgotten.' But there is another way to write 'Suyuan.' Sound exactly the same, but the meaning is opposite." His finger creates the brushstrokes of another character. "The first part look the same: 'Never Forgotten.' But the last part add to first part make the whole word mean 'Long-Held Grudge.' Your mother get angry with me, I tell her her name should be Grudge."

My father is looking at me, moist-eyed. "See, I pretty clever, too, hah?"

I nod, wishing I could find some way to comfort him. "And what about my name," I ask, "what does 'Jing-mei' mean?"

"Your name also special," he says. I wonder if any name in

Chinese is not something special. "'Jing' like excellent *jing*. Not just good, it's something pure, essential, the best quality. *Jing* is good leftover stuff when you take impurities out of something like gold, or rice, or salt. So what is left—just pure essence. And 'Mei,' this is common *mei*, as in *meimei*, 'younger sister.' "

I think about this. My mother's long-cherished wish. Me, the younger sister who was supposed to be the essence of the others. I feed myself with the old grief, wondering how disappointed my mother must have been. Tiny Aiyi stirs suddenly, her head rolls and then falls back, her mouth opens as if to answer my question. She grunts in her sleep, tucking her body more closely into the chair.

"So why did she abandon those babies on the road?" I need to know, because now I feel abandoned too.

"Long time I wondered this myself," says my father. "But then I read that letter from her daughters in Shanghai now, and I talk to Auntie Lindo, all the others. And then I knew. No shame in what she done. None."

"What happened?"

"Your mother running away—" begins my father.

"No, tell me in Chinese," I interrupt. "Really, I can understand."

He begins to talk, still standing at the window, looking into the night.

After fleeing Kweilin, your mother walked for several days trying to find a main road. Her thought was to catch a ride on a truck or wagon, to catch enough rides until she reached Chungking, where her husband was stationed.

She had sewn money and jewelry into the lining of her dress, enough, she thought, to barter rides all the way. If I am lucky, she thought, I will not have to trade the heavy gold bracelet and jade ring. These were things from her mother, your grandmother.

By the third day, she had traded nothing. The roads were

filled with people, everybody running and begging for rides from passing trucks. The trucks rushed by, afraid to stop. So your mother found no rides, only the start of dysentery pains in her stomach.

Her shoulders ached from the two babies swinging from scarf slings. Blisters grew on her palms from holding two leather suitcases. And then the blisters burst and began to bleed. After a while, she left the suitcases behind, keeping only the food and a few clothes. And later she also dropped the bags of wheat flour and rice and kept walking like this for many miles, singing songs to her little girls, until she was delirious with pain and fever.

Finally, there was not one more step left in her body. She didn't have the strength to carry those babies any farther. She slumped to the ground. She knew she would die of her sickness, or perhaps from thirst, from starvation, or from the Japanese, who she was sure were marching right behind her.

She took the babies out of the slings and sat them on the side of the road, then lay down next to them. You babies are so good, she said, so quiet. They smiled back, reaching their chubby hands for her, wanting to be picked up again. And then she knew she could not bear to watch her babies die with her.

She saw a family with three young children in a cart going by. "Take my babies, I beg you," she cried to them. But they stared back with empty eyes and never stopped.

She saw another person pass and called out again. This time a man turned around, and he had such a terrible expression— your mother said it looked like death itself—she shivered and looked away.

When the road grew quiet, she tore open the lining of her dress, and stuffed jewelry under the shirt of one baby and money under the other. She reached into her pocket and drew out the photos of her family, the picture of her father and mother, the picture of herself and her husband on their wedding day. And she wrote on the back of each the names of the babies and this same message: "Please care for these babies with the money and valuables provided. When it is safe to come, if you bring them to Shanghai, 9 Weichang Lu, the Li family will be glad to give you a generous reward. Li Suyuan and Wang Fuchi."

And then she touched each baby's cheek and told her not to cry. She would go down the road to find them some food and would be back. And without looking back, she walked down the road, stumbling and crying, thinking only of this one last hope, that her daughters would be found by a kindhearted person who would care for them. She would not allow herself to imagine anything else.

She did not remember how far she walked, which direction she went, when she fainted, or how she was found. When she awoke, she was in the back of a bouncing truck with several other sick people, all moaning. And she began to scream, thinking she was now on a journey to Buddhist hell. But the face of an American missionary lady bent over her and smiled, talking to her in a soothing language she did not understand. And yet she could somehow understand. She had been saved for no good reason, and it was now too late to go back and save her babies.

When she arrived in Chungking, she learned her husband had died two weeks before. She told me later she laughed when the officers told her this news, she was so delirious with madness and disease. To come so far, to lose so much and to find nothing.

I met her in a hospital. She was lying on a cot, hardly able to move, her dysentery had drained her so thin. I had come in for my foot, my missing toe, which was cut off by a piece of falling rubble. She was talking to herself, mumbling.

"Look at these clothes," she said, and I saw she had on a rather unusual dress for wartime. It was silk satin, quite dirty, but there was no doubt it was a beautiful dress.

"Look at this face," she said, and I saw her dusty face and hollow cheeks, her eyes shining back. "Do you see my foolish hope?"

"I thought I had lost everything, except these two things," she murmured. "And I wondered which I would lose next. Clothes or hope? Hope or clothes?"

"But now, see here, look what is happening," she said, laughing, as if all her prayers had been answered. And she was pulling hair out of her head as easily as one lifts new wheat from wet soil.

•

It was an old peasant woman who found them. "How could I resist?" the peasant woman later told your sisters when they were older. They were still sitting obediently near where your mother had left them, looking like little fairy queens waiting for their sedan to arrive.

The woman, Mei Ching, and her husband, Mei Han, lived in a stone cave. There were thousands of hidden caves like that in and around Kweilin so secret that the people remained hidden even after the war ended. The Meis would come out of their cave every few days and forage for food supplies left on the road, and sometimes they would see something that they both agreed was a tragedy to leave behind. So one day they took back to their cave a delicately painted set of rice bowls, another day a little footstool with a velvet cushion and two new wedding blankets. And once, it was your sisters.

They were pious people, Muslims, who believed the twin babies were a sign of double luck, and they were sure of this when, later in the evening, they discovered how valuable the babies were. She and her husband had never seen rings and bracelets like those. And while they admired the pictures, knowing the babies came from a good family, neither of them could read or write. It was not until many months later that Mei Ching found someone who could read the writing on the back. By then, she loved these baby girls like her own.

In 1952 Mei Han, the husband, died. The twins were already eight years old, and Mei Ching now decided it was time to find your sisters' true family.

She showed the girls the picture of their mother and told them they had been born into a great family and she would take them back to see their true mother and grandparents. Mei Chang told them about the reward, but she swore she would refuse it. She loved these girls so much, she only wanted them to have what they were entitled to—a better life, a fine house, educated ways. Maybe the family would let her stay on as the girls' amah. Yes, she was certain they would insist.

Of course, when she found the place at 9 Weichang Lu, in the old French Concession, it was something completely different. It was the site of a factory building, recently constructed, and none of the workers knew what had become of the family whose house had burned down on that spot.

Mei Ching could not have known, of course, that your mother and I, her new husband, had already returned to that same place in 1945 in hopes of finding both her family and her daughters.

Your mother and I stayed in China until 1947. We went to many different cities—back to Kweilin, to Changsha, as far south as Kunming. She was always looking out of one corner of her eye for twin babies, then little girls. Later we went to Hong Kong, and when we finally left in 1949 for the United States, I think she was even looking for them on the boat. But when we arrived, she no longer talked about them. I thought, At last, they have died in her heart.

When letters could be openly exchanged between China and the United States, she wrote immediately to old friends in Shanghai and Kweilin. I did not know she did this. Auntie Lindo told me. But of course, by then, all the street names had changed. Some people had died, others had moved away. So it took many years to find a contact. And when she did find an old schoolmate's address and wrote asking her to look for her daughters, her friend wrote back and said this was impossible, like looking for a needle on the bottom of the ocean. How did she know her daughters were in Shanghai and not somewhere else in China? The friend, of course, did not ask, How do you know your daughters are still alive?

So her schoolmate did not look. Finding babies lost during the war was a matter of foolish imagination, and she had no time for that.

But every year, your mother wrote to different people. And this last year, I think she got a big idea in her head, to go to China and find them herself. I remember she told me, "Canning, we should go, before it is too late, before we are too old." And I told her we were already too old, it was already too late.

I just thought she wanted to be a tourist! I didn't know she wanted to go and look for her daughters. So when I said it was too late, that must have put a terrible thought in her head that her daughters might be dead. And I think this possibility grew bigger and bigger in her head, until it killed her.

Maybe it was your mother's dead spirit who guided her Shanghai schoolmate to find her daughters. Because after your mother died, the schoolmate saw your sisters, by chance, while shopping for shoes at the Number One Department Store on Nanjing Dong Road. She said it was like a dream, seeing these two women who looked so much alike, moving down the stairs together. There was something about their facial expressions that reminded the schoolmate of your mother.

She quickly walked over to them and called their names, which of course, they did not recognize at first, because Mei Ching had changed their names. But your mother's friend was so sure, she persisted. "Are you not Wang Chwun Yu and Wang Chwun Hwa?" she asked them. And then these double-image women became very excited, because they remembered the names written on the back of an old photo, a photo of a young man and woman they still honored, as their much-loved first parents, who had died and become spirit ghosts still roaming the earth looking for them.

At the airport, I am exhausted. I could not sleep last night. Aiyi had followed me into my room at three in the morning, and she instantly fell asleep on one of the twin beds, snoring with the might of a lumberjack. I lay awake thinking about my mother's story, realizing how much I have never known about her, grieving that my sisters and I had both lost her.

And now at the airport, after shaking hands with everybody, waving good-bye, I think about all the different ways we leave people in this world. Cheerily waving good-bye to some at airports, knowing we'll never see each other again. Leaving others on the side of the road, hoping that we will. Finding my mother in my father's story and saying good-bye before I have a chance to know her better.

Aiyi smiles at me as we wait for our gate to be called. She is so old. I put one arm around her and one arm around Lili. They are the same size, it seems. And then it's time. As we wave good-bye one more time and enter the waiting area, I get the sense I am going from one funeral to another. In my hand I'm clutching a pair of tickets to Shanghai. In two hours we'll be there.

The plane takes off. I close my eyes. How can I describe to them in my broken Chinese about our mother's life? Where should I begin?

"Wake up, we're here," says my father. And I awake with my heart pounding in my throat. I look out the window and we're already on the runway. It's gray outside.

And now I'm walking down the steps of the plane, onto the tarmac and toward the building. If only, I think, if only my mother had lived long enough to be the one walking toward them. I am so nervous I cannot even feel my feet. I am just moving somehow.

Somebody shouts, "She's arrived!" And then I see her. Her short hair. Her small body. And that same look on her face. She has the back of her hand pressed hard against her mouth. She is crying as though she had gone through a terrible ordeal and were happy it is over.

And I know it's not my mother, yet it is the same look she had when I was five and had disappeared all afternoon, for such a long time, that she was convinced I was dead. And when I miraculously appeared, sleepy-eyed, crawling from underneath my bed, she wept and laughed, biting the back of her hand to make sure it was true.

And now I see her again, two of her, waving, and in one hand there is a photo, the Polaroid I sent them. As soon as I get beyond the gate, we run toward each other, all three of us embracing, all hesitations and expectations forgotten.

"Mama, Mama," we all murmur, as if she is among us.

My sisters look at me, proudly. *"Meimei jandale,"* says one sister proudly to the other. "Little Sister has grown up." I look at their faces again and I see no trace of my mother in them.

Yet they still look familiar. And now I also see what part of me is Chinese. It is so obvious. It is my family. It is in our blood. After all these years, it can finally be let go.

My sisters and I stand, arms around each other, laughing and wiping the tears from each other's eyes. The flash of the Polaroid goes off and my father hands me the snapshot. My sisters and I watch quietly together, eager to see what develops.

The gray-green surface changes to the bright colors of our three images, sharpening and deepening all at once. And although we don't speak, I know we all see it: Together we look like our mother. Her same eyes, her same mouth, open in surprise to see, at last, her long-cherished wish.